ANCESTORS

AND

DESCENDANTS

This is a work of fiction.   All of the characters, organizations, and events portrayed in this novel are either products of the author's imagination or are used fictitiously.

ANCESTORS AND DESCENDANTS

Published by Damn Fool Press
www.damnfoolpress.com

ISBN 978-0-9950434-6-6 epub
ISBN 978-0-9950434-5-9 mobi
ISBN 978-0-9950434-7-3 trade paperback

First Edition : November 2018

This is for Lynn and the cats.

CHAPTER ONE
Knight Errant

A pack of young children ran along the dusty road shrieking with glee, their scraps of dirty clothing fluttering behind them. It wasn't that their parents were poor or the children mistreated, for this was a civilized place. It was simply the most practical outfit for active children to wear on a warm day as they played in the fields surrounding the town. Today, however, they were running away from the fields and back to their homes bearing news of great importance. Well, something different at any rate.

"A knight is coming! A knight is coming! We saw him at the pond, watering his horse!" they proclaimed to all they encountered. Being the bearers of such tidings caused their small chests to puff out with importance.

"A knight?" called out a middle-aged woman sitting next to her stall. "What makes you think he is such?"

"You'll see, grandmother, you'll see," they yelled in passing. Their cries continued, but faded from her hearing as they ran further into town. The woman snorted in disbelief, but patted the dust from her clothing and checked that her hair was arranged neatly.

A few minutes later she heard the clopping of shod hooves moving smartly along. The slight bend in the road and arrangement of the buildings prevented her from seeing who was coming, but the sounds were getting louder. The clatter of the hooves was just beginning to echo from the buildings when the horse and its rider came into view.

She caught her breath at the sight of the stranger. His armour shone like the sun and the trappings on his warhorse were of the finest quality. He was handsome, tall, well-muscled without being stocky, and held himself as one to the nobility born. His demeanour was friendly, but his eyes missed nothing as he rode through. The townsfolk waved at his cheery greetings, and the street urchins shrieked with joy as he tossed coins among them. The lack of insignia or heraldic device on his armour and trappings went unnoticed in the happy confusion that followed him.

By the time he reached the mayor's office, a small crowd had gathered about him. The stranger dismounted, took a sheathed sword from the saddle, and knocked upon the door with the pommel. When the mayor opened the door, the stranger said in a strong voice, "Where is the dragon that is plaguing you? I have come to deal with him."

The mayor shrugged with tired resignation and pointed down the road. This was not the first knight who had come to fight the dread creature. The cost of burying them was becoming a burden. "Half a day's journey to the next village if you ride at a good pace, my lord knight."

"My thanks, good sir," answered the sturdy young man, who then promptly remounted. All the young, and not so young, women waggled their eyebrows at him as he continued on his journey. Several were rather more forthright with what they waggled, but the stranger kept his gaze on the road before him.

Once past the town, he kept the horse's speed to a steady trot. He'd ridden for several hours when he smelled smoke up ahead, and saw a hint of flame beyond the next rise. Increasing the horse's pace to a canter, he soon reached the top of the rise and came to a halt as he viewed the horrific scene below him. A small group of buildings, too few to be called a town, was ablaze. The inhabitants had gathered to one side safely out of the fire's reach. A peal of laughter from on high drew his attention upwards, and he spotted a winged form cartwheeling about. It paused in its antics long enough to reveal itself as a dragon.

The rider's face was a study in stone as he rode towards the ruined buildings. He stopped in front of the assembled group and asked softly, "Is everyone safe?"

From the mumbled replies he gathered that everyone was, indeed, uninjured. However, their homes, livestock, and food stores were gone.

"Did the dragon do this?"

Again the mumbled replies answered in the affirmative. Then one older man spoke up, "It came roaring from the sky. Demanded that all assemble here or face death. We came out, and it said that we'd been chosen as an example for the others. That we should feel blessed for the honour." The last was spat out.

The stranger gave a small shake of his head as his face hardened. He glanced at the dragon cavorting in the sky, then back at the huddled victims. "Stay here," he said over a shoulder as he urged his warhorse down the road and closer to the dragon. There was a slight rise ahead which he reached in short order. Dismounting without bothering to take any weapons, he strode forward to the centre of the rise. Once there, he stood in a neutral stance facing forward with his hands folded in front of him.

"Oh ho!" came a cry from above. "Another brave knight come to test his mettle against me."

A sudden rush of air and the flapping of wings heralded the arrival of the dragon, who landed just ahead of the stranger. "Tell me your name, brave knight, that the villagers may carve it on your tombstone."

In response, the warrior removed his helmet and said,

"Hello, Freddy. Fancy meeting you here."

The dragon reared back as if struck. "You? What are you doing here?"

"Following rumours. Protecting the powerless. Defending the defenceless. You know—the usual. How about yourself?"

The dragon regained its composure and leaned forward, peering at the man through slitted eyes. "You shouldn't be here. He won't like it. You'll ruin everything."

The man tilted his head slightly to one side, and in an innocent voice asked, "Me? Ruin things? You're the one who destroyed those buildings. You're the one who put all those innocent lives at risk."

"I got them out of harm's way first, you know," said the dragon petulantly. "I was careful."

"You burnt their homes. Destroyed their stocks of food. Destroyed their ability to work the land and fend for themselves."

"The large towns can take care of them. Lots of people there and lots of food to spare. No-one got hurt. Just some property damage. Now go 'way."

The man shook his head slowly and said in a stern voice, "Can't do that, Freddy. You of all people should understand that. At least, you used to understand that." Then he added in a soft voice, "What happened to you? You look rough. And doing this low-level enforcer crap? You're better than this, Freddy. A lot better."

The dragon reared its head up in anger. "What do you know? What do you know about anything? You don't know what it's like," was the hissed reply.

"Freddy, this has to stop. You know that."

"Is this a formal warning?" asked the dragon in a neutral tone.

The warrior stared hard for a moment, let out his breath, and shook his head. "No. It's just me. But if I caught wind of this nonsense, the word is getting around. It'll get to the wrong ears, sooner or later. You don't want that, Freddy. You really don't. Listen to me, please. For old times' sake."

"Oh, sure ... friend." He spat that last word like a curse. "He wants the message to get around. He's giving us all what we want—all we have to do is ask for it. Do a few favours. No biggie. But not you. Oh, no. Not mister special high and mighty." The dragon's head was weaving, and ropes of drool were dripping off its fangs. The pupils of its eyes were large, but not to the same diameter. The air above the back shimmered as waves of heat rose up from the body.

"Yes, Freddy, I am your friend. Always have been. You know that. And as your friend, I need to ask you about that gemstone you've got on your forehead."

The dragon let loose a roar as it reared back. "No! It's mine. He gave it to me. You can't have it."

"It's killing you, Freddy."

"No," shrieked the dragon as it shook its head. Then it stopped and looked down at the man, fear in its eyes. "Mine," shrieked the dragon once again. Then it drove its head and neck towards the stranger. Its mouth was agape, exposing a formidable array of deadly teeth.

With no time to grab a weapon, the warrior stood waiting. When the dragon's head was an arm's length away, he snapped up the helmet in his hand and slammed it against the oncoming head. Spinning in place so that the jaws missed him by a hairbreadth, he swung again. This time an uppercut with the helmet snapped the dragon's head back. The dragon staggered back and settled heavily on its haunches shaking its head to clear it. The man knelt and placed the helmet on the ground, brushing the ground with his hands as he did so.

After a couple of seconds the dragon lowered its head and emitted a low growl. The scaled mouth opened wide to expose saliva-slicked teeth as ripples of heat arose from within the throat. As the dragon began to inhale deeply, the warrior's hand blurred as he flicked a stone into the beast's left eye. A fraction of a second later his other hand flicked a stone into the right eye. The dragon screamed in pain as the stones impacted. The armoured head reared up for a moment but came down, with the mouth open to blast its enemy.

The man, however, had taken the opportunity to run forward and close the gap between them. The momentum of his motion added extra strength to an upward kick that slammed into the bottom jaw of the oncoming head. The dragon's mouth snapped shut with a force that shattered teeth. The impact also caused the beast to stumble back and settle heavily on its haunches. Dust rose up around the dragon as it sat there stunned. Stepping forward, the warrior slammed a gauntleted fist into the exposed midriff. An enormous sudden exhalation greeted the blow as he danced off to one side to avoid the randomly flailing limbs.

The dragon shut its eyes and wheezed with pain in a high-pitched tone as its head sank until it was almost touching the ground. Pressing the attack, the warrior grabbed his helmet off the ground and sprang upward onto the beast's neck. He slammed the helmet against the dragon's head several times until the creature collapsed and stopped moving. With his free hand, he grabbed the dagger from his belt and pried out the jewel embedded in the dragon's armoured head. Handling it as if it burned like fire, he tossed it into the now-dented helmet and slid off the dragon. Placing the helmet on the ground, he stomped the open end shut to seal the jewel inside.

"You took it," wheezed the dragon. "You weren't trying to help me; you were only taking it for yourself."

The warrior held up the now-sealed helmet and waggled it. The encased jewel rattled inside, making it sound like a child's rattle.

The dragon moaned soft and low. "You spoiled it. All that

iron. It's spoiled." Tears began to fall from its eyes, and its words had a slight slur due to the broken teeth. "That was all I had to keep me going. He'll never give me another one, and I'm still bound for another five cycles. Why are you doing this to me? Why are you ruining everything—for me, for everyone? Why? Why?" The dragon sobbed large tears, and mucus was flowing from its nose.

"To save you, Freddy. This was killing you. You know that. You're in bad shape—surely you can see that. Go home and get healed."

"Can't. Even if I weren't bound to your brother, I couldn't go back."

The man sighed. "Then go to a sanctuary planet. There are still a few around. They're not much, I know, but better than doing this." He waved his hand around to encompass the burning buildings and frightened inhabitants.

"No," screamed the dragon. It reared up and brought down its two front legs towards the warrior. He rolled back out of the way, then leapt up and over a sweeping tail. The warhorse was not so lucky, and fell to its side screaming as the tail hit it. The warrior turned to help his mount, but a flurry of blows from the limbs of the dragon forced him to concentrate on saving his own skin. When the flurry ended, he risked a look at his opponent. The dragon had turned away from him and was eating the warhorse, tearing chunks out of the still-living horse and gulping them down.

"Stop it, Freddy."

The dragon turned its head towards the man, blood dripping from its muzzle. "He'll come for you. I'm going to tell him what you did here. He'll come for you, and I'm going to enjoy it when he does."

With that the dragon took to the air and flew away. The man watched, his face sad and his shoulders sagging slightly. Then his face took on a puzzled look as he detected a faint but distinct discordant note in the levitation energies of the dragon. Swivelling his head from side to aside allowed him to detect a harshness in Freddy's energy flows that hadn't been there earlier. To the best of his limited knowledge, that wasn't an effect of mind gems.

In any event, within seconds the dragon was too far away to be seen or sensed. This new mystery would have to wait. There were more pressing issues to deal with. He turned and walked back to the villagers, his steps slow and thoughtful.

Just before he got to a group of villagers who had gathered to watch the battle, he tossed the helmet and the enclosed jewel off to one side before continuing on. A few people moved to look at it. "Don't," warned the warrior. "It's dangerous." The few brave souls gaped at him and kept moving, although with somewhat more care.

"Stop," he bellowed. In a more moderate tone he added, "It is cursed. The iron of my helmet dims its powers, but not enough to make it safe." A couple of young men shrugged and tried to sneak closer. The warrior sighed. "If you touch the helmet, you will become unable to ... perform. Ever again. My armour protects me." That got their attention, and they both reluctantly moved back with the rest of the crowd.

The warrior scanned the crowd and spotted the old man he'd spoken with upon his arrival. Catching the old man's attention, he motioned the elder towards him and off to one side. "Your pardon, old one, do you have any iron or steel plate?"

The elder shook his head and pointed at the one of the most-damaged buildings. "I'm sorry, but that was our smithy."

"Ah," said the young man in a soft tone. "I don't suppose you have a hammer that I could borrow?" Once again he received a sad look and an apology. "No matter, sir, my armour will serve my purpose, and a stone will do as a hammer. More importantly, though, can I help you with salvaging your belongings?"

"Thank you, sir knight, but there's nothing to be done until the fires have died down. Many have injured themselves trying to retrieve what they could."

"Will the town receive you, do you think? Give you shelter?"

"Perhaps, sir. Some of us have relatives there. But the town is an expensive place to live—that is why we live here."

The warrior thought for a moment then said, "Send men to my warhorse. Salvage whatever you can from what remains. My supplies included food and medicines. If they are still usable, distribute them amongst your people. If nothing else, the warhorse itself will serve as food. Anything else of value, including the harness, is yours. To help pay for your future. I wish that I could do more."

The old man looked upon the warrior with wonder. "Sir, that is more than generous. I wish we could repay your generosity." Having said that, the old man turned towards the crowd and sent a handful of men towards the remains of the warhorse.

"No, elder, the honour is mine," said the warrior. "Still, perhaps you could repay me with information. I am new to these parts, and know not the lay of the land. Would you happen to know of a volcano in the area?"

The old man examined the stranger carefully. "You must be from very far away, indeed. No, there is nothing like that anywhere near here. However, there is a legendary pit of fire beyond the great inland sea. I've always assumed that the ancient texts were describing a volcano."

The warrior's eyebrows raised in surprise and astonishment.

"Heh. I was a scholar and a traveller in my youth, young sir. Studied in the great university, too. But there was no way to earn a living with scholarship, so I wandered about and came back to the family village. It's not much, but a good place to live. Was a good place to live." The old man ended on a sad note.

"The land is still here, old sir," said the stranger in a firm tone. "Your people are still here. If luck holds, my gear will be worth enough to see you all through the winter. Anything you can salvage will help you re-build."

The old man's mood brightened as he nodded in agreement. "We've seen hard times before. As you say, with luck we'll be able to rebuild. Now, are you very sure that you want to go to that volcano you seek? It is a goodly distance away through very difficult terrain. At least several months of hard travelling with a string of horses and extensive supplies. Considerably more difficult and time-consuming for a man on foot."

The warrior shrugged as he said, "It is what must be done."

"Well, the ancient texts might be somewhat flowery in their descriptions of the geography, but they are quite explicit about the dangers. As I said, there is the inland sea to cross. And cross it you must, as it is impossible to go around due to numerous sinkholes, mud pits, and toxic gases."

"Of course," grunted the warrior.

"Oh, and the sea is inhabited by a fearsome creature. Some say that is a demon that has attacked and killed our people throughout the centuries. The only thing that the descriptions agree upon is that it is large and vicious."

"Aren't they all?" was the murmured reply.

As they spoke, the salvage crew at the warhorse were making happy sounds and waving others to bring over baskets. There were enough knives to make quick work of the butchering process. There was, of course, no shortage of fires upon which to roast the meat.

The two men turned back to each other, grins on both their faces. "Well, sir knight, there seems to be some good news. Would you stay and eat with us?"

The warrior shook his head. "I need to beat more steel

around the jewel right away. Preferably after heating it up—heat helps to further deaden its powers. After that, I'd like to head out as soon as possible. If you have a sack you can spare and a gourd for water, that'd be useful. Which way is this inland sea of yours?"

The old man pointed, "That way. Where the dragon flew."

"Of course," sighed the warrior. "Well, I'd best set about sealing up the jewel in steel. Is there a place where I can make a fire and work without getting in the way?"

The old man pointed towards the end of the row of burning homes. "Anyplace beyond those homes will be fine, sir knight. Are you sure that we cannot offer you any food? Shelter for the night?"

The warrior politely refused, picked up the encased gem, and headed to the assigned area. Once there he found a nice flat area and dropped the encased gem. Then he dragged some of the partially-burned wood from the ruined buildings to use as fuel, and built a large fire. These proceedings had drawn a curious crowd gathering to watch him work. Leaving the fire to burn down to hot coals, he took a stick and drew a circle around the fire. He gave it a radius of about twice his height, figuring that would leave him enough room without being excessively large. He noted that the crowd of curious onlookers was growing, so he sketched out various complicated symbols at various points around the circumference.

Turning to the crowd he intoned, "The mystic circle will protect you while I attempt to neutralize the dark magic of the gem. This is dangerous work, so for your own protection stay well back." He noticed the crowd included the old scholar, who looked to be struggling to hide a smile.

Keeping his expression neutral, the warrior approached the circle, stopping short of crossing it. He raised his eyes skyward, and made what he hoped looked like mystical motions while muttering incantations. When the crowd grew silent, he slowly stepped inside the circle, stopped, and repeated the process. Moving to the fire he found a completely-burned log and scraped some charcoal from it. Taking the charcoal, he moved to three points on the circle and with great ceremony tapped some of the charcoal off his hands at each point. Moving back to the fire he was pleased to notice that the crowd had pulled back.

With the basics taken care of, he doffed his armour and allowed himself a satisfied grunt and a small smile. The smile became a sour look as he examined the encased gem. Even encased in the helmet, he could feel the damnable thing's allure. The fire had burned down to a satisfactory amount of hot coals, so he used a stout stick to manoeuvre the helmet into the fire. A few drops of white fluid dripped out of the helmet onto the ground. That was odd, but his knowledge of the gems was limited so he shrugged and made sure to toss those bits of soil into the fire as well.

While it all baked, he surveyed his discarded armour, weighing the different pieces. A shout from the crowd caused him to raise his head to look at them. They were pointing towards the fire, so he turned to see what the problem was. A cloud of white vapour was arising from the inside the helmet, and to a lesser extent from the fluid-drenched bits of soil. He yelled at the crowd to get back, while at the same time he watched the movement of the vapour. The heat of the fire had neutralized or dissipated most of it, and no more was being emitted from the helmet.

The warrior took a long stick and fished the helmet out of the fire. Using a large stone he hammered the helmet solidly shut and moulded it more tightly around the gem. The heat had softened the metal nicely, and the effects of the gem were lessened but still noticeable. Even diminished in strength the gem was still dangerous and needed to be destroyed in the volcano.

A sudden shift in the direction of the wind caused him to

raise his head. The breeze sent a wave of heat into his face, as well as a wisp of the white vapour. Every muscle in his body locked up, and he toppled to the ground. "This shouldn't be happening," was his last coherent thought as waves of ecstasy overtook him. After what seemed like an eternity, he lapsed into unconsciousness.

* * *

When he awoke, it was morning and he was on a bed with the sun beating upon him.

"Awake at last. It took you long enough, young sir."

The warrior swivelled his head to view the speaker, surprised to see the old scholar he had met earlier. "Yes. How long was I asleep?" Surveying his surroundings showed that he was on a rough mattress outside of a burnt building.

The old man smiled, although his face showed some concern. "Just the night. You're a lot heavier than you look, you know. Took four of the stronger lads to carry you."

The warrior smiled for a moment before his face turned grim as he sprang to his feet. "The gem! What about the ..."

The old man made soothing motions with his hands. "Taken care of, never fear." He paused for a moment then added, "We exercised caution, I assure you."

At the warrior's doubting look the old man laughed. "I told you that I had trained as a scholar. I know enough of the chemical arts to take precautions. Even when some would dress up such things as magic." He shot a baleful glare at the warrior.

The young man smiled and offered a slight bow. "My apologies, Master Scholar. Time was of the essence and I dared not waste time with explanations. Also, the people of the Great City exhibited no love for learning."

The old scholar smiled as he replied. "A fair point, young sir knight. Those in the city tend to value commerce and the accumulation of wealth above all else." Then waggling a finger he added, "Still, don't go assuming that country folk are simples. But I accept your apology. Now, how are you feeling?"

The warrior frowned as he answered. "Somewhat weak and dizzy, if truth be told. As if I'd run a long distance in full armour."

"Perhaps some water would be in order. And some food, if you feel up to it. Do you know what that foul white smoke was?"

The old scholar offered a gourd filled with water. The stranger gave a grateful nod as he accepted it, then quaffed the contents. Lowering the gourd, he smiled broadly and said, "That helps. Thank you." A plate of cheese and bread was offered and he was about to take it, but then stopped. "I hate to take food when you have so little."

"Not so little, as it turns out," the old man said. "Much was lost, true, but we have found more than we dared expect. And your gift of the horse went a long way to filling our bellies. We owe you for that, if nothing else."

The warrior took the food and ate slowly but with gusto. When the meal was finished, he accepted another gourd of water and quaffed that.

"Your appetite seems good," the old man said as he grinned. "That's a good sign. Feeling better?"

The warrior stood up and took a few tentative steps. "Much better, thank you. I am in your debt. Now, I really should be seeing about that gem and making sure that it is safely sealed."

"No fear of that, young sir. After it had cooled sufficiently to be handled, the smith wrapped it in several layers of pitch-soaked cloth, then did a final dip in pitch. It's as well sealed as human hands can make it. Let us go examine it so you can set your mind at rest."

The old man led the warrior to the site of his fire. "After you collapsed, I realized that you had been exposed to some noxious substance. The winds quickly dispersed it, so I deemed it safe to approach. I made the appropriate incantations before entering it to check on you, of course. The incantations were to convince some of the lads that it was safe enough to enter and carry you out. When nothing untoward happened, the smith and I dealt with the encased gem."

"Incantations?" murmured the young man.

The old scholar chuckled. "Yes, yes. The old beliefs are still widely held, especially in times of turmoil. And, as you said, time was of the essence."

In a few minutes they had reached the site of the incident. Inside the circle, but away from the remains of the fire, sat a dark-coloured ball. A rough handle was embedded into the pitch wrappings. The stranger squatted, sitting on his heels in front of the ball and examined it with care. Then he half-closed his eyes and stared at it.

"You act as if you are listening for something," came the quiet voice of the old man.

"I have a sensitivity for the magics contained in the gem."

That got a derisive snort out of the old scholar. The warrior smiled and turned to look at him. "I mean no disrespect. That gem was made to contain subtle and powerful energies."

"Made? What manner of learning was used in the making?" The old man leaned forward, eager to learn more.

The warrior shook his head. "Great learning turned to evil ends, I fear. Such things are not common, but I have heard of them. They are powerful and addictive, but can be contained and diminished by iron or steel."

"But not destroyed by them?"

"No. That takes something much more powerful."

"Ah. The volcano."

"Indeed, Master Scholar."

"Why do you not sell it? Even if its powers are diminished,

I am sure there are those who would pay a handsome price for it. In the Great City, for instance."

"Indeed. Which is why I won't be returning there. Also so that no-one finds out that the gem was ever here. It must be destroyed as soon as possible. "

"The dragon has allies?"

"Yes, I'm afraid so. He is part of a larger scheme that I have sworn to investigate and put an end to."

"But, sir knight, the dragon knows of us."

"I'll take care of him," came the reply, in voice of ice and steel and judgement. "This was just a minor scouting mission, but I'll make sure he tells no-one of it."

The old man stared at the younger with sadness. "It appeared that you were speaking with him. I could not understand the language, but you seemed to know each other."

The warrior sighed. "Yes. We were friends once. Grew up together."

"But now he is a dragon?"

Another sigh. "It was his choice, freely made. I made different choices."

Neither spoke for a time. Then the old man cleared his throat and asked, "What of that white smoke that affected you so strongly? Do you know what it was?"

The younger man shook his head and frowned. "Never heard of a gem doing such a thing. I've no idea what it is."

"That bothers you greatly." It was not a question.

The warrior nodded. "It does. Such things should not affect me. I have ... call them 'charms' for lack of a better word. They are supposed to protect me from such things."

"These charms of which you speak ..."

The young man laughed. "Not magic, learned sir, I assure you. Advanced learnings."

"Very advanced. More so than any learnings I have heard of."

The warrior smiled and shrugged.

That got an unhappy sigh from the old man. "Well, once a scholar always a scholar. Still, there are things that I can teach you despite your fancy learnings. Come."

The young man followed the old scholar, puzzled but intrigued.

"I was digging through the remains of my home and found some maps and old books that may be of use in your journey. You need more rest, in any event." He held up a hand to forestall any protests. "No, no, please humour an old scholar who has seen too many accidents. You heal quickly, but waiting until tomorrow would be best."

The warrior considered that. In truth, he was still feeling somewhat off, and that bothered him. His healing factors should have not only neutralized whatever that chemical was, but also brought him back to full strength by now. Waiting until tomorrow was out of the question, but another hour or two couldn't hurt. Besides, the old scholar might have some useful information.

Several minutes of brisk walking brought them to a small, burnt-out house. Off to one side was a rough lean-to made of partially-burned timbers, packed with various items from the ruined house. In a soft voice the warrior said, "I am truly sorry for this."

"The fault is not yours, young sir, but that of your former friend. You saved us from much worse by driving him off. Many of the buildings are ruined, 'tis true, but many of the contents are salvageable. The timbers will suffice to build sturdy, if somewhat cramped, living quarters. As is often the case, the morning makes the evils of the previous day not so dire."

As he spoke, he led the young man to the lean-to, and knelt to burrow within. "I placed some items close to hand for you, and ... ah, here it is." He pulled out a sturdy-looking staff, then with a snap of his wrist flung it towards the warrior who caught it easily. The force of the toss was surprising for one so old.

"Examine that, if you will, young sir," said the old man. "That was my own staff many years ago."

The warrior's hand fit easily around the shaft. It was a simple long length of wood with no decoration. He hefted it and found that it weighed rather more than he would have guessed. He gave an approving grunt, then the young man stepped back and gave it a one-handed twirl. "Good balance," he said. Then with rapid, precise motions he went through an increasingly complicated pattern of thrusts and parries, ending by standing at attention as the butt of the staff slammed down next to his right foot. The old man smiled with satisfaction—it was always a pleasure to watch skilled staff-play.

"You have some training, I see."

"My father insisted on it. Drilled me daily until his blows no longer hit me. Then he taught me the advanced moves."

"A brusque, but effective, technique. The university insisted that we learn the basics, and the knowledge served me well."

"It is a fine staff, learned sir. I'd hate to take it from you, given that it is unlikely that I'll ever pass by here again."

"Better to be lost in use than rot in storage. Not that it will rot for many decades. That's ironwood. Grows only in the South, and very difficult to work. Took me the better part of a year to shape it. My philosophy master suggested the project as a way for a hot-blooded youth to still the mind. It saved my skin on more than one occasion, and I hope it will aid you on your quest."

Turning back to the jumble he pawed around for a moment before pulling out a large chest, which bore scorch marks from the fire. "Ah, yes. You'll need this," he said as he opened the chest to reveal several bound volumes and several rolled-up scrolls.

"Maps and histories. Part of my studies at the University, and I updated the map over the years." He took one scroll and unrolled it, motioning his companion to join him.

"See ... we are here. The University is down there. See how our land juts into the ocean? And the shoals that surround us on all sides?"

"This map is very detailed," said the stranger as he knelt to view it. "Is this based on verified information or travellers' tales?"

"The University has several maps that have survived from the Golden Age. Those were quite detailed and have always proven to be correct, so far as they went. Anything north of here, however, becomes rather more vague very quickly."

"How so?"

"A week's journey to the north of here gets you to the mountains. All but impassible, they are ... as I can attest. I once climbed to the peak of the nearest one to see what was beyond. As bad as the climb was, what lay beyond was worse. In many of the valleys and to either side of the mountains were swamps."

"You have exceptional eyesight, Master Scholar."

The old man laughed. "Not really, but I do have a far-seeing device." He reached into the chest and carefully unwrapped a package, revealing a tube as long as his forearm. "You look in this end, and far scenes appear to be closer." He handed it to his companion, who took it carefully and used it as instructed.

"This is ... amazing." In truth he was very impressed with the level of technology the old man had achieved with minimal tools. The optics were not the best, of course, but offered a magnification factor of about six. He lowered it and carefully examined it. "The workmanship is masterful."

The old scholar shrugged. "Not really. Just a basic tube. Nothing fancy. I have seen some that are works of art."

The younger man shook his head. "Mere ornamentation.

This ..." he held up the tube, "is a product of skill and insight."

The old man was moved by the sincere compliment, and turned towards the chest to hide his embarrassment at the praise.

He cleared his throat and took a bound volume. "This explains some of the history of what little is known about what lies beyond the mountains. Aside from a few rumours and legends, there is a single documented expedition. During the Golden Age a king sent a regiment out to explore the lands beyond the mountains. One man returned, and not entirely whole or sane."

"You've mentioned a Golden Age before. What was it?"

The old man looked thoughtful. "How is it that you do not know of this?"

"My father kept me at training for most of my life. He had little patience for legends and rumours, preferring to deal with the here and now."

"And yet you help an old scholar?"

The young man grunted. "I learnt better after leaving to see the larger world."

"How did that sit with your father?"

"We no longer speak."

"Ah. I am sorry to hear that. One word of advice—don't put off speaking for too much longer. Fathers aren't around forever." A look of pained regret flashed across the old man's face, leaving sadness.

The stranger cleared his throat. "Tell me about this survivor."

"Ah, yes," said the old man, happy to focus on something else. "Well, as I said, the expedition was to explore the lands beyond the mountain. In those days there were legends of a monster--a demon of sorts--that periodically came to ravage the lands. It first appeared at the peak of the Golden Age ... a time of learning and wonders. There were great cities filled with people, and traders ensured that the wonders of each spread throughout the land. Then the plagues came and many died. Shortly after that the demon rose up and the plagues returned. Whole towns were destroyed. Some legends say it was the plague, and some say 'twas the demon who blasted them. Finally the plagues ended, and the survivors rebuilt. Generations passed without further incidents. Eventually, though, the demon returned and slaughtered many of the royal families. Chaos reigned for a time before order reasserted itself. That was centuries ago, of course. Much knowledge was lost or garbled in the re-telling."

"Pretty specific for a mere legend. These plagues ... how many people died?"

"Many. It is not known for sure. Some scholars at the University attempted a study of that ancient time. They estimated at least half the population was lost, probably more. That would explain the breakdown in the social structures."

"And the so-called demon?"

"Has never been seen since those times. But there is an oddity about it that might interest you." The old man took a scroll and unwound it. It proved to be a short one, with illustrations showing something with wings spewing what looked like fire at a burning village. Another drawing showed the winged creature blowing a cloud towards an intact town. "This is a copy of one of the few drawings of the demon made in the plague years. Keep that in mind while I tell you the story of the expedition." He placed the scroll, still unwound, off to one side. He then took up the bound volume, flipping through the pages with careful hands.

"Now, the survivor claimed they made it past the mountains after losing a quarter of their number. They came to a great lake. Beyond the great lake was a mountain of fire—obviously a volcano. Within the lake were large creatures, three or four times the size of their horses. At least one came ashore and slew many of their number before it was driven back into the lake, badly wounded. Another approached but was driven off with arrows and spears." He stopped flipping pages to point at a drawing of something coming out of the water onto the shore. It had an oversized head on a snake-like neck. The body was a stocky cylinder, with four legs and splayed feet that ended in long claws.

"Nasty-looking things," commented the stranger. "How accurate are these drawings?"

The old scholar shrugged. "Impossible to say. The survivor described the scene to artists who created what you see. It looks too unbalanced to be accurate, I think. Still, the general idea of something aquatic with formidable teeth and claws seems possible. Nothing like that has ever been found, but beyond the mountains anything is possible."

"Hmm. Was that the demon of legend?"

"Oh, no," said the old man, shaking his head. "Those were just guards ... or perhaps local pests." He flipped the page to show another drawing. "The demon came on wings, spewing fire upon them. Compare this drawing with the Golden Age drawing."

The warrior made a careful examination of the two illustrations. Both showed a generally cylindrical creature with one end tapering, much like a short, stout snake. The face shown on each was vaguely human, with two eyes and what looked to be tendrils spaced around it. The mouth was a gaping maw with no teeth showing. Each drawing had small wings coming off from about one-third down the length.

"Why is it that on the Golden Age drawing, the demon is shown spewing fire and something else? A wind?"

"No. That's an interesting point. The legends are careful to describe two different types of attack. One of fire and another of a fog or liquid that would coat the countryside."

"A poison?"

"That is unclear. However, some historians note that the areas sprayed with the fog became clear of the plague before any of the others. Perhaps a coincidence."

"Hmm. Those wings seem awfully small."

"You have a keen eye, sir knight. Yes, that is a point of some debate. All references of the demon mention, or show, small wings. In some quarters that is taken as a sign that dark magics were involved. As with your friend, the dragon."

"Excuse me? The winds produced by the dragon were strong enough to fan the fires most effectively."

"I'm not surprised that you would make that mistake, young sir." The old man was in full-on lecture mode now. "Scholars have long determined that wing size must grow faster than the size of a body. That is, larger birds have larger wings, proportionally, than do smaller birds. It is a deep mystery that few are aware of, but there it is."

"Which means?"

"What it means, young man, is that for the demon or your dragon to fly, something must be assisting their wings."

"Dark magic?"

The old man nodded, then grew thoughtful. "Or advanced learnings," he said in a sly tone.

"Hmm," the warrior responded as he examined the drawings of the demon with more care. His visage grew thoughtful.

"Do you see something else," asked the old scholar. "Or ... maybe you recognize another friend?"

The warrior shook his head. "Hard to tell," he said in a soft faraway voice. Then he took a deep breath and raised his head. "I need to go to this lake of yours."

"Now? You need to heal more than you have."

"I'll heal up along the way. This is important. I must destroy the gem. As for the demon ..." His voice trailed off for a moment before continuing. "I'll deal with that when I get there."

"And those lake creatures?"

"Them as well."

The old man sighed. "I wish you would tarry for a while longer. You need to heal, and ... I find that it is joy to discourse with such a keen mind as yours."

The warrior smiled kindly. "If I could, I would stay. But duty calls me to go."

The old scholar gave a heartfelt sigh. "As you say, duty calls. Very well. The staff is yours, of course. Do you wish to take the map or books?"

The warrior hesitated before answering. "No. My task is too dangerous to take along such valuable historical items. All I require is a knapsack to carry the gem, and my dagger. If you can spare it, I'd appreciate a water gourd and length of rope. In return you can have my armour in addition to everything else."

"What about food?"

"I can forage for that along the way. My father's training was most extensive."

Less than an hour later, the warrior was set to travel. The villagers had created a rough knapsack from some scraps of burlap and short lengths of rope. The only weapons he took were his dagger and the staff. After a lengthy series of goodbyes, he set off on his journey to the inland sea.

"Wait, sir knight," cried the old scholar. "What is your name and house that we may inform them of your great deed?"

The warrior smiled broadly. "I am no knight and belong to no house. But you can call me Bob." With that he set out on his quest.

CHAPTER TWO
Demons of the Lake

Bob strode away from the village at a steady pace. The emanations from the gem had diminished to a slight tingle which could be safely ignored for the time being. The staff swung from his right hand, thudding against the ground with every other step. His spirits brightened the further he got from the village. The air was fresh and contained only the scents of untouched wilderness. The sun was warm upon him. Life was good.

After a couple of hours he took a break. The road had become a trail, which in turn had become a vague path. Taking a small sip of water, he surveyed the area. Nothing aside from the usual wildlife could be seen or detected by his other senses. Recalling the map, he modified his route slightly and used a distant mountain peak as a reference. He settled his load carefully, then began a ground-eating lope. He kept this up knowing that if anyone happened to see him it would be accepted as normal for a man in good condition. Once past human habitation he could increase the pace to something faster.

After several hours of running, the sun was beginning to set. His breathing was still even and unlaboured. There was a copse of trees up ahead next to a stream, a good place to rest and check his bearings. Once there he dropped his pack on the ground and approached the stream. It was quite dark by now, as only a mountain area can get. That didn't impede his progress, as he could adjust his vision to use the starlight and infrared.

Bob walked with care along the bank of the stream, not wanting to chance a fall or twisted limb. Within a few minutes he caught a couple of fish and ate them raw, bones and all. He finished up by washing up and drinking deeply from the stream. The sketchy meal completed, he gathered up the pack and resumed his journey.

This time he increased his speed to a fast lope, the fastest he felt was safe over unfamiliar rough territory. He used his staff as a third leg to assist in keeping his balance and to vault over the large rocks that were becoming more prevalent. His breathing was still even and easy, and he was feeling rather good about life. Still, after a few hours of this he felt much weaker than he should have. His breathing became laboured and he was forced to halt when he began to stumble. Something was definitely not right—he should have been able to maintain that pace for at least another day without any problems.

As he stood resting, he felt sweat pop from his brow as a wave of dizziness came over him. Bob clamped his eyes shut and took several deep cleansing breaths. That helped, but he still felt a bit weak. Looking around he saw some large boulders nearby, one several times his height. He walked over to it and clambered to the top taking care to keep low. He surveyed the area, but saw nothing that would be dangerous, not even local predators. Slipping back to the ground, he squatted down and shrugged off his pack, kicking it a body-length away. The gem's emanations hadn't gotten stronger but had attained an annoying level of irritation. In fact, despite his strange tiredness he felt jumpy and irritable.

Forcing himself into a meditative state, he queried his

healing factors. They told him little that he hadn't already noticed except that they saw no issues to be addressed. That meant they did not attribute his state to any foreign influence. Which was strange since there was the influence of the nearby gem, not to mention the mysterious white smoke from yesterday. The latter had knocked him out—a potent strangeness in and of itself—then left him still somewhat weak after he woke up. Whatever the substance was, combined with the gem it made for a powerful influencing agent.

Or did it? Was it traces of the substances in his body that were still affecting him, or was it the absence of it after being exposed? That was an interesting, if disturbing, thought. First of all, his healing factors should have neutralized it within seconds or minutes after exposure, not allowed him to be knocked out for hours. Secondly, substances that would cause withdrawal symptoms to his kind were very rare. All the known ones could be dealt with by his healing factors, which meant this was something new and nasty.

Which brought to mind Freddy, who'd been exposed to the euphoric effects for some time. That thought caused Bob to curse his own carelessness—he should have been paying more attention to attacks from the sky. Freddy was injured and angry; not a good combination for one of his size and powers. On the other hand, withdrawal symptoms typically increased with exposure, so Freddy probably wouldn't be at peak fighting form for some time.

His cogitations, and the realization that this was now a combat mission, had steadied Bob's nerves to some extent. He took out the small amount of cheese and bread the villagers had gifted him with and munched on them thoughtfully. He was no medical specialist, but his training included some mention of obscure conditions such as withdrawal. He recalled that severe cases would include physical pain and impairment of bodily functions. Lesser cases would impair higher-level functions, to a greater or lesser extent. The only cure was time or a session with trained medical personnel.

Bob sighed. Perhaps he should have paid more attention during the medical training. Of course, that would have taken time away from the training his father had been giving him. Much of Bob's knowledge of medical matters came as a result of learning to heal himself after his father's training sessions. One of the hardest lessons to learn was that sometimes healing takes time. Not that one necessarily has the time to do it, so best to make use of what little time one has. Another important lesson learnt the hard way. So he finished the food, drank the last of his water, and relaxed as much as his jangling nerves allowed him.

By the time the first traces of sunrise appeared, Bob felt much better. He stood up, took a deep breath, and started out at an easy lope towards his target mountain. The air was cool, but not chilly, and felt most refreshing. Less than an hour he came to a stream and spent a few minutes catching and eating several fish. He also took the opportunity to drink deeply and fill his water gourd. With his nutritional needs taken care of, Bob started out at a faster lope to make up for the time spent resting during the night. He had to moderate the pace at times in deference to the increasingly rocky conditions, but was still making far better time on foot than a man on a horse could.

By nightfall, though, he was beginning to puff with the effort of running, so he stopped when he came across another of the numerous streams that were appearing. He ate his fill of fish, and topped it off with a large helping of leaves. His nerves weren't as jangly as they'd been the previous night, which was encouraging. Still, he had hoped for a faster recovery. To pass the time, he tried focusing on the route ahead, but his vision had problems focusing at long distances in the low light. That was a good test that verified the degradation of the higher-level functions. It also meant that for the time being he couldn't apport. Not that his apporting skills were very good, but he hated having limited options. Especially when there was a pissed-off dragon around.

His equilibrium returned after a couple hours of rest, which he took to be a good sign. His night vision was almost back to normal, so he decided to carry on at a walking pace until sunup. He paused only long enough to catch and eat a few fish before heading out.

Dawn found him at the base of his target mountain. Taking a long, careful look around at the highest magnification his eyesight allowed, he decided to take the climb at some speed. Pausing to take several deep breaths as he surveyed his path, he charged forward at increasing speed. He jump-bounced off smaller rocks, used his staff to vault over larger ones, and scrambled around anything taller. As his training demanded, his path was a random zigzag to confuse potential snipers. He also took advantage of the larger rocks to do a controlled tumble that allowed him to scan the sky for potential hostiles.

After a non-stop couple of hours of effort, Bob reached the top of the mountain. He was breathing a bit heavily from the exertion, but not as badly as before. He paused at the top, lying flat to present the smallest target, and examined the route in front of him. The mountain descended into a series of small, scrubby trees—not enough to be considered a forest or even a copse. The valley itself was a fetid swamp. Bob snorted in disgust. It wasn't that travelling through swamps wasn't something he hadn't trained for, but it wasn't his favourite thing to do.

He stared at the peak of the next mountain, attempting to view the scene to the point of synchronicity. The necessary quantum entanglement teetered on the verge of completion for nearly a minute before he gave it up. That failure was more than a little discouraging. It meant that not only were the withdrawal effects still active, but he'd have to walk through the swamp. He tried to brighten his spirits by reminding himself that sometimes tasty creatures inhabited swamps. Not often, but sometimes. It turned out that this was not one of those times. The creatures inhabiting this particular swamp were voracious, nasty, and not worth eating.

Bob sloshed his way through the swamp and was in a foul humour by the time he reached dry land. He decided to deal with his sodden clothing before making the climb up the mountain, so he stripped and began wringing the water out as best he could. This proved to be a mistake, as a large fanged creature took the opportunity to lunge out of the water at him. Bob sighed. He'd had the impression that something was stalking him but had hoped that it would give up once he reached dry land. He rolled the staff with his foot and flipped it up into his hand just before the creature reached him. A quick twist of his body, first one way then the other, slapped the staff across the snout of the creature resulting in a loud *crack* each time. It dropped at his feet, puzzled at the refusal of its prey to cooperate. The creature gave its head a shake then lunged forward. This time it was met with the base of a staff driving its snout into the ground.

"Bad predator," said Bob in a stern voice. The creature hissed and lunged again. Bob slid the staff under the creature's body and heaved, sending it sailing backwards into the water. After hitting with a large splash, the creature righted itself and glared at the prey that refused to accept its position in the grand scheme of things. Then it exhaled strongly enough to raise a plume of water as it huffed away into the swamp.

"I hate swamps," Bob muttered as he dressed in the still-damp clothes. "The stupidest predators, the ickiest parasites ..." he paused to flick off several dead string-like creatures dangling from his body, "... and nothing worth eating." The latter was not strictly true, as his digestive system could process almost anything organic. Still, some things were more enjoyable to eat than others.

After dressing he turned and trotted up the slope. He passed through the typical scrubby shrubs and trees, and breathed a sigh of relief when he got back to rocky terrain. The air was cleaner, smelled better, and the sun felt warm enough to lift his spirits. It didn't take him very long to reach the top, and he crawled the last distance so as to not stand out against the skyline. Peering around a large rock, he surveyed the route ahead with distaste. Once again the valley held a dank-looking swamp.

Hoping for the best, Bob concentrated on the next peak beyond the swamp. To his delight he felt the stirrings of a synchronistic pairing. Exerting extra effort, he achieved the required depth of simularity, took a deep breath, and apported. His effort was a little rough, and he ended up tumbling when he arrived at the destination. He managed to control the tumble within a couple of rolls, and lay on his back grinning. It was only by exerting his full self-control that he stopped himself from whooping with joy, and he laid there for a few seconds savouring his triumph.

He rolled over onto his stomach and wiggled up to the top, once again staying low. Looking back the way he had come revealed no surprises, and neither did the way ahead of him. He tried to focus on the next peak, but was neither surprised nor disappointed when he failed to achieve a synchronistic pairing. The degradation of the withdrawal was nearly cleared up, and it wasn't as if his apporting skills had ever been very good. He turned and headed down the slope to the next swamp at a speed that was higher than his father would have considered wise. Especially since Bob indulged in his favourite game of leaping, tumbling, and bouncing off obstacles in his path. He was even looking forward to the meagre food offerings of the swamp.

He managed to get across without incident— although several of the predators he encountered would remember the incident with no satisfaction and some pain. One of them would never remember anything ever again, as it ended up being a meal. After wringing out his clothes, he clambered up the slope to the top of the current mountain.

By the time he got to the top his apporting ability was back to operational levels, and he arrived at the next peak in short order. This time his arrival was rather more controlled, resulting only in some swaying on his feet until he caught his balance. This was close enough to normal that he was tempted to declare himself fully recovered. The only thing that tempered that diagnosis was the unexpected level of fatigue he felt. Rather than push things too hard, he decided to descend to the level of the next layer of scrub trees and spend the night there.

After putting a layer of branches and leaves over the rocky ground for bedding, he returned to the swamp to catch a meal. The hunt took only a few minutes, and he carried the catch back to his crude nest to devour it raw. He would have preferred to cook it to improve the taste, but didn't want to draw unwanted attention to himself. The stories of the last expedition through here had spoken of enough nasty creatures that he would rather take some care, even if those creatures were some distance away. Recalling the map, and accounting for the crudity of it plus the stories, he figured he was about half way to the inland sea or whatever it was. If his recovery continued at its current rate, he figured to reach it in a day or two.

* * *

It ended up taking the better part of two full days, with his rate of apporting increasing each day until it was finally back to normal. The sun was setting as he lay on the peak of the last mountain, viewing the expanse of water ahead of him. The lake, or inland sea, stretched as far as he could see. To either side of his location were swamps, and his lips curled at the thought of crossing those. Across the water he could just make out a hint of mist-shrouded land in some areas. Whether those were the far shoreline or islands he could not say. Perhaps the better light of the morning would make it more obvious. In any event, the distance and mist prevented seeing well enough to apport.

Two important things came out of his examination. First, he saw no signs of the water monsters that had bedevilled that early expedition. Secondly, now that night had fallen he could see a distinct red tinge that indicated a large fire—hopefully the volcano he sought.

Given the proximity to the alleged dangerous creatures Bob decided to slip back towards the valley for the night. That would eliminate any chance of being seen on the mountain skyline, and give him access to food and water. Tomorrow promised to be a busy day and he wanted to be fully recharged. He also needed to figure out a good way to reach the other side of the lake. He decided to shelve that problem until after he fed.

Just before dawn, he crawled back to the top of the peak and carefully peered at the lake. His head was now covered with leaves and mud so that only his eyes were exposed—the better to minimize his infrared signature and blend in with the ground. He watched for a time but only saw a hint of ripples. It was unclear if they were the result of a creature moving or the wind. Several times a fish-like creature jumped out of the water but it didn't appear to be trying to escape a predator. It was all nicely boring. The only oddity was the lack of birds. In his experience all worlds had birds or something equivalent in their ecosystems. Now that he thought of it, there seemed to be a dearth of creatures outside of the swamps. That was very odd.

Speaking of odd things, he hadn't seen any trace of Freddy around. Enhancing the infrared sensors of his eyesight, he took a good look around but saw nothing untoward. The fireglow on the horizon stood out even more strongly, and Bob was convinced that it was the volcano. Shaking his head to reset his eyesight, he looked away from the brightness of the volcano and examined the lake but found no heat signatures. It was possible that Freddy had left the planet but Bob thought that unlikely. Even as a child Freddy was not one to let a real or imagined slight pass by without reprisal, and age hadn't mellowed his outlook in the slightest. The odds were that he was still around, somewhere.

Bob pondered the question of Freddy some more. There was a portal near the tip of the south coast, which was the only way to and from this world. Freddy's flight speed, even if diminished by withdrawal symptoms, would allow him to complete a thorough aerial search between the village and the portal by about now. Not finding Bob, what would he do? Head back to village and search there, and then head to the mountains. There really was nowhere else to go. Which meant that Freddy might be flying in any time now, if he weren't here already.

Giving his head a shake to reset his vision, Bob carefully scanned the sky again. There were no heat signatures, which meant that Freddy was either not yet here or had gone to ground. Given the withdrawal he must be enduring, the latter was likely. Even so it would be prudent to expect a visit from him at any time. Evading him would be difficult, given that the dragon aspect he had assumed typically had a good suite of battle-quality sensors. The only bright spot was that the fire-breath weapon, although impressive, precluded the inclusion of more effective weapons. Bob sighed—that was Freddy, favouring flash over effectiveness. Still, a dragon aspect was large and powerful even without the addition of weapons. Not to mention that the levitation-enhancing flight modules gave him a distinct advantage.

Bob gave some thought to his options if a confrontation could not be avoided. He was beginning to regret leaving behind his armour, especially the gauntlets. Those had added some heft to his punches and offered protection for his hands. On the other hand, he had a good staff and the experience to use it to best effect. Freddy's aerial advantage could be partially negated by damaging his wings, which were used as control surfaces. Bob smiled. As children, Freddy had always enjoyed using his larger size to knock Bob around—something that had found favour with Bob's older brother. Freddy still seemed to enjoy being a bully, but he'd find that Bob was no longer as defenceless as he'd once been.

Dawn came later to the flat land of the lake than to the mountain peaks. The gradual brightening gave Bob a good chance to note how the local ecosystem reacted to the coming of daylight and to view the lake itself in varying light. Once again, he noted the absence of birds—they would normally begin singing as the sun rose. On the plus side, he saw a few small animals scurrying about the water's edge. Not many, but it made the ecosystem seem less barren.

The sun had just risen above the horizon when Bob decided to head to the water's edge. There had been no sign of large aquatic predators of any sort, so perhaps the creatures mentioned in the history were dead or gone. Given the battle, either was a possibility. At any rate, he'd decided on a plan of action. There were some decent-sized logs on the beach, and those combined with his rope and vines from the swamp could be used to make a small raft. Given that he'd be paddling, he wanted something as light as possible.

It took the morning to finish, but he managed to make a suitable craft. It wasn't much wider than his own broad shoulders, and floated rather lower in the water than he would have liked, but it would do. Using his knife he managed to slice slabs off a log to make two paddles. The staff he reserved for poling in the shallows.

Once finished with that, Bob took a brief rest to catch and eat some food. He managed to take down some of the small land animals by throwing stones. It was an effective technique, as he could throw stones at just under subsonic speeds, making them silent but deadly weapons. As expected they turned out to be small mammals, and much tastier than the creatures of the swamps. He washed them down with some seaweed from the lake. His healing factors were low on various trace minerals and the seaweed served to fulfil those requirements.

With preparations completed, it was time to go. Bob took a look around to establish landmarks. He couldn't see the far shore from the surface, and wanted to have a backup check for his normally unerring sense of direction. His training and experience had drilled that into him.

He pushed off from shore, knelt on his raft, and began paddling. Slowly at first to get a feel for his craft, he gradually increased the rate and strength of his strokes. He found the physical effort required to be an enjoyable change from all the walking he'd been doing. Not so much so that he forgot to scan the sky and water for dangers—he'd not forgotten that he was being hunted.

Bob made good time and arrived at his destination just before dark. It turned out to be an island of moderate size covered with small shrubs. Bob pulled the raft ashore and hid it in the underbrush. As enjoyable as the paddling had been, he hadn't enjoyed being so exposed for hours at a time. The Precepts of Survival taught the value of having as many options for escape as possible. Also, the night would show off his heat signature to anything—or anyone—sensitive to such things. All in all, it was probably prudent to spend the night on the island. If nothing else, it would make it easier to survey what lay ahead.

After hiding the raft, he kept the pack and the staff as he explored the area. Once again he detected no birds and little in the way of wildlife aside from some small rodents. They were too small to make a proper meal, so he munched on berries that he stripped off the bushes as he walked. Few were ripe, but his digestive system was more than capable of processing them.

He arrived at the far side of island and looked around. The topography was rather flat, with only a few larger rocks to gain height advantage. However, climbing those would leave him seriously exposed, so he contented himself with peeking above the scrub brush. He was rewarded with the sight of the far shore that he was aiming for, and estimated it to be about two or three hours away by raft. It was too far away to pick out details, given the mist and darkness, but it looked very rocky along the entire length that he could see. That could make landing a bit of a challenge, but that was a worry for tomorrow.

Bob finished his cautious circumnavigation of the island and returned to where he had hidden the raft. He debated whether to leave it here or paddle to the far side. On the one hand he wanted to keep an eye on his destination to see if anything untoward awaited him. On the other hand he needed keep an eye out for anyone following him. In the end he compromised. Checking to make sure that the raft was secure for the night, he went to a point on the island's shore where he could see both locations. Like most compromises it didn't offer the best view of either, but would be good enough. Bob smiled at the remembrance of his father's views on "good enough". The smile became something grimmer at the memory of the pain that followed the enforcing of those views.

To keep his mind off the past, Bob listened to the rhythms of the waves on the shore. It was a complex pattern, modulated by the winds, the far shore, the near shore, and the several other small islands he could see in the distance. Patterns were important and understanding them could be the difference between life and death. So said the Precepts of Survival, and Bob's own experiences tended to agree with that assessment. So he sat and listened as he scanned the sky and horizon. Within a couple of hours the patterns of the waves began to make sense, and Bob relaxed enough to pay more attention to his destination. The glow of the volcano was a beacon on the horizon, and Bob amused himself by trying to estimate its distance.

His deliberations were interrupted by a change in the pattern of the waves. Right away Bob focused his attention on the lake. The change was slight, both in frequency and intensity, which meant that the cause was probably some distance away. He slowly swung his head back and forth, attempting to get an idea of the source of the disturbance. However, things soon returned to normal and stayed that way for the rest of the night.

Bob was mildly concerned, but not too much so. Transient phenomena were always difficult to interpret. Whatever this was seemed to have occurred some distance away in the direction of one of the distant islands. It could have been caused by any number of things. Perhaps an animal larger than the small mammals he had seen had entered or left the water. Perhaps there was a slight, localized shift in the wind. Or perhaps—just perhaps—something large and stealthy had taken a quick peek before returning underwater.

With no obvious signs of threat, he allowed himself to relax a bit. Tomorrow promised to be an interesting day.

* * *

Dawn came and Bob waited until the sun was just above the horizon before setting off again. He had remained motionless during the night but there were no further oddities. The sunlight glancing off the water gave him a good chance to catch anything lurking at the surface, but nothing was visible. There was a heavy morning mist along the near shore, making an examination of possible landing areas—much less apporting-- impossible.

Taking care to be silent he put the raft into the water and continued his trek to the near shore. He kept the paddling strong but quiet, trying to time it with the pattern of the waves. That slowed him a little, and it took nearly four hours to reach the shore. Lying flat on the raft, he surveyed the shore with care. The beach was rocky and narrow. There were large boulders jutting out of the water and he could see swirls indicating rocks just below the surface. Laying the paddles on the raft, he used the staff to pole his way to shore taking care to minimize any noise that he made.

The raft nosed its way onto the rocky beach, making a soft rasping sound as it slid on the pebbles. Bob stepped off into the water then pulled it as far onto the beach as he could. To his left rose a sheer cliff that looked like it would be a difficult climb. To the right ran a narrow beach, widening some distance further along. He had begun walking towards the wider beach when an unexpected shift in the wind, followed by a soft lapping of waves, caused him to turn around. A large head with a mouth full of long, sharp teeth was making a soundless lunge at him.

Bob flipped up the staff to catch the head under its chin and, using the creature's momentum against it, directed the head against the cliff face. The impact resulted in a wet-sounding *thud* that brought a pained whine out of the creature. The head was attached to a long serpentine neck, and both flopped to the ground as the creature moaned in pain. Bob quickly scanned the water, and saw a v-shaped wave heading towards him. He began running towards the wider beach area in hopes that it would offer a way further inland and away from these creatures.

The ground was rocky but firm, allowing him to trot at a

reasonable speed. A hiss behind him suggested that his speed might not be fast enough, so he concentrated on looking ahead for a solid patch of ground. A waft of rank breath warned him of another attack, so he put on a burst of speed for a couple of steps then launched himself up onto the vertical cliff face. He continued running along the cliff, using his momentum and the staff to keep his path horizontal. A large head flashed alongside him, just beneath his chest. Bob skidded to a halt, and as he dropped he used his fist as a hammer against the creature's head, causing its face to hit the ground. As the creature skidded to an abrupt stop, Bob landed just ahead of the jaws and continued running. Despite the predicament he found himself grinning—this was all rather fun. Well, so long as those creatures didn't catch him, of course.

The sound of wet flesh slapping together followed by angry growls hinted at a collision between the two creatures. Bob chanced a quick look backwards before snapping his head forward again. The creatures had, indeed, collided. What's more, the lake bottom was becoming shallower, which would force the creatures to run after him rather than swim. On the bad side, it sounded like the creatures were back on the hunt. A quick look back confirmed this, and allowed him a better look at their bodies. The necks were attached to barrel-shaped bodies about twice his height in length and as wide as he was tall. They had broad, powerful-looking flippers with large claws. The creatures might be water-based, but they could run well enough on land it would seem. Escaping them could be tricky.

Up ahead the beach was widening out as the water became shallower, but was still rocky. The cliff face offered no obvious or fast way up. There was, however, a grouping of large boulders overlapping the beach and shore up ahead. Most were about his height, and some much taller. A plan began forming, but was interrupted by the sounds of two sets of powerful flippers slapping water and stones racing after him.

Bob angled his path towards the middle of the array of boulders, arriving just as the sound of flippers became close. The first boulder was slightly shorter than he was, and he leapt up landing on his left foot. Pushing off from there he hopped up onto a slightly taller boulder, then onto the tallest one. He used his momentum to leap straight up, spun around, and brought his staff down on the head of the creature directly behind him. The creature's head slammed against a boulder with a wet *crunch* that caused Bob to wince at the sound. The creature whined in pain as it slid to the ground and lay there gasping for breath.

Scrambling to the top, Bob crouched in a position that offered him a means to dodge in any required direction. The one creature was still flat on the ground below him. Soft, wet sounds coming from his left indicated the other was circling around. Bob grinned and moved silently to his right, quickly enough that he caught up to the tail end of the creature as it stalked him. A wound at the top of the head indicated that it had been the first attacker. The creature stopped, and its posture indicated that it was moving its head along the surface of the boulder, edging its way to the top. Bob was impressed by the cleverness.

Alas for the creature, Bob had clever tactics of his own. By the time the creature's head had reached the top, it was met by Bob's staff slamming down on its snout. Uttering an angry hiss, it reared up and attempted to strike again. This time it was met by a flurry of blows from the staff to either side of its snout. The creature backed away huffing and snorting. A scraping sound alerted Bob to an attack by its partner, and he spun around to see the other head bearing down on him. He was out of position to use the staff, so he brought his right leg around and delivered a roundhouse kick to the beast's head. The creature reared up and took several steps back to regain its balance. It cast a baleful glare at Bob through narrowed eyes as it shook its head slightly.

"No," said Bob in stern voice. The creature made to move towards him, so Bob repeated the command, but this time waggling the index finger of his right hand in a meaningful fashion. A sound from the other side caused Bob to glance there, where the other beast was beginning to move towards him. "Sit," Bob commanded as he pointed a finger. He raised the finger vertically then brought it down slowly until it pointed at the second creature. "Sit," he repeated in a stern voice. This time he added a layer of infrasonics to his voice. To his surprise and relief the creature lowered its body until its stomach rested on the ground. Turning around, he repeated performance with the other creature, who behaved in the same manner. The two of them began to move slowly towards each other.

"Bad," he added. "You have been very bad doggies." They stopped in their movement, and actually looked somewhat guilty. Time to try something else, Bob reasoned. "Back. Go back into the lake." He made shoo-ing motions with his free hand, holding the staff motionless in the other. "Go on," he urged. "That's a good doggie. Go on." Their movements were tentative at first, but at Bob's continued glaring and shoo-ing motions they slid back into the water and moved slowly away. He watched them as their wake showed them moving some distance from shore and eventually submerging.

"That was interesting," he murmured.

He took the opportunity to look around from the vantage point the boulder offered. The shoreline curved away from him but looked much the same as where he had come. There was a rocky beach, of varying width, edged by a steep cliff reaching up at least a dozen body-lengths or more. He couldn't get a clear look at the top, so apporting was ruled out. The beach offered little or no protection, so continuing along it would be very risky. Taking a careful look to ensure that the local wildlife wasn't trying to sneak back, he clambered down the boulder, walked to the cliff, and began climbing.

The first couple of body-lengths went easily enough, but soon became more challenging. All the more so given the requirement to keep glancing behind at the lake to keep watch for playful predators. They were actually kind of cute, and he felt a bit sorry for having to rough them up. Still, they had been trying to hunt him, so he had used the minimum necessary force. The Precepts of Survival strongly encouraged the use of minimal force. For one thing, it kept open the possibility of a more positive relationship. For another, it masked one's full capabilities.

As he climbed, Bob was tempted to toss the staff aside, given that it made the climbing more difficult. However, it had been a gift and as such deserved better consideration. Also, Bob liked the feel of it. So he kept it despite the problems it presented, and eventually made it to the top and clambered over. He lay flat as he wormed away from the edge to get away from the weathered portions. That done, he got his feet under him and squatted to minimize his profile as he looked around. There were fern-like plants covering the ground all around him, a scattering of shrubs, and a few trees interspersed here and there. Real trees, not the scrubby specimens he'd seen in the mountains. He increased the sensitivity of his hearing to get a feel for the rhythm of the ecosystem. He'd heard no changes in response to his passing, nor any indications of birds. He had detected the scurrying of small creatures in the underbrush and the sounds of larger things, some of which were following the small things. There were a few different types of insects, but no clouds of blood-suckers. That was an odd, if welcome, development—his bodily defences would kill them as they bit, but not keep them away.

Resetting his senses to their normal levels he stood up and

carefully made his way along, following the edge of the cliff. The ground rose steeply to some indeterminate height and he wanted a better look at the perimeter of the shore. He walked at a careful pace for nearly an hour and found nothing of note. The shoreline was much as he'd already seen, as was the cliff. That was enough of that, so he decided to head up to see what he could find. As before, he walked at a steady pace being careful to minimize the sound of his passing. There was none of the leaping and jumping he'd indulged in while in the swamps or mountains on the other shore.

Night was falling so he tweaked his vision to low-light mode and kept moving. The local sounds changed somewhat as night approached, but not as much as he would have expected. Now and again some of the local animals would dash in front of him, not realizing that he was there. After this happened a few times he clubbed one with the staff and after examining it, ate it raw. That sat so well that he clubbed and ate another couple, washing them down with the water in his gourd. He decided to drink the entire contents of the gourd to minimize the sounds a partially-filled one would make. Given the foliage around, he expected to find a stream sooner or later.

It was local midnight by the time he got to what appeared to be the top. Kneeling alongside a tree he surveyed the area around and beyond. Locally, the only change was the increased density of trees of varying types. The night sounds indicated that the local small fauna was more plentiful. Off on the horizon was a glow from the volcano. It was brighter now, and Bob judged to be perhaps a day or two's march away. Closer if he apported, of course, but he was beginning to wonder where Freddy was. It might be prudent to minimize the use of the alternate energies, as they could be sensed.

Then there was the problem of the legendary demon. It

might be nothing but a storyteller's imagination turned meme, or it might be based on something rather more substantial. There were plenty of dangers and horrors scattered amongst the stars, as Bob's people had learned to their immense sorrow. Then again, some of those horrors were his own people.

To that end, Bob had kept his own senses attuned to any strangeness, either of natural or artificial sources. He decided to spend the night on the top of the ridge, as there was lots of cover and it gave him a good view of the land, sea, and air. On the water, he thought he detected a faint v-wake or two travelling along the coast. He still felt a small pang of regret at having to harm such lovely creatures, despite their predatory nature. That thought brought a twinge as he recalled how his father had tried very hard to eliminate that sense of empathy from his youngest son, but without much success despite the increasingly severe punishments inflicted.

That sense of victory brought a small, tight smile to his face. Then memories of a time when that empathy had been lost on a planet of eternal war caused the smile to be replaced by a chill that filled his soul. It had been a bad time—a time of horror and madness—that he'd tried very hard to forget. It was with some difficulty that he stilled his shaking limbs and controlled his breathing. His clothing was soaked with sweat, but he let the night breezes dry it. His head dropped onto his arms and he let the tears flow, careful not to make any sound. That part of his training had been learnt well.

Morning found him in the same position except staring out at the lake. Nothing untoward had happened during the night so he got up, brushed off the dew, and headed out in the direction of the volcano. He'd put away the self-pity that had threatened to consume him, and was fully alert and focused on the task at hand. It had taken him many years to learn how to bounce back so quickly.

As the sun rose, so did the temperature. It wasn't hot and muggy like the southern lands could get, but pleasantly warm. Once again he moved as quickly as a silent passage allowed. As expected, he came across several streams and used the opportunity to drink his fill. He decided not to bother to fill his gourd, both to lighten his load and to help maintain silence. Just before nightfall he came to another ridge and decided to camp there for the night. There was a stream nearby, with fish, so he caught and ate several of them. His normal appetite and good spirits had returned during the day's march.

The volcano's light was noticeably nearer, which also improved Bob's mood. The emanations from the encased gem were beginning to annoy him, like an itch that refused to go away. It also heightened his conviction that the decision to destroy the gem on this world, rather than off-world, had been the correct one. There was something strange going on here. Mysteries to be investigated. The human population isolated on a single continent, the series of plagues, the sparse ecosystem ... all very strange. Then to top it off, his brother's interest in this world as evidenced by Freddy's enforcer nonsense. Oh, and the demon of legend. It wouldn't do to forget that. The first task, though, was to destroy the gem. Not only was it an abomination, destroying it would embarrass his brother. Not a minor consideration these days.

Night came and went with nothing of interest occurring, not even hints of activity on the lake. That made Bob sigh, but wasn't unexpected. For breakfast he caught and ate a couple of fish before resuming his trek.

Towards the end of the day he turned a corner and caught his first glimpse of the volcano itself. There was a shallow valley between him and the base of the volcano, which was perhaps half a day's hiking away. The volcano cone was dark in colour, strewn with boulders and lava tubes. It was semi-active, which Bob had already known, and he could feel the heat from it even from this distance. The most striking characteristic was a large torus-shaped cloud which slowly rotated above the cone. The base of the cloud glowed a bright orange—that must be what he'd been seeing at a distance. All in all, it was an impressive sight.

The big question was, should he continue on or wait until morning? As he was idly contemplating the conundrum, it hit him—what was that cloud doing there? It had been there for all the time he'd been able to see the volcano, and had been mentioned in the accounts of that ancient expedition. No natural cloud formation would do that. Which begged the questions of "who" and "why", and those could only be answered by closer examination. Onward, ever onward, it was then.

On the plus side, the warmth of the volcano would help to mask his infrared signature as he climbed. On the negative side, it'd help to hide the heat signatures of any hostiles. Those were the sorts of odds that Bob was fine with, so off he trotted towards the volcano.

The trip to the base of the volcano was uneventful, and he began his climb upward. It was a straightforward hike, for the most part, with only a few detours to go around lava tubes and large boulders. He was tempted to use the opportunity to clamber over them, but decided that discretion was the better option. The higher he went, the hotter the ground became until he began to feel the heat through his boots. It wasn't enough to cause concern, but was indicative of the active nature of the volcano.

When he achieved the summit of the cone he surveyed the inside. There was a thick crust some distance down, with pockets of liquid magma bubbling up. The heat was very intense from those areas. Bob looked up at the cloud torus. There was something strange about it, some strange emanation of energies. He focused on it and became suddenly dizzy. Squatting to regain his balance, he again focused on the cloud trying to discern what it was. The patterns of energy he could sense from it were tantalizingly familiar, yet not quite recognizable.

Sudden realization caused him to blurt out loud, "Oh, Dad. Really? Is this one of yours?"

The more he examined it, the more he was convinced that his conclusion was correct. The rotating cloud was one of his father's private portals, using the volcano as an energy source. On the one hand, it made sense. The energy of the semi-active volcano would be sufficient to maintain the cloud used to mask the portal. Using the volcano as an energy source instead of something more high-tech meant that it would be very hard to detect, which was very much in keeping with his father's view of things. Still, using it without dying in the attempt would be a severe test of control and ability—also in keeping with his father's view of things. The only way to use it would be to drop into the centre of the torus from the correct height—there would be a maximum height for activation of the portal—and set the coordinates before dropping below the activated doorway. Anyone arriving at the planet would be shot upward, and would have to be capable of apporting or flying within a few seconds.

Bob stood admiring the workmanship—if not the demands on the operator—of the portal for several minutes. Then he took a deep breath and shrugged off his pack. Opening it up, he took out the encased gem and threw it into one of the pockets of liquid magma. When it hit he felt the emanations from it terminate, and he let out a deep breath of relief. That was one problem solved, once and for all.

The next question was why his father would have a private portal on this planet. In and of itself, that wasn't much of an issue. Private portals weren't unusual, just not overly common these days. His father, though, was a portal engineer—something rather rare—and this could be something he had done for amusement. After thinking about it for a minute, Bob decided that it would be safe enough to do a low-level query of the system.

He took a deep breath, hardened his defences, and issued a query at the cloud. The mechanism issued a standard identity challenge, and Bob responded with his identification signature. The system accepted that, then demanded proof of family affiliation. Bob smiled—that was standard for a private portal—and allowed the system to do a deeper scan of him. Once his identification was accepted, he was given access to the interface. That allowed him to check what features had been implemented, and in fact do anything short of actually transiting out.

Bob checked out the system with great interest. His father had given him some training in portal engineering and instilled an appreciation for the subtleties involved. The regular public portals allowed anyone of Bob's people through, of course, but with strict security measures to ensure that hostile forces couldn't make use of them. That had been a lesson hard-learned during the Great Wars.

The public portals offered a number of services to travellers, including local histories and sociologies, samples of local identification and currencies, and the leaving of messages. The messaging features were as important as the travel functions, allowing messages to be left for specific people or the general public. Messages or physical items could also be sent to specific individuals on specific planets via the dawn boat system. All in all, the public portals allowed people to keep in touch over long distances and times.

Private portals were something else again. The basic ones simply allowed movement from place to place. The same security measures as used in the public portals were used, of course. Beyond that, it was up to the designer. In this case, it was a basic system with a messaging function tied only to the other private portals of his family. However, when Bob tried to check the usage logs he found access to them restricted. Not entirely unexpected, but not something his father normally did for his private portals. Which meant that this was something more than a test system. Another mystery. However, at the very least it meant that he could use this to exit the planet, and keep the destination off the books. A use of private portals that he'd learnt to appreciate.

There was nothing more to be learnt here, so he terminated the connection with the portal. His current location offered a good view of the surrounding area, so he hiked around to the opposite side of the cone. Once there he sat on the ground and surveyed the area below him. It turned out to be similar in fauna, but somewhat different in terrain. The biggest difference was that the cone's base became a good-sized flat area, one side of which offered a gentle slope down to the water. He could see some shimmering that would indicate streams. The real shock was when he saw what looked like areas of cultivated fields, and off to one side a large crude shelter. The seemingly-cultivated areas weren't large, certainly not large enough to serve as a primary food source for more than one or two people at most. That made him aware of his exposed position, so he moved down the cone to an area where a collection of boulders formed a good hiding spot. For the rest of the night he stayed on high alert, carefully monitoring the ground, water, and sky for any activity. It didn't seem like the type of thing Freddy would go in for, but it never hurt to be careful.

The night evolved into morning with no sign of any activity. Bob decided to go down and take a closer look. On the one hand, he didn't want to make himself a target for the wrong sort of person. On the other hand, he didn't want to look like a threat. So a careful, but not overtly stealthy approach was called for.

He reached the edge of the cultivated plot and paused to survey the area, but detected no-one. The plots looked to have been undisturbed for at least several days, but that didn't mean anything in and of itself. He examined what was being cultivated and discovered a root-bearing plant plus a couple of short shrubs. He sniffed at them and decided they might be used for flavourings for cooking or a hot drink. Whatever they were, they were pleasant enough. That might mean nothing, but tastes were considerably different from one culture to another, and the fact that someone was growing something that he might like was indicative.

A low barking sound drew his attention to the slope leading to the beach. He approached carefully, making sure to keep out of sight of anything below. Approaching the knee of the slope, Bob knelt behind some bushes and peered out. To his surprise he saw two creatures similar to the ones that had attacked him upon his arrival. Squinting to zoom in, he saw wounds on their heads that matched the ones he had inflicted. This was getting a little bit beyond strange.

A sound from behind and above him drew his attention. Staring up he saw a shape fast approaching. Not a dragon, it was cylindrical, tapered at one end, long and wide. The end facing him was a distorted visage of a human face. The mouth was proportional to the size of the face, and filled with sharp teeth. Small wings beat furiously as it bore down upon him at a speed too fast for him to run away to safety. So he stood up with his legs slightly apart, the staff carefully placed at his feet, with his hands folded in front of him.

The creature rushed on a collision course towards him, but Bob maintained his neutral stance. Just as it reached him it decelerated to a halt and swooped up until it hovered a body-length above him, blocking out the sun. Her eyes bored into Bob's own, and he returned the intense stare with one of his own.

"What have you done to my pets, you little monster?" it demanded.

"Hello, Aunt Freida. Imagine meeting you here," said Bob.

CHAPTER THREE
The Lady of Healing

"I recognize you, young Bob. You've not changed much, I see. Now answer my question ... what did you do to my pets?"

"Oh, those aquatic predators that tried to eat me? Those were yours?"

"Well ... ah ... yes. Tried to eat you, you say? What did you do to provoke them?"

"Nothing, Aunt Freida. Shortly after I arrived on the shore they tried to sneak up and eat me."

"Nonsense. Floppsy and Smidgen are the gentlest of creatures. High-strung and easily frightened. Quite harmless unless provoked."

Bob sighed. As a young boy, he'd had unfortunate encounters with several of Aunt Freida's "harmless pets". In a firm, but gentle, voice he replied, "I'm sorry, Aunt Freida, but they did try a sneak attack. Perhaps they were having an off day, but they did attack. The wounds on the top of their heads are the result of hitting a rock when I dodged out of the way."

"Harrumph. Well. Be that as it may, but what about the bruises on their jaws? How did they come by those?"

Continuing his patient tone Bob said, "They kept coming, I'm afraid. I tried to dodge away but they wouldn't stop. I gave them a rap across the chops to get their attention."

"And then?"

"I scolded them and told them to go back into the lake. They were smart enough to listen, and nothing more needed to be done."

Freida harrumphed again and snorted several times. "Well, I'm sure they didn't mean any harm. As I said, they are normally very gentle. Something must have riled them up."

Bob opened his mouth to say something soothing, but then closed it with a snap. "What's their normal range, Aunt Freida?"

"Eh? What's that got to do with it?"

"You said that something must have riled them up. What if something, say, chased them?"

"Hmm, that would do it. But there's nothing around here that can do that." After a brief pause she said in a thoughtful tone, "What made you think of that?"

After clearing his throat for a moment Bob said, "I had a run-in with Freddy a few days ago. You remember him, don't you? He and I used to play together when we were kids."

"Freddy ... Freddy ... oh, yes, now I remember him. A somewhat disagreeable child, as I recall. Not the best of playmates, was he?" The last was said in a soft, kindly voice.

"No, although he did have his moments."

Freida nodded. "Yes, and as I recall he began hanging around your brother. A bad seed that Freddy. Never approved of him. Never terribly fond of your brother, come to that."

Bob made a wry face. "Can't disagree with you on either count, Aunt Freida. For his Naming Day, Freddy took on the aspect of a dragon and went off on a Grand Tour. That was the last I saw of him until the other day."

"A dragon, you say. I never agreed with that aspect, I must say. Very pretty, but with limited combat capability. Not at all practical. And a great irritant to our relationship with the

True Dragons. I've always preferred the tried-and-true combat forms, myself." A slight wave ran along the length of her bulky form as she gave her head a slight shake. "But as for yourself, young Bob, I see you chose a very traditional aspect. But ... uhm ... forgive me for saying this, but it is little different from your original body. Were there ... ah ... problems?"

Bob's face grew impassive as he gave a curt nod. "Yeah. Something like that."

Freida's face fell and she made fluttering motions with her various limbs. "Oh, I didn't mean to be rude, Bob. Please don't think that of me. Ah, can I offer you some tea?" She pointed towards her rough shelter.

Bob forced himself to relax and smile. "Tea would be lovely, thank you, Aunt Freida."

They went to the shelter, and Freida puttered about getting water boiled and preparing a pot of tea. While waiting they spoke little, preferring the comfort of their own thoughts. Finally the tea was ready and they settled down to drink it.

"My apologies for the lack of furniture, Bob. I get so few visitors here, you know."

Bob nodded as he sat cross-legged on the ground. "Not at all, Aunt Freida." He gave a genuine smile. "Dad never was one for 'fancy living', as he liked to call it."

That got a laugh from his Aunt. "Oh my, no. Not him. Very much an old-school follower of the Precepts of Survival. A good man, though. A very good man."

Bob tipped his head in agreement. They drank in silence for a minute.

"Tell me about Freddy's activities here, please," asked Freida.

Bob lowered his cup and placed it carefully on the ground in front of him. Then he folded his hands in his lap and looked directly at his Aunt. "I don't have the whole story, I'm afraid. Heard some off-world rumours about this place, so I decided to take a look. As you know, the major city isn't too far from the public portal."

Freida nodded as she sipped her tea.

"Well, I poked around and heard stories—recent ones—about a dragon flying around destroying buildings in the outlying areas. Odd thing was, it was taking pains not to hurt the inhabitants, just their buildings. The only casualties were the ones who tried to stop him. That sounded like something a criminal enforcer might do, so I purchased some armour and headed out to take a look. Found Freddy torching a village in one of the northernmost settlements. We discussed the matter, and he decided to leave."

After several seconds of silence Freida asked in a quiet voice, "He decided to leave, did he? Just like that?"

Bob sighed. "We had words. And I had to hit him a few times to convince him."

"And?" Her tone was gentle but insistent.

Bob took and released a deep breath before replying. "I removed a mind gem from his forehead."

"Oh, no! What was he doing with one of those horrid things?"

"Apparently Set gave it to him," Bob replied in a grim voice.

"Your brother is dealing in mind gems?" Her face mirrored her shock at the news.

"Yep. And Freddy was here on Set's orders. I don't know why, exactly, but I put a stop to it."

"Oh, dear. What did you do with the gem?"

"Encased it in steel at the village, then heated it a hot fire."

Freida nodded. "Well done, Bob. That would certainly disable the worst of its effects. Then what did you do with it? Dispose of it off-world?"

Bob shook his head. "No. Using the portal would leave a clear trail if someone wanted to get the gem. Or trace my activities, of course. Another concern was to keep Freddy's employers from learning about this planet for as long as possible. I heard about the volcano and decided to toss it in there. Walked from the village to here."

"Walked? Why not levitate or apport?" She covered her mouth with a pair of tendrils. "Oh, I do apologize, Bob. I forgot that you lack those skills. Please forgive me."

To her surprise, Bob just laughed. "Not a problem, Aunt Freida—truly. Still can't levitate worth a darn, but I can apport well enough these days. Not long distances, but anywhere within clear sight."

"I am so glad to hear that. But why not simply do a series of apport hops?"

"Couldn't. When I heated the gem it released a cloud of white gas. Very intoxicating and knocked me out for hours. Took days for the effects to wear off."

Before Bob could react, a tentacle shot out and wrapped itself around his left wrist. He resisted the urge to jerk free. For several seconds he felt subtle energies pulsing through his arm as Freida interrogated his healing factors. She was a highly trained medical professional, but even after all this time her bedside manner still needed work.

"Dear boy, why didn't you say so immediately? How much of this gas did you inhale? How did you escape it?"

"Not much. It was almost dissipated when a gust of wind flung some of it at me. As for escaping, the locals dragged me away then coated the steel-encased gem with pitch."

"Describe your symptoms." It was not a request.

Bob described in detail what had happened, and allowed his healing factors to transfer their detailed analysis to her.

Freida unwrapped her tendril from Bob's wrist and shook her head. "You were very lucky, young Bob." Then she asked hesitantly, "How often have you used mind gems?"

Bob was shocked. "Never, Aunt Freida. On my honour. Never saw a real one until Freddy's; just images in my medical studies. Dad taught me how to neutralize them, of course."

"Of course." Freida nodded absently. Then she turned her gaze on him as she asked, "And that white smoke? Did you see what caused it?"

"Not sure, but there was white liquid inside the gem that was leaking out. Why? Is that not normal for mind gems?"

She shook her head. "No. And it is a very disturbing development. The use of mind gems is relatively uncommon, but not unknown. They were developed as a medical treatment, during the Great Wars, to produce a feeling of general contentment for badly injured people. They went out of use when our current level of biotechnology was developed, but a few people every generation seem to find satisfaction with them. But that white fluid, Bob ... that's a true evil thing." She paused until Bob encouraged her to continue.

"It is called 'pure quill'. Have you heard that name?"

Bob shook his head.

"I am very glad to hear that, Bob. Very glad, indeed. It is an extremely potent euphoric ... as you found out. That makes it psychologically addicting. The real danger from it is that it bypasses our healing factors, both in its effects and withdrawal symptoms. This is the first time I've heard of it being used in conjunction with a mind gem or continuously dripped into a person. Normal use seems to be to ingest a drop of it now and again, although I've heard reports of groups burning it to create a smudge-cloud."

"Where is it from? Why haven't I heard of it before now?"

Freida heaved a great sigh. "It is--or has been--very rare. It was decided long ago to limit knowledge of it to an inner circle of medical professionals. Little is known because apparently no user wants to take a chance on losing their source. I've never heard of one of our kind using it, though. It has always been assumed to be a vice of the lesser races.

As for the source, rumours say that it is something supplied by the Ravens."

"The Ravens? No-one's seen anything of them since shortly after the Great Wars, so far as I've heard. That doesn't make sense."

Freida nodded gravely. "Exactly. No sense whatsoever. But consider this. The occasional recreational use of mind gems began shortly after the end of the Great Wars. Not surprising, I suppose, but it went out of favour within a generation. Then its use began popping up again after ... after ... well, after my home planet was destroyed. Pure quill, though, didn't show up until later."

Bob shook his head. "No. That still doesn't make any sense. After the Great Wars, humanity was all but exterminated. Secrets like that couldn't have been hidden. Our ancestors would never have allowed it, given the small size of the gene pool back then."

"True enough, Bob, but what about the lesser races?"

Bob snorted. "Nothing *lesser* about them. They're as human as we are, just not as technologically or genetically advanced."

"So where did they come from?"

"Ah, a trick question." Bob gave an easy laugh. "We don't know. Yes, yes, I know the usual guff about how they are descended from lost colonies and isolated military bases. Some are, sure, but not all." He rose to his feet and began pacing back and forth. Freida hid a smile as she watched him.

"I've been to a lot of worlds, Aunt Freida, and many off the beaten paths. Too many human-inhabited worlds with long histories to be explained away so easily. No, there's something else at play here. Don't know what or how, but I'm looking."

"Ever curious and never trusting established wisdom. Very much like your father and his father before him. You do credit to your ancestors, young Bob."

Bob stopped his pacing and cleared his throat in embarrassment at the unexpected praise. "You knew my grandfather? I never met him."

"Yes, but he was very old and I was very young. He died shortly after we met."

"Dad never said much about Grandfather, aside from happy generalities. Never talked about what happened to him."

"Your father is about my age, you know, so they never had a great deal of time together. I remember him as being stern but caring. Oh, and people were always annoyed at his habit of poking around and asking questions. My elder siblings knew him somewhat better, but we never talked much about him. Now of course ..."

Bob remained silent, realizing that the conversation had taken a painful turn.

Then Freida perked up and said, "We must have fresh tea." She hurried away and busied herself brewing a new batch. The silence between them lasted for the several minutes it took for the tea to brew, and they sat with their respective cups.

Freida broke the silence. "I'm sorry that I missed your Naming Day, Bob. I ..." She fell silent.

"That's alright, Aunt Freida," replied Bob in a gentle voice. "Dad explained it to me. He didn't tell me that you'd come to this planet, though."

She looked around. "This is one of his worlds, you know."

Bob shook his head. "He never mentioned it to me."

"Perhaps it isn't so surprising. Like you, he questioned accepted wisdom and this was one of his Mystery Worlds, as he liked to call them. He called on me to investigate and help out."

"He did?"

Freida looked far off into the distance. "Yes. I was lost and angry and his request came at a good time. You know that my family's world was destroyed, yes?"

Bob nodded.

"Well, only my brother and I escaped. Actually, the two of us were tossed into the portal by our mother. An emergency bounce-jump to random locations. I was lucky and ended up on the world of a family I was on good terms with but didn't know well. The rest you know, I would think. Except for poor Sid—no-one ever heard from him again."

Bob nodded. "Yes. Did they ever find out who the attackers were?"

Freida's smile became predatory. "There wasn't enough left of them to make a determination. Bits of wreckage indicated that it was probably one of the oppressor species left over from the Great Wars. Before I was born such things happened every now and again. Never this bad, mind you, but it did happen. Everyone thought such things were over and done with. We were wrong."

Bob let her remember those painful times for a minute before he cleared his throat and asked, "How did you get in touch with Dad?"

She shook her head as if to clear it. "Oh, he was one of the ones who came in answer to our distress call. Everyone was much too late, of course. But he detected the signs of portal usage, and managed to narrow down the destination probabilities. I'd moved on to one of the sanctuary planets by the time he found me, and had almost given up. He convinced me to help with this little mystery and has let me stay on. I wasn't too sure about staying here, at first ... not after having an entire planet at my disposal. But this ..." she waved a tendril to encompass the lake and the land. "... is all I require. A mystery to solve and a place to quiet my soul."

"And this mystery was ..." Bob prompted.

"Oh, didn't I say? A plague. Or, rather, a series of plagues. When I first arrived, a plague was tearing through the local population. It was highly contagious, had a zero survival rate, and had an unknown but effective transmission vector. To save the remaining population I had to eliminate all sources of the infection."

Bob recalled the pictures he'd seen. "You burnt entire towns."

"They were already doomed, dear. Everywhere the infection cropped up resulted in the death of every person, without exception. I stopped the progression using the only means available to me."

"Then you developed a cure and spread that."

She gave him a curious look as she replied. "A vaccine, not a cure. But how did you know?"

Bob gave her a grin. "There are drawings of you breathing on towns. Some showing fire and some showing a cloud. But you mentioned a series of plagues."

Freida nodded. "Yes. Subsequent ones were variants of the original, but each required a slightly different vaccine. Until that was developed I made sure the plague didn't spread too far."

Bob rested his chin in a hand and gave a thoughtful nod. "How extensive was this plague? It sounds as if there was more to it."

"Indeed there was. Notice anything strange about the ecosystem?"

"No birds," he answered without hesitation. "And very few animals aside from those in the swamps. The plagues?"

Freida nodded. "Very good. Yes, all that was caused by the plagues. It is very unusual for a disease to cross from one species to another like that and maintain its kill rate. Yes, the avian population was destroyed, along with much of the animal population. I've repopulated some of it from the few surviving pockets I found elsewhere on the planet. Best I could do, I'm afraid."

"How did the plague start?"

"Your father came here because it was listed in old records as a minor supply depot. There were hints that bioweapons had been stored here at one time, so he used caution when checking things out. Everything seemed to be fine. The human population was expanding outward from the original base near the portal, and was rebuilding after a severe social collapse. That collapse wasn't terribly surprising, given that the natural geography limited their spread to a single large isthmus. Then the plagues hit and your father decided to bring in a medical expert."

Bob considered that for a moment then asked, "OK, but why the changes in the original plague? Could that be due to natural causes? Something from the non-human part of the world?"

Freida smiled. "Excellent questions. Yes, in theory it might be possible."

"I'm hearing an 'except' in there."

"Except that all the usual disease vectors and incubators had been all but destroyed in the first plague. No birds, no small animals, no obvious way for the disease to be modified naturally. And the disease was too human-specific to be alien in origin."

"Malice, not nature."

Freida nodded, then frowned. "A very strange type of malice, though. Almost like a puzzle to test our wits. Once solved, the problem never re-appeared."

Bob answered her frown with one of his own. "A malicious puzzle, if that's what it was." He paused for a moment then asked, "That is all well and good, Aunt Freida, but local records indicate that after the plagues ended you selectively killed off much of the nobility. Is that true?"

She nodded. "Yes, it is. In the course of my investigations I had conducted a genetic mapping of the human population. The ruling class had an unfortunate tendency towards inbreeding, with some nasty recessives cropping up."

"Yes, but ..."

"Recessives that affected mental stability for the most part. Well-formed and attractive physically, but became dangerously psychopathic after puberty. Since the royal houses of all the little kingdoms interbred, the result was social instability that threatened to turn into a general all-out war. I had spent all that effort saving them from the plague, and wasn't about to let some mental defectives ruin it all."

"A bit harsh, perhaps?"

Freida shrugged. "Not really. We were far more ruthless with our own people when rebuilding after the Great Wars."

"True enough. Anything else from the genetic analysis?"

She smiled and leaned forward. "Oh, yes. The original ruling class were from a single small stock of humans. Probably from a small supply base left on its own, with the resultant genetic problems. But then another group of humans showed up, and then some centuries later another group."

"Excuse me? How? I've seen no signs of spaceflight ability of any sort, much less FTL capability."

"Exactly. The three waves show up socially as well as genetically. The original ruling class were, as I said, from one source. The minor nobles and upper classes from another, and the bottom rung from the third genetic source. Oh, there's been mixing to some degree, of course. People will be people, after all."

"When did all this take place?"

"Well before I got here, that's all I can say for sure. At least several centuries, judging from the pre-plague social structures as well as the genetic mixing."

"Who else knows about this?"

"Your father, of course. He verified that the public portal had not been used to transport these new populations. And I've sent a report to the Central Archives."

Bob snorted. "In other words, no-one."

Freida gave Bob a stern look. "Now see here, young Bob. The universe moves in slow cycles, and there's more complexity in life than someone your age can appreciate."

"Aunt Freida, please. Whatever Dad used to do or be, now he pretty much sits at home and does what Mom tells him to. Which is to sit at home and not make waves with the other families. And almost no-one reads the Archives."

Freida smiled serenely as she gazed at him.

Bob blushed. "Alright, alright," he mumbled. "Sometimes bored and lonely kids read them. Very few others, though. You have to admit that."

She sighed and nodded.

They sat in awkward silence for a few moments. Bob decided to break the ice. "Any leads to finding your brother? I only met him a few times when I was a kid."

Freida shook her head. "No. Your father did try, though. Sifted through the probabilities to find likely worlds. He visited several of them, but found nothing. Your mother put a stop to the wandering, I'm afraid. We never did get along very well."

"Did you try ..."

"... leaving messages?" Freida finished his thought. "Of course. No replies. It has been a very long time, and a bounce-jump can be dangerous. I'll admit to almost giving up hope."

An awkward silence dragged on until Bob tried again to say something without putting his foot in his mouth. "Uhm, so, how have you been spending your time? What with the plagues and such being sorted out."

"Well, I've been focusing on healing myself these days. To my surprise I rather enjoy living in a smaller environment and the depth of focus it can afford. My pets give me a lot of joy, of course. Such loving and devoted creatures. And my gardening, as well. Not just here—I've got some rather extensive plots elsewhere on the planet. Been trying to encourage the local fauna to regenerate here and there. With some successes, I might add." She sounded very pleased with herself.

Bob's astonishment must have shown on his face, and Freida gave a hearty laugh. "Don't look so surprised, young Bob. Sometimes even an old follower of the Precepts of Survival can change. To be honest, I've been finding myself more and more aligned with the contemplative nature of the Precepts of Philosophy. To my surprise, there's been an upsurge of interest in it, especially among the folks my age. Why, even your Aunt Gertrude has shown an interest. Now there's a hard-core Survivor that I'd never thought would change. Apparently many of the Eldest Ones have been quietly expanding upon those teachings, and have begun reaching out. A few years ago they sent out a detailed communication to many of us who'd begun sharing our ideas. It's been dense going, but we're managing to make some good progress on it. In fact ..."

Her enthusiastic monologue was interrupted by a series of loud hissings from the lake shore. Freida turned to the lake and crooned soothing sounds to her upset pets. Bob scanned the sky.

"Give me back my gem, you thief!" screamed Freddy, as he dove out of the sun towards where Bob was standing. "Give it back to me *now*."

"That will be quite enough of that," snapped Freida, her voice intense enough to make the air shimmer. Both men winced in pain at the sonic assault. "The Precepts of Survival are honoured here. Do not forget that. Either of you."

Freddy landed rather heavily, taking care to be well outside the reach of Freida's tendrils.

"He stole from me, Aunt Freida," whined Freddy. "He hit me and he stole it."

"Bob tells me that you were bothering the locals, Freddy. That was very unkind of you. Now, sit yourself down and we'll all have a nice cup of tea and discuss this calmly."

"No. He stole from me and I want it back."

Bob sighed. "Sorry, Freddy, but I can't do that. I tossed it into the volcano. It's gone for good."

Freddy raised his head and let loose a bleat of anguish. Then he turned to face Bob. "Then I demand satisfaction. Right here, right now."

"Now, Freddy ..." interjected Freida.

"No. The both of you are followers of the Precepts of Survival, and they clearly state that thieves must provide compensation."

"No, Freddy," Bob replied in a calm voice. "I will not provide you with another mind gem. Especially not one that ..." his voice trailed off at a glare from Freida. "That causes harm to you," he finished lamely.

"Then you must face me in a Judgement of Battle. I demand it, as is my right."

Freida turned to face Bob, despair written plain on her face. "He is correct, Bob. You must face him or renounce the Precepts, shaming your family and ancestors."

"I'll face him," replied Bob in a calm voice.

"Very well," said Freida sadly. "But the mismatch in aspects is too great. Bob is allowed a weapon."

"I choose my staff."

Freddy chortled. "Fine. But you can't have anything else. Throw away your knife."

Bob shrugged, removed the knife from his belt, and tossed it aside. He walked over to the staff and flicked it into his hands with the flip of a foot. "Where do you want to start?" asked Bob. "Here or the beach."

"Beach," came the immediate answer.

Bob repressed a grin. Freddy had obviously chosen on the assumption that the rocky shore would impede Bob's movements.

Freida gave both men a mournful look, turned, and

without a word led them to the beach. Her pets were half out of the water, looking at Freddy and snarling. Freida crooned a command to them, and they reluctantly eased back into the water to retreat some distance away.

The two men assumed positions along the beach, standing apart at a distance roughly three times Freddy's length. At this range, Bob could detect a slight discordant note in Freddy's energy flows. It wasn't as severe as after their first meeting, but would nonetheless help to take the edge off Freddy's abilities. As the Precepts of Survival said, "Victory can be built upon a foundation of small advantages."

"Are you very sure about this?" Freida asked in a quiet but firm voice.

"I demand my compensation," said Freddy.

"It'll be alright, Aunt Freida. Thank you for the tea," said Bob.

Freida rose up and floated out over the lake until she was hovering above her pets. "Begin," she intoned.

Freddy sprang at Bob with his head lowered, attempting to ram him with the bony protrusions that were sticking out of his armoured crown. Bob sprang forward as well. He knelt and planted one end of the staff under his right foot while angling the staff low. The free end of the staff was positioned perfectly to hit Freddy in an eye. Freddy saw this and attempted to stop, but the rocky beach gave him little traction. He lifted his head up, but not quickly enough to prevent the staff from giving him a solid hit to the throat. Freddy uttered a pained wheeze and reared his head and neck back out of reach of the staff. While Freddy reared up and back, Bob picked up a pair of pebbles before standing up again.

Freddy took another step back before snapping his head forward with mouth agape. Bob executed a pair of swift underhand throws and sent the rocks slamming against Freddy's left eye. The momentum of the lunge was such that

Freddy couldn't stop it, so Bob leaped out of the way using the staff as a fulcrum. As Bob assumed a neutral stance with the staff acting as a third leg, Freddy's head bounced off the rocky ground.

"Had enough, Freddy?" asked Bob in a quiet voice. "We don't have to do this."

In reply, Freddy gave a rapid sweep of his tail. It was fast enough that Bob couldn't entirely avoid it, so he used the staff to push himself above the sweep. That saved his legs, but the bottom end of the staff was knocked out from under him. That left him off-balance enough that he had to tumble to regain control, but was then met by a foot attempting to stomp him.

Bob made a fast roll to one side, the impact against the sharp stones bruising and cutting his back. The pain quickly receded and the injuries were healed by the time his roll was finished. Using his momentum to come to his feet at a squat, he planted one end of the staff against the nearest leg and vaulted up onto Freddy's back. He lifted up his staff and slammed it against the side of Freddy's head.

Screaming with pain and rage, Freddy sprang up into the air, his wings beating strongly. "That's going to cost you, Bob. I was just going to damage you—now I'm going to toss you into the volcano. Poetic justice, don't you think? Your brother will reward me, too."

Bob said nothing, choosing to concentrate on not being flung off. As Freddy's speed increased, the wind began to whip at him causing his eyes to tear. Using a sleeve to wipe his eyes, he saw Freida silently following their flight. He risked a quick wave, and was rewarded with a flash of annoyance on her face.

They reached the volcano within seconds and Freddy circled the caldera. "Enjoying the view, Bob? Here, have a closer look." With that, he tucked one wing under his body and executed a snap roll. Bob barely managed to hang on and pressed himself closer to Freddy's body. Freddy laughed and did another snap roll. Again, Bob struggled to hang on. Freddy had lost some altitude with his antics, and straightened out to flap up to a higher altitude.

"Remember how we used to float on the wind when we were kids, Bob? Oh, right. We floated, but you had to run on the ground after us. Poor, crippled Bob. Couldn't levitate. Couldn't apport. Just a crippled loser that we all laughed at."

Freddy was still gaining altitude, but at a slower rate. Bob took a quick look at the torus cloud, and estimated that they were half-way between it and the magma. He did a quick query of the portal control system, and it confirmed that he needed to drop from above to actually active it.

"Hey, Bob, what say we go a bit higher? That way when you drop you'll have more time to enjoy the view."

"No, no, Freddy. Let's go back to the beach. That was a fair fight. Going above the cloud just makes everything in your favour. You know I've never liked heights." Bob tried to put an edge on his voice without going too far overboard. He needn't have bothered—Freddy was enough of a bully to thrive on a victim's fears, real or faked.

"Oh, gee, Bob. I'm so sorry. Of course I want to be fair about this." He flapped harder, rising higher and higher until he was above the cloud. Bob queried the portal but was told that he was still not high enough to instantiate it. By this time Freddy had levelled out and had begun a tight circle about the inner portion of the torus. "Wonderful view, isn't it, Bob?" crowed Freddy.

Bob sighed. It looked like this was as high as he was going to get by doing things the easy way. Gripping with his knees, he sat up and grasped the staff firmly in his right hand. Then he whipped it around and struck the base of the right wing. Freddy's gasp of pain proved the effectiveness of the attack, so he repeated the strike several times. Freddy levelled out as best he could and screamed curses. Bob released the grip his knees had, twirled around to stand on Freddy's back, and began using the staff to slice at the right wing's membranes.

"What are you doing? You'll get us both killed!" screamed Freddy, who turned his head to survey his injuries. Bob's said nothing, but gave a series of sharp blows to the head with his staff, causing Freddy to make an involuntary dive. This threw Bob off Freddy's back, but he managed to whip the staff one more time against the middle of the injured wing. There was a sharp *crack* and the wing folded in half. Freddy screamed as he frantically tried to use his remaining wing to make a controlled glide back to the ground. For his part, Bob twisted until he was facing up, spreading his limbs to stabilize his fall.

"Are you quite sure you know what you're doing, Bob?" Freida's focused communication boomed in his ears.

"I'm working, Aunt Freida," replied Bob as he gritted his teeth.

"Well, get on with it, dear. You're running out of altitude."

Bob didn't bother replying to that as he tried to focus on a piece of air above the torus cloud. It was very difficult to select something that couldn't be seen, and heat from the magma wasn't helping. That gave him an idea—he could use the heat to see the air above more clearly. He activated his infrared vision and scanned the sky above. If he was correct, the cloud would block the heat, and give a cylinder of cooler air. Of course it wasn't a perfect cylinder, and the warm air would eventually merge with the cool to form a sharp-ish edge and ... there it was. A quick scan to achieve simularity and he apported above the cloud-torus.

The sudden difference in temperature made him inhale sharply, and reminded him that he had a limited time window. He executed a roll and resumed his spread-limb attitude. It required a little fine tuning to adjust his fall to the centre of the torus, but he managed to do that without wasting too much time. Then he contacted the portal control system and told it to instantiate the doorway. There was a slight delay that gave him something of a start before a film of darkness deeper than black began forming and the system prompted him for a destination. Trying to be helpful, it also showed him a countdown timer indicating the time he had left. Bob uttered a brief growl at the cussedness of his father to add extra pressure to an already tricky portal activation.

On the other hand, he had forgotten to decide on a destination. It had to be somewhere he hadn't been recently and somewhere no-one would think to look for him.

"Try one of the waystation worlds, dear. But do it quickly, please."

Acquiescing to his aunt's superior wisdom, Bob transmitted the coordinates of one he hadn't used in many years, and was gratified that the system accepted it. "Thank you, Aunt Freida," he told her in a meek voice.

"You did very well for a first time on this portal, Bob. It is one of the more difficult ones. Oh, before you go. Here's a list of the worlds that your father thought Sid might have landed on. I've marked the two that he wasn't able to visit. If you have the time, I'd greatly appreciate it if you could check them out. Just in case."

"I'll look into it, ma'am. Thank you, again."

"Drop by any time, dear boy. And don't worry about Freddy. I'll take care of him—he won't be going anywhere for a while."

Bob spared the time to take a brief look around for Freddy, and saw him make a heavy landing amongst a stand of trees. Then he entered the doorway and contact was broken. After an instant of time that seemed to stretch on forever, he popped out of the destination portal. He stumbled forward, taking several steps to regain his footing. He turned and watched as the portal deactivated and slowly de-instantiate as it made the transition into hyperspace to wait for the next activation.

It had all gone rather well, he thought. The portal should have handled the velocity differential more cleanly, but he wouldn't put it past his father to have done that on purpose. Still, it would be unwise to linger. He needed to find a public portal.

Bob sent out an anonymous query-request, and received a response showing its location in absolute and relative terms, as well as a local map. The portal looked to be about an easy half-day's hike away. That would give him a chance work out some of the kinks and bruises he had suffered during his fight with Freddy. Even with healing factors a brisk walk was the best cure for many ills.

Thinking of the fight brought a lop-sided smile to his lips. He was glad his childhood sort-of-friend had survived, but was certain that Freddy wasn't going to be thanking him for that anytime soon. After a quick look around to get his bearings, Bob headed off towards the public portal at an easy walk.

CHAPTER FOUR
A Throw of the Dice

Bob took several steps then halted as a thought occurred to him. He was, after all, being hunted by his elder brother. Would Set have set traps around a portal? The obvious answer was "yes", of course. On the other hand, he'd not want some random stranger to be setting off traps. Did this mean that Bob could assume that the way was clear? The Precepts of Survival were very clear on that, stating "assumptions are the path to failure and death". Not the most uplifting of sayings, but correct more often than not.

Still, lethal traps were not very likely. On the other hand, monitoring devices were a distinct possibility. All the more so since he'd used them to good success against Set in the past. His brother was many things, but stupid he was most definitely not.

He considered the problem while standing motionless. Recalling the map of the area, he could see that the private portals were arranged in a rough circle around the public portal. About a third of the portals were marked as "offline" or "repairs required". Status of the latter indicated that state had existed for some time. That made Bob feel rather sad. Even given his relative youth, he remembered a time when no portal was left unrepaired for any length of time.

It turned out that even the public portal had not been used

in some time. That, in itself, wasn't unusual for the galaxy was large. Still, waystation planets used to be a place for families to meet and mingle. Children were introduced to peers and elders, to ensure that ancestors and descendants knew one another. It was also used as neutral ground when tensions between individuals grew too large.

Bob shook his head to dismiss those thoughts so as to better focus on the issues at hand. His private portal was bounded on either side by unrepaired ones. The map indicated the families owning them, and that was another surprise. Those families were both active and flourishing, so why would they leave a private portal inoperative? Bob gave another slight shake of his head as a sigh forced its way out. It was a time to move, not ponder new mysteries.

One answer might be to leave an obvious path from the active portal to the public portal, or to offer a pair of unused paths that would appeal to a sneaky person. Or perhaps both were true—that would be something he'd do. Had done, in fact. Traps were unlikely, but monitors should be taken as a given. However, this was a world with a rich ecosystem, which meant that any monitors would need to ignore the local wildlife. That implied (Bob could hear his father growling a warning about assumptions) that the monitors looked for usage of the alternate energies. If he refrained from using active sensors or apporting or accessing a portal control system he could probably walk to the public portal without worrying. That was good enough for him, so off he went once more.

A couple hours later found Bob alongside a stream, munching on some raw fish and drinking his fill of the cold water. Although not a gastronomic libertine, he enjoyed good food and was getting somewhat tired of eating raw wildlife. He'd been trying to decide where to go next. Despite Aunt Freida's attentions Freddy would probably get a message off to Set sooner or later. That meant a very good chance that

Set would interrupt his plans to deal with an annoying brother. The thought of interrupting Set's plans without actually having to do anything appealed to Bob's sense of correctness. It also meant that going to an out-of-the way world for a time would seem to be a very good idea.

Bob mulled the list of worlds that his Aunt had sent to him. Of the two unvisited worlds, only one was familiar to him. It took him a bit of thinking to figure out why, but it finally came to him. His favourite relative, Auntie Gertrude, was very fond of the tea there and would often talk about it. That decided it—he'd go there for a few weeks, pick up some tea, take in the sights, and plan his next move. That required, of course, that he stop lazing about and get to the public portal. Pushing himself up using the staff, he brushed the dirt off his clothes and continued his journey. His destination was an hour's brisk trot away.

As he got closer to the portal the trees grew thicker, as did the underbrush until the path eventually petered out. That didn't worry Bob at all, as this was the standard defensive perimeter for a public portal on all worlds. He'd always considered it rather pleasant, and it was always well populated by the local wildlife. Any life-form above a certain level of sentience found the area unnerving and would avoid it. Pushing on regardless would result in feelings of blind terror and the need to flee. Bob, of course, was not affected by any the defences as he pushed his way in.

There was a path, of sorts, for those that knew what to look for. The map sent by the portal could be used, but Bob always enjoyed testing his own skills whenever time allowed. Every portal forest was different, and in any event was changed over time. To his delight he only had to backtrack a couple of times before reaching the grove at the centre.

This was where Bob expected problems, so he halted just outside the grove and examined the area carefully using all the passive senses available to him. There was nothing obvious to be seen, which meant that either there was nothing or the potential opposition wasn't insulting him by using anything obvious. Whatever the case, he needed to use the alternate energies to summon the portal, and there was nothing he could do to mask that. Although the summoning was anonymous, the portal would keep a record of his identity and his destination. On the other hand (he was using a lot of hands recently) not many people had the skills to access or understand a portal log. Set did, if only to a limited degree, but that would take time away from his main goal. Bob shook his head in mock grief. It was so sad when setting up a galactic empire interfered with life's simpler pleasures like stopping an interfering younger brother.

With that happy thought, Bob sent the activation command to the portal. The ground became darker as the form of the portal began to take shape. Bob always enjoyed watching the instantiation process. Each portal was slightly different, and his father had taught him to appreciate the subtle differences and what they meant. In practical terms, it was a means to gain some diagnostic information without leaving traces in the portal logs. In this case, the process revealed that this was an older type of portal, of a type unfamiliar to him. Normally he could get a sense for how long a portal had lain dormant, but in this case its unfamiliarity made it difficult. Bob leaned on his staff as he waited until the instantiation was complete. Humming softly to himself he walked around the structure while examining it. It was a basic series of cubes within cubes, which placed it from the time of the First Expansion. Or perhaps it was a minor outpost from the Second? Bob decided that was close enough for an age estimate, for in either case the instantiation spectrum was similar. His humming stopped as he pointed a finger at the portal and proclaimed, "Not used in over a local century, at least. Maybe three."

His curiosity piqued, he decided to check the logs. His

identity was already on record, so no real harm could be done. To his delight, the portal's last use had been two hundred and twenty three years ago. Checking the identity of the user would send an alert to them, so Bob decided to deny his curiosity that piece of information.

Portals automatically checked for personal messages for the user, but there were none for him. After a moment's hesitation, he decided to send a message to his youngest sister. There was no way to hide the fact that he'd been here, so he might as well make use of the opportunity. He quickly composed a short message, keeping it light on specifics. It was a certainty that the messages were being intercepted and read by others in his family. That much had become evident shortly after he left home. Since then he'd had a few messages from her, but none in a very long time.

Of all his family, she was the only one he truly missed. As always, he concluded his message by promising to be there for her Naming Day. That was a promise that he intended to keep, family quarrels or no. The trick would be to stop his mother and brother from slaughtering him on the spot. Still, that was a problem for another day. He posted the message and confirmed that it had been accepted by the portal. From there it would be automatically routed from portal to portal until it reached his family's home. Up until that point it was encrypted and untouchable.

On a whim, Bob decided to get a précis of the news and gossip. As expected, there was little of note. There was the usual handful of birth and Naming Day notices. He skipped over the taunts and hissy fits left by the children for each other. Only two news items stood out. The first was a call for anyone interested in something called the Philosophy of Change. There were a number of names attached, and Bob was surprised to see several Eldest Ones included. It was normally unheard of for them to take part in social events of any sort. The other was a notice for something calling itself the Society of Change that simply called upon people of good breeding to contact them. Bob recognized many of the names, but the ones that stood out were Freddy and Set. So his elder brother was finally coming out the shadows and making a public declaration.

Why Set had chosen to go public was something of a puzzlement to Bob. There had been several rather messy and embarrassing setbacks, which Bob had made sure were well publicized. His smile turned into a frown as he remembered Freddy's mind gem and that pure quill substance. That marked a new side to Set's operations, and one which Bob decided needed to be looked into and stopped.

Putting all that aside, he closed the news and prepared to leave. A wisp of thought stayed his decision, and he opened up the news again. There was something not right, and it took him several passes through it before he figured out what had bothered him. First of all, the news was rather thinner than he remembered. Thinking back, he realized that the news had slowly been getting thinner over the years. This was the first time it had been this sparse.

The second oddness was the lack of death notices. His people were very long-lived, but people still died from any number of causes. A few of old age, a few by accidents, and a few by suicide—but there were always a death notice for someone. This set of news had none, and that was very strange. Fewer deaths and fewer people doing anything of note. Perhaps he needed to start taking a more active interest in the news, rather than looking at it after increasingly long intervals.

With that thought in mind, he closed the news and prepared the portal for a transit. He sent the necessary pattern of symbols that defined the address of his destination. A film of darkness beyond blackness appeared before him and he stepped through it. This time the transition was perfect and there were no missteps as he arrived.

Looking back at this new portal he saw that it was a Middle Period design. It featured a mixture of spheres and cubes in the overall structure, with some stylish yet subdued ornamentation around the control surfaces. The colour, like the previous one, was a muted pearl white.

Bob contacted the control system and obtained a précis of this new world. After assimilating that, he made queries for information about the local political and cultural conditions. He was pleased to see that he'd be able to pass as a foreigner of indeterminate origin, so long as his identification papers were in order. The portal would be able to create suitable identification, currency, and clothing. It would all be somewhat dated, which was odd.

A check of the summary logs showed that there had been a few visitors over the centuries, but recent ones hadn't bothered to update the portal's information banks. That was considered quite rude, and Bob muttered darkly to himself for a moment.

Giving his head a shake, he decided to do an in-depth examination of the logs to see if he could spot Sid's arrival. He knew the date, and after some serious digging found an arrival at that time. It was marked as an emergency bounce-transit, which was rare enough that it had to be Sid. Tracking the terminus of the bounce was rather more difficult. By design, an emergency bounce was supposed deposit a person at a random location on a planet with a portal. In practise, the bounce took extra energy that varied with the distance from the portal. A knowledgeable person could probe into the diagnostic functions and determine the efficiency of the portal, and thanks to his father Bob had that knowledge.

Given the energy efficiency of the portal and the energy used, Bob could determine a maximum and minimum destination radius. The bounce algorithm was supposed to keep people away from oceans if at all possible, so that eliminated about two thirds of the possible area. Some further digging indicated the altitude the person had been bounced to. That was useful because the algorithm had an optimum height above the ground, to avoid structures and flying wildlife. That height indicated that the bounce took place over a mountainous area, which eliminated most of the remaining areas of interest. He queried the portal for details of the narrowed search area and assimilated that for later perusal.

For now, his first steps were to exit the protective zone and head to the nearest town. From there he would establish himself and get up to speed on current conditions before deciding how to proceed. Uttering a small sigh of regret he left his staff behind, as indications were that such things would cause unwanted interest in the cities he would need to go. The portal had a small storage area for travellers, so he put it in there and protected it using a lock-code that would restrict access to himself.

He stepped back and dismissed the portal. Without even bothering to watch it fade away, he began marching out of the forest. Bob was eager to see what this geopolitical unit called "Great Britain" had to offer.

* * *

Bob began walking in a northwesterly direction, walking across the spot where the portal had been. His destination was a town called Talgarth, some seven distance-units—kilometres they were called—away. He continued walking, but stopped when he almost stepped in the remains of a small campfire. Even stranger than finding a campfire within the protected zone were the complex symbols carved into the ground around the fire.

This wasn't just strange, it should have been impossible. The warding defences of the portal were designed to send any sentient creature screaming away in terror. In fact, getting as close as a half kilometre should have been impossible. Yet here were obvious signs that someone had been here, and stayed for some time judging by the amount of ash in the old fire.

He squatted to feel the remains of the fire and found it to be cold. He poked at it with a stick, but the inside of the ashes were as cool as the outside. Whoever had been here was long gone. He leaned forward to view the area from ground level and saw hints of footsteps, but nothing recent. Judging by those, it appeared that someone had walked in, made a fire and the symbols, and done little else. There was nothing to indicate a general wandering about. It looked as if the intruder had come for a very specific purpose.

Next he took a closer look at the symbols. They weren't mere scratchings, but made with care and deliberation to nearly a finger's width of depth. The symbols themselves were complex, and some of them vaguely familiar. He concentrated for a few moments, but no memory came to mind. Still, their general form and shape were familiar enough to him—someone was attempting to cast a magic spell.

Bob almost laughed at the incongruity of it. Every human world had created its own systems of symbologies intended to invoke and control larger-than-human forces. Yet this particular invocation had been performed next to what was the most advanced technology ever created. The smile vanished from his lips as he turned to look at the symbols again, especially the ones that looked vaguely familiar. Destination addresses sent to a portal were complex patterns representative of a time-insensitive routing through the complex of alternate spaces. Perhaps these crude drawings were an attempt to mimic that? Try as he might he couldn't make those patterns fit into any representation of a portal address, no matter how sketchy he made it.

It was very tempting to recall the portal and examine its

logs to determine who had used it last. The fire and the symbols weren't more than a month old—perhaps as little as a week depending on local weather conditions. He decided against it, as it might be safer not to alert anyone to his arrival or awareness of this incident. His lips pursed with frustration he walked past the mystery—taking care not to disturb it—and went on his way. His training ensured that he left no traces of his own passing.

After an hour's leisurely walk he walked into Talgarth and began a cautious reconnoitre. There weren't many people living there—about two thousand—but they'd be sure to notice anyone skulking about. It all seemed pleasant enough. His clothes drew some curious looks, but nothing beyond mild curiosity. Fashions had changed in the several decades since the portal's last update, but not enough to elicit much attention. He did a meandering circuit of the town before walking into an establishment that appeared to have clothing similar to what most people were wearing.

"May I be of assistance?" a young woman asked.

"Why, yes, I hope you can," Bob replied with his most charming smile.

The young woman gave him a warm smile in return. "I certainly hope so. Are you looking for anything in particular?"

"I need some new clothing." He gestured at what he was wearing. "Through an accident too tedious to go into, this is all I have. So I'll need everything, and something to carry it all around in. Not too much, of course. Something to wear plus some spares. Perhaps a rucksack or some such to carry things around in."

There were no other customers present, so Bob had the full attention of the young lady. Within an hour Bob had the clothes he needed and a tote-bag. In addition, he found out that the young lady's name was Nell, she was 22 years of age, single, and her shift ended in a couple of hours. She'd also given him a good thumbnail sketch of who was who, and who they did it with, in Talgarth. All in all, a standard sort of place in Bob's extensive experience.

"Look, Nell, I don't want to lead you on. I'm not in town for very long, and likely to leave at a moment's notice."

Nell made a pretty pout.

"Oh, don't be like that," he said with a laugh. After a moment Nell joined in.

"That's all right, Bob. You've not been leading me on, but ta for saying. In truth, though, is there anything else you'll be wanting?"

Bob thought for a moment. "Is there a travel agent in town or someplace to make bookings for trips outside the country?"

Nell nodded. "My cousin, Tara, works at one just down the street there." She pointed to his left. "Tell her I sent you."

Bob nodded his thanks as he asked, "I'd also like to pick up some tea for a favourite aunt. She's always raved about oolong black dragon tea. Would there be any to be had around here?"

Nell frowned and pursed her lips in thought. Bob thought it was a charming look on her, and was forced to remind himself that he had more important things to attend to. Then her face smoothed out and she said, "Not sure about that specific type, but Tara's mam runs a tea shop next street over. Got all sorts there. It might be worth stopping by."

"Great," said Bob. "Thanks so much for your help, Nell. I need to check with your cousin right away."

"Might you be back?" asked Nell somewhat shyly.

"Can't say for sure," Bob said in a kind voice.

"Well, at least you're honest about it, Bob. You know where I am," she said, smiling shyly.

"Thanks again, Nell," Bob said. He paid her out of the limited store of currency he had and exited the store.

A few minutes later Bob entered the travel agency that Nell

had directed him to. He was greeted by a young woman who gave him a professional smile and asked if she might be of service.

"I certainly hope so. Are you Tara?"

The young lady nodded.

"Your cousin, Nell, suggested that you were the one to see about getting trip details sorted out."

Tara's smile became friendlier. "She's absolutely correct about that, Mister ...?"

"Just call me Bob," he said, adding a charming smile.

"Alright, Bob. Whereabouts are you needing to go?"

"Romania."

"Family visit or just to see the sights?"

"A little of both, actually. An uncle of mine went there some years back, and I've taken it into my head to retrace his footsteps. The usual tourist stuff, of course."

"You'll be meeting him there?"

"Oh, no. He passed away shortly after that. I'm doing this trip partly out of respect for my aunt, his sister. She's getting on in years, and wanted someone in the family to keep the memory of his travels alive. He was quite the traveller, I've been told. Only met him a couple of times, when I was very young, but I remember him making me laugh. Not many of us left, and I've got the time, so here I am."

"Well, Bob, that's a lovely thing for you to do. Though I am curious about why you are starting your journey from Talgarth? We're not exactly on the main path."

"We all have to start somewhere, Tara. And, as I explained to Nell, I've had a bit of unfortunate run of luck lately. Hadn't planned to be here, but now that I am I figured to make the best of it."

Tara seemed not entirely convinced, but the prospect of a sale kept her moving things forward. "Very well, Bob. How were you planning on travelling? Rail, air, private car ...?"

"I've got no real preferences, Tara. But now that I've

started my journey I'd like to proceed as quickly as possible. How about checking the fastest route? Oh, and first class, of course."

"Of course," murmured Tara, pleased that her cousin had sent her a decent lead for once. She turned and tapped rapidly at her keyboard for a minute, then turned back to Bob. "Well, Bob, it appears that I can get you a direct flight to Bucharest out of London tomorrow morning. Business class, of course. I can book a hotel for you, too, if you wish?"

"An excellent idea, Tara. It's just myself, so nothing terribly grand. A small suite perhaps? Something close to the downtown area?"

Tara smiled broadly as she tapped away. "Yes, as it happens I can book something along those lines for you. How long would you be staying there?"

Bob frowned. "I'm not sure. A lot depends on how accessible the various sights are. I've got references from the postcards and letters my uncle sent, but I have no idea how long it will take to see everything. Why don't you book it for at least three weeks? On second thought, make that four weeks. May as well pay for it all now, too."

"That sounds like a lovely idea, Bob. Now, how were you planning to get to London? Do you have a car?"

"No, I don't. Perhaps you could arrange a transportation service to get me there?"

"I know just the man for you. My fiancé, Alun, runs a limousine service. Would that do?"

"That sounds perfect. What time would we need to leave to get to London in time to catch the flight?"

Tara pursed her lips as she thought for a moment. "First thing tomorrow morning. And I do mean first thing. Crack of dawn, if not before. You need to be at the airport at least two hours ahead of the flight to get through security and check in. Do you have a place to stay here in town?"

"Ah, no. Do you know of ..."

"Aunt Wynny runs a B&B down the road. That would be perfect, I think."

"Sounds grand, Tara."

"Uhm, just one thing, Bob. How will you be paying for all this?"

"How much is it all?"

Tara scribbled furiously on a pad of paper for a minute and handed the calculations to Bob. "That's a rough estimate, but should be close. Can your credit card handle it?"

"Don't have one. Don't believe in 'em. Can I arrange a transfer through a bank?"

Tara gave him a strange look. "No credit card?"

"Nope. There is a bank in town, I assume."

"Uhm, yes. Just down the road a piece. My uncle Dyfan is the manager."

"Excellent. Why don't you give him a call to let him know I'll be popping by in a few minutes? Tell him how much you'll be needing from me, just to make sure he knows. Oh, better double that amount, just to handle incidentals and taxes. Don't want you getting shorted."

Tara just stared at him. Bob got up and smiled as he said, "I'll pop over to the bank now, deal with the money, then pop back. Will that give you enough time?"

Tara burbled for a moment then shook her head. "No. It's rather a lot to do in just a few minutes."

Bob considered that for a moment then said, "Alright, how about this. First I'll deal with the bank, then I'll arrange for a room with your Aunt Wynny. Could you give her a call to let her know to expect me? I have a couple of errands to run after that, so why don't you just drop all the paperwork off with her when you're done? Oh, and give your Alun a call to coordinate a pickup time, and leave a note to let me know when that is? Anything I've forgotten?"

She shook her head, looking a bit numb.

"Grand," exclaimed Bob. "I'll be off to see your uncle at the bank."

He turned and walked out the door, proceeding along the street at a slow pace. He needed to stall for time. Whenever possible, the portal control system set up ties to a world's financial system. He could only hope that something of that sort had been set up here.

Bob established a link with the portal system and explained his request. It turned out that there were a number of financial resources available to him. He selected one in London and one in Bucharest that were sufficiently well-established as to probably avoid any issues. The portal gave him all the necessary passwords and access codes for both. By this time he was drawing alongside the bank, so he terminated the contact and walked inside.

An official greeted him and enquired how he might be of service. Bob asked for Dyfan, and a portly, middle-aged man came out of an office.

"My niece, Tara, just called me. You must be the young fellow she mentioned. Bob, was it? Come in, come in." The man led Bob to an office, directed him to a chair, and shut the door. Sitting in his own chair Dyfan leaned back, steepled his fingers, and asked, "Now, how may the bank be of assistance to you, Mister ..."

"Just call me Bob," he replied, a slight smile tugging at the corners of his mouth.

"As you wish, sir. As you wish. Now ... er ... Bob ... Tara wasn't very clear about what exactly you might be needing. Perhaps if you explained it to me."

"Not much to it, actually. Tara is making some travel arrangements for me and I need to ensure that she has access to the funds necessary to pay for everything. I don't have a credit card, but I do have access to more than ample financial resources at other institutions. I'm not sure how best to do this, though. I'd suggest a direct transfer of fund, but the total amount isn't determined yet. Perhaps setting up an account here that she could draw from might work? I'll be guided by what you think is best."

Dyfan's steepled hands tapped against his pursed mouth for a moment. "Well, Bob, this is somewhat irregular."

Bob smiled. "I've got all the necessary access codes to make the transfer happen immediately. You'll be able to confirm that the account is part of a much larger financial group, with ties to several well-established businesses. I'm merely looking to establish a small source of local funds."

Dyfan tapped at his nose with the tip of a stubby forefinger. "I see."

It was obvious that Uncle Dyfan was not a trusting man. Still smiling, Bob asked to borrow a pad and pen, which were handed to him. He wrote a series of access codes and passwords, then handed the pad to Dyfan. The gentleman took it gingerly, as if handling a counterfeit bill, and examined what Bob had written. His eyebrows rose up as he recognized the bank identifiers.

"Sir ... I mean, Bob ... I'll get this handled right away. As you suggested, we could set up an account here. Ah, would that be a personal account?"

Bob frowned a moment before replying. "Which would make it easier to get payment to anyone requiring it?"

"A business account, certainly. But it pays less interest."

Bob waved a hand. "Not a concern. I only wish to pay for services rendered in a way that gets them paid as quickly as possible."

"I understand, sir, and can appreciate your attitude. Tara implied there was some urgency to this."

Bob nodded. "Yes. I'll be leaving first thing tomorrow morning to catch my flight. Could this all be set up now?"

"Yes, I believe it can be. It's somewhat irregular, but as you say the amount being transferred is negligible compared to the parent account. There will be some papers to sign and perhaps a delay in transferring the funds. Oh, no great amount of time. Just that it might not happen until tomorrow."

"That will be fine. Just so long as you can get confirmation that the funds are available for transfer. I want no question about that. Or much of a delay in paying those who have provided services."

"That won't be a problem. Now, why don't I get this started while we get you those papers to sign. Would you like a cup of tea while you wait?"

Within half an hour all the papers were signed and the wheels set in motion to transfer the funds. Bob had enjoyed the tea and biscuits provided by Dyfan, who turned out to be an enjoyable conversationalist. He shook Bob's hand warmly as they concluded their business.

"A pleasure meeting you, Bob. I do hope you'll drop by after completing your trip. It sounds like it should be quite an adventure."

"I'm very much looking forward to it, Dyfan. Now, if you'll excuse me I need to arrange for a room for the night."

"Be sure to tell Wynny that we've been speaking, and that she's to send the bill here."

"I will, Dyfan. Thank you very much for your assistance. Good evening."

Bob left and headed to Wynny's house and arranged for the room. She showed him to a smallish room on the main floor.

"I hope this will be suitable for you, Bob. It's a bit cramped, but it's got the longest bed. You're a good-sized lad."

"Not at all, Wynny," Bob replied as he beamed at her. "It's perfect."

"Glad you like it. Now, will you be wanting something to eat?"

"Now that you mention it, I am beginning to feel a little hungry. Is there a place to get something to eat around here?"

"Oh, Bob, don't be silly. I can fix you up something."

"Alright, Wynny, that would be lovely. Say, I've heard that Tara's mam runs a tea shop. Would it still be open, do you think? I want to pick up a present for an aunt."

"Ooh, it'd be closed about now. But never you mind. I'll just give Eiriana a call and she'll open it up for you. No, no, it'll be no problem. It's just out the door, turn right, and left at the first corner. There's a big sign, you can't miss it. Dinner will be ready by the time you're back."

Bob thanked her and left. It was a short walk and he found the shop with no problem. Upon opening the door he was assailed by a wave of wonderful scents.

"You must be Bob," said a middle-aged woman, who beamed up at him as she rose from her seat.

"Why, yes. Eiriana?"

"I'm pleased to meet you, Bob. I understand that you're looking for a present for an aunt? An oolong blend, perhaps?"

"Yes. I've heard her raving about oolong black dragon tea. She hasn't had it in ages, and I'd love to get some for her, if you have any."

"Hmm. I believe we do. It's rather a speciality item, you know." She rummaged about in a bin behind the counter. "Ah, yes, here it is. Was ordered special for a local who decided she didn't want it. A full kilogram of it, too. Last time I take special orders from her, let me tell you."

Bob was saved from a long and detailed tale by the ringing of the phone. It turned out to be Wynny saying that Bob's dinner was ready and he should come back right sharpish.

"Well, I'd best wrap this up for you Bob. Apparently you're paying with that new account you've opened up at Dyfan's bank?" Word had certainly gotten around about that.

Bob nodded. "If that's no bother."

"No, no. That will be fine. Could you just sign the receipt here and here, please? Lovely. Now run along. Wynny sets a good table, and you'll not want to keep her waiting."

Bob took the package of tea and headed back to his room. After a very satisfying meal he said that he'd like to take a walk before turning in.

"Don't be staying out too late, Bob. You've got an early start."

"I won't. Besides, I can't leave until Tara drops off all that paperwork."

"Oooh, true. I'll give her a call to remind her. Now off you go, and mind you stay on the main streets. It's getting dark."

Bob thanked her and left. Walking briskly, he reached the edge of town. Looking around to make sure no-one was watching, he headed along the road and eventually into the woods. He trotted at a good clip back to the portal. Once there, he instantiated it and put the tea into the storage compartment along with his staff. He took some of his new money and gave it to the portal as reference. He'd also brought a sample of current clothing and gave that to the portal as well. As an afterthought he gave details of his new account, just in case some future traveller might require it. It was always a good idea to provide for the future, even if it wasn't one's own.

That done, he released the portal and trotted back to town.

Several packages were waiting for him. Two were from Tara, one with his flight information and another with his hotel information. There was an envelope from Dyfan containing a plastic bank card and a note encouraging Bob to use it despite his distrust of such things. Bob smiled and added it to his wallet. Then he stretched out on the bed for a few hours of sleep. Tomorrow promised to be an interesting day.

CHAPTER FIVE
Unexpected Revelations

Bob managed to get to Bucharest with minimal difficulty over the somewhat dated documentation that the portal had provided for him. Having a verifiable paper trail that included well-established banks kept those problems to a minimum, though. It was all enough to make Bob long for a low-tech planet, even if that meant battling Set's minions.

By the time he got to the hotel it was late afternoon and his nerves were somewhat frayed from the hassle and noise of the primitive air transports he'd been forced to use. The hotel turned out to be an older building, and he found the architecture decorative without being ostentatious. The staff were attentive but not clingy, and adjusted their presence to suit his obvious need for privacy. He declined the offer of a porter to carry his luggage, explaining that the light exercise was what he needed after the long trip.

Tara had done a good job in selecting the hotel, in Bob's estimation. The suite wasn't overly large, and consisted of a sitting room, bedroom, and bathroom. All the furnishings complemented each other and were sized to fit the room perfectly. He took his time putting away his few belongings, and took a leisurely walk around the suite. It would have taken a careful observer to note that Bob's wanderings took him past every section of the walls and every piece of furniture. Satisfied that there were no listening devices, he washed up and went downstairs to find something to eat. He ignored the elevator in favour of the stairs. In his experience it was always a good idea to check out all potential escape routes.

Bob walked up to the duty manager at the front desk. "Hi, is there someplace nearby that you'd recommend for a meal?"

"There are many fine establishments near here, sir, both large and small. It really all depends on what you are looking for."

Bob smiled. "Where do you eat when you are on break?"

The manager laughed. "There's a small restaurant halfway down the block, sir. It's not fancy, but the food's first-rate. If that's the type of thing that appeals to you, there's none better in the city."

Bob detected a note of pride in the description. "Family owned is it?" he said in a teasing tone.

The manager shrugged and grinned. "My aunt and uncle own it. But it really is good."

"It sounds like a fine choice. I'll let them know that you recommended it."

"Thank you, sir, I appreciate that. Was there anything else I can help you with?"

"Perhaps later. Best not to keep your aunt and uncle waiting."

That got a chuckle out of the manager, who gave detailed directions on how to find the restaurant. Bob gave a cheerful nod, then turned and left the hotel. The restaurant turned out to be not only small, but also tucked away on a small side-street. It certainly wasn't the sort of place a casual tourist would have found.

When he entered, the first thing that struck Bob were the delectable aromas emanating from the back where the kitchen was. A short, bald man on the late side of middle age came out of the kitchen. Wiping his hands on the apron around his waist, he greeted Bob warmly.

"Welcome, welcome. How can I help you?"

"Actually, I'm looking for something to eat. Are you the owner of this establishment?"

"Yes, sir, I am. With my wife, of course."

"Are you the chef?"

That got a laugh from the old man. "Oh, no, sir. My wife does all the magic with the food, but she allows me to do the heavy lifting and cleaning."

"I heard that," came a woman's voice from the kitchen. "The man came to eat, Mihai, don't let the poor soul starve while you talk his ear off."

Both men grinned at that, and Bob took a seat at a small table. "Your nephew at the hotel recommended this place to me. Said it had the best food in the city."

The old man gave a slight shrug and tilted his head to one side. "Piotr is a good boy. Very loyal to family. But I can only promise good food and plenty of it."

Bob laughed. "I can ask no more than that. Well, I'm a stranger to your country and would love to try food that you enjoy for yourself. It's been a long day of travelling and I'm in no rush. What would you recommend?"

After a brief discussion, a series of dishes was decided on. The old man brought a plate of nibbles and a tankard of beer to keep Bob busy while the main dishes were being prepared. As he sampled the appetizers and drank beer, Bob watched the parade of people through the window. He always enjoyed watching patterns of behaviour, and everyday interactions gave valuable insight into a culture and locale. He was the only sit-down customer, although several people dropped by for takeout orders. After not too long a wait the main dishes began to arrive, and he turned his attention to the food. As promised, it all turned out to be both tasty and plentiful.

At the end of it, Bob leaned back with a contented sigh and

sipped on his coffee. There was no-one else in the restaurant, so he invited the old man and his wife to join him for an after-dinner drink. They were happy to do so, especially since Bob insisted on buying an entire bottle of their best plum brandy.

They sat in companionable silence for several minutes before the old man asked, "So, what brings you to our fair city, Bob? You mentioned that you've been travelling a lot."

Bob explained his desire to follow in the footsteps of his uncle. The elderly couple nodded in sympathy.

"That is a fine idea, Bob, but a difficult research task for an outsider," said the woman. "You should let Mihai help with the research."

Bob raised an eyebrow as he looked at the old man. The latter shrugged and said, "I used to be an historian. Then there were cuts at the university, so we took over this restaurant from her parents when they retired."

"That might be very useful," said Bob in a thoughtful tone. "Hmm. What if I dropped off a list of the names and places I know about, and you take a look at those over the next few days. I'm in no rush, and am happy to tour the city while you find out what you can. I'll pay standard rates, of course."

The old man tried to wave off any mention of payment, while his wife looked conflicted. Finally Bob said in a firm voice, "I always pay my debts. You'll be performing a professional service for me, and I insist on paying the standard rate for that service. Fair is fair. If there are going to be expenses involved, I am willing to advance you those funds. Hmm, wait a moment." Bob took out his wallet and extracted the bank card that Dyfan had given him. "Here, take this. Use it as necessary for expenses, including meals or transportation. Or use it to transfer funds into your own bank account, whichever is easiest for you."

The two oldsters looked at him in shock. Then they began arguing with him, both at the same time. Finally Bob held up a hand and said in a firm voice, "Enough. Please." That silenced their protests for the moment.

"I appreciate that you are trying to be fair about this." His mouth quirked as if suppressing a grin as he added, "And possibly trying to protect me from my own folly. But I assure you that I am sincere in all this. I want to track the movements of my uncle. That is going to take someone with both local knowledge and the skills to track down old information. If you say that you have those skills, then I am willing to take you at your word for the time being. All I ask is that you give it a few days of effort and then get back to me. We can decide what to do from there."

The old couple looked at each other and nodded in acceptance. "That sounds more than fair, Bob," said the old woman. "However," added the old man while waving the bank card, "This is not something you just hand out to people." With that he put it on the table and slid it towards Bob.

"Alright," said Bob, "let's try a different way. Tomorrow I go and open up a local bank account." After seeing both of the oldsters open their mouths to speak, he hurriedly added, "With limited funds, of course. There will be other expenses that I will no doubt incur, and it might prove useful to have a local bank assist me with that. Probably your own local bank would do as well as any ... would you recommend it?"

The old woman nodded. "Putting it that way, yes, that might be useful. Especially if, as you say, you'll be dealing with other local businesses. Our local bank is just down the road, and opens at ten in the morning. Mention us when you go in and everything should go smoothly."

Bob nodded. "That sounds like a good idea. But there's just one minor detail left."

The two looked at him with quizzical expressions.

"What time do you open for breakfast?"

A week passed before Mihai had any detailed news to report. Bob passed the first couple of days touring the city, but soon grew bored with that. He tried doing some research on his own but with little success. In truth, he expected little else given the primitive nature of the planet's data systems.

He dropped by the restaurant several times each day, more for the company and good food than a need to check on Mihai's progress. It turned out that the project was absorbing more and more of his time. His wife, Ioana, was pleased to see her husband engrossed in historical research once again, but was straining to keep up with the demands of the restaurant. When Bob found out he insisted on helping her. Ioana protested, of course, but Bob simply donned an apron and began working. There were dishes to wash, floors to sweep, and garbage to dispose of. Soon he was greeting customers and taking orders.

During one of the daily lulls she finally voiced her concern. "Bob, you're a good boy and a credit to your parents for helping me out. But you really shouldn't. Not when you're paying Mihai to do your research."

Bob continued sweeping the floor. "Nonsense, Ioana. If it bothers you so much, then consider it as a cheaper alternative to hiring temporary staff. Besides, I enjoy it. It's been a long time since I've had to do chores like this. Makes me feel useful. Brings me peace of mind."

Ioana looked at him carefully. In truth, he did look somewhat more relaxed than when he first arrived several days ago. She sighed and insisted that he sit and join her in a cup of coffee. Bob grinned, put the broom to one side, and sat across the table from her. He knew when it was time to bow to superior wisdom. It also helped that Ioana's coffee breaks always included her mouth-watering pastries.

She waited as Bob wolfed down a couple of pastries and a large cup of coffee. It did her heart good to see a young man with a good appetite. Her little restaurant had never been so clean. Mihai was a dear who worked hard, but sometimes the energy of youth was needed for physical labour.

"Oh, Ioana, I forgot to tell you. The parts we need should be arriving today. I'll pop out and pick them up before lunch. Then I'll replace those faulty taps, fix the loose couplings, and replace those broken tiles. Should be done before the evening crowd shows up."

She smiled happily. "That will be lovely, Bob. Truly. Mihai works very hard, but somehow the work piles up faster than we can do everything."

Bob nodded. "I know how that is." He looked around with some pride. "The two of you have done very well here. All you needed was a little bit of extra help to take care of the little things that pile up. I'm pleased to be able to help out. Truly."

"I'm glad to hear that. It's been a pleasure to have you around, and not just for the help you've given us. You're a good man, Bob. There's just one thing ..."

Bob looked at her, a puzzled expression on his face. "Yes? Feel free to ask me anything."

"I don't want to offend you. But ... well, it's this quest of yours. You're putting a lot of effort, and money, into it. It all seems rather quixotic." She squirmed slightly in embarrassment.

To her relief, Bob smiled broadly. "I'm not offended in the slightest, Ioana. Not at all. It's very kind of you and Mihai to worry about me, and very flattering." His expression became serious as he sat back in the chair with a soft sigh. "Your characterization of this as quixotic may not be entirely untrue. I never knew my uncle very well, but my memories of him are good ones. A while back his sister, my aunt, helped me out of a tight spot. She had lost track of her brother when they were younger and after many years of not hearing from him had begun to assume the worst. I promised to look for him. One of the several possible places to begin looking was here. It's as simple as that."

Ioana gave Bob a calculating look. Despite her limited experience with him, she suspected that neither he nor his quest were as simple as he made them out to be. But nothing in Mihai's research indicated anything untoward. Still, Mihai had been hinting at historical oddities that he'd uncovered that demanded more research. The research work had given him a much-needed boost, and she was willing to forgive much of Bob for that gift.

At that moment the door banged open and Mihai barged in, clutching an array of documents to his chest, very excited about something. "Oh, there you both are. Good, good. So much to show you."

He dropped his armload of documents onto the table that Bob and Ioana were sitting at. It was only Bob's reflexes that saved the dishes from being sent crashing to the floor. While he dealt with that, Ioana took Mihai's coat and sat him in a chair.

"Mihai, sit and catch your breath," she said in a stern voice.

"Yes, yes," he replied while waving her off with his right hand. "Stop fussing, woman. I'm fine."

"Then why are you puffing like a steam engine? Sit. Breathe. I will get you a coffee."

"No coffee. Fetch the brandy, Ioana."

Both Ioana and Bob stared at him in surprise. He just sat there grinning and puffing. "Trust me, you two. You'll need a healthy glass before you're ready to hear what I have found. In fact, I will join you. Now, please, fetch the brandy."

Ioana fixed a reproving glare on her husband of many years, sighed as one long martyred, and went to fetch brandy and glasses. Mihai winked at Bob, then closed his eyes and concentrated on calming his breathing. By the time Ioana had returned, Mihai's breathing and colour were both almost back to normal.

"Pour out the glasses and don't be stingy."

Ioana shot him a glare but did as he asked.

"Drink, everyone. Drink it all down." He led by example. The other two looked at each other, shrugged, and followed suit.

Mihai took a deep breath and placed both his hands on the table, palms down. He turned slightly to face Bob. "OK. First of all, yes, I've found some references that seem to be of your uncle. And those point to other references. And those point to ... well, I'll get to that in a moment. First, let's get that map unrolled out here on the table."

It took a minute to move their now-empty glasses and unfurl the map and get it adjusted just so. Then Mihai leaned back, made a contented sound as he settled into the chair, and pointed a large index finger at Bob. "First of all, don't lie to an historian. No, no, don't deny it. Just shush and let me talk. Okay? Historians are trained to sort through falsehoods and bullshit to find as close an approximation to the truth as possible. It's what we do. Some falsehoods are total fabrications, some play games with the truth, and some are honest mistakes. And, yes, time tends to wash away everything, whether true or false. But echoes remain, if nothing else. Think of history as a tapestry composed of many threads. Some threads are original, some are forgeries, and some are missing. Historians seek out the patterns of the tapestry, whatever the nature of the threads. We follow those patterns wherever they may lead."

While Mihai spoke, Bob was leaning back in his chair with steepled fingers, watching with polite interest. Inside, though, his excitement was growing. This may or may not be a dead end for finding Uncle Sid, but there might be an interesting mystery here. In his experience trained researchers rarely got this excited over nothing.

Mihai paused for a moment as he leaned forward to stare

intently at Bob. "My first question to you is, when did your uncle arrive here?"

Bob gave him a puzzled look before answering. "I'm not exactly sure of the date."

To his surprise, Mihai smiled before asking his next question. "And how old are you, Bob?"

Despite his attempt at calmness, Bob's head jerked back. "Excuse me?"

Mihai leaned back in his seat. "Also, where are you and your uncle from?"

Ioana had placed a hand on her husband's shoulder and was beginning to squeeze with some pressure. Mihai patted her hand before resting his own upon it. He turned to her and said, "We're safe enough, I think." Then he turned to Bob. "Am I right?"

Bob sighed, but was otherwise silent for some seconds. "This is not going the way I thought it would," he said. Then he saw his friends tense up and hurried to add, "Oh, don't worry. You have nothing to fear from me."

"So where are you from? Is 'Bob' your real name?" asked Ioana with some hesitation.

Bob chuckled and smiled as he faced them. "Yes, that's my real name." At their disbelieving looks he hurried to add, "Truly. I chose it myself, as is the custom among my people." He shook his head and said with a hint of defensiveness, "It's a good name, with a proud history. Really."

Sensing that there were some deeper issues, Ioana asked, "And what do your parents call you?"

To her surprise Bob laughed. "My father called me 'youngest son'. My mother would often refer to me as 'accursed spawn of the Nameless Ones'. I prefer to be called 'Bob'".

"Ah," was all Ioana said. She sensed that he might come from a family with serious issues.

"And your uncle?" asked Mihai in a soft voice.

Bob turned to look at him, still smiling. "He came here about eight hundred years ago, plus or minus. And, yes, he might still be alive. And no, he was not a young man when he arrived here. Yes, he is older than me."

"Where do you come from?" asked Ioana in a quavering voice.

"Ioana. Mihai. You are my friends. Please, I am not here to hurt anyone. Not you, nor anyone on this planet. I'm only searching for my uncle. Nothing more."

"But why did he come here, Bob? To this country? To this planet?" asked Mihai.

All trace of humour was gone from Bob's face as he looked at his friends. "There was a war. My uncle's planet was attacked by a vastly superior force. His family saved him and his sister before destroying their planet to eliminate the invaders. She was found, and is safe. Better than safe, actually ... she saved another planet of humans from being exterminated by unknown enemies. Her brother remains lost, after all this time. He came here—if he came here at all—by an accident of fate."

"Being out of touch for so long is not normal?" asked Ioana.

"No. It is most definitely not."

"This war of which you speak ..."

"Fought and finished a very long time ago. The attack on my uncle's planet was an aberration that occurred long after the war was over. Assumed to be the last gasp by enemy forces."

"And what about that other planet? The one your aunt saved?"

Bob shrugged. "It might have been natural causes, but she had reason to believe that there was outside interference. She—and her whole family—were medical researchers. Very respected among my people, actually. But even with her expertise, all she found were hints. Still, I put my trust in her hunches."

"And your uncle? Was he a medical expert as well?"

Bob cleared his throat. "Not exactly. I don't have the whole story. No-one really talked about his family after the attack. Still, I gather he was something of a black sheep. I don't know the details. But as I said, my memories of him are good ones."

Mihai grunted. "Your people sound like us. Sound human."

Bob smiled broadly. "We are. It's complicated, but we are."

"Why do you think he is here?" asked Mihai.

"This was one of two planets that he might have been sent to. If he was sent here, this area is where he most likely would have arrived."

"That is a lot supposition."

Bob shrugged. "It's all I have at this point."

"Why wasn't a full-scale search done centuries ago?" asked Ioana.

Bob cleared his throat. "It gets complicated. We—my people—are not numerous, and are far-flung. When nothing was heard from him most people assumed him to be dead. There was a search of the most probable destinations. It's a big universe. People move on."

"But your aunt survived?"

"Yes, but she had lost everything. Not just her home, but her entire family. That's the type of loss my people don't recover from."

"But she did."

"Yes, she did. Apparently my dad helped her. I only found out about it when I stumbled onto the world she was living on."

"Your father never told you?"

Bob sighed. "No. But then, we never talked about such things when I was young. Then I left home."

"I'm so sorry to hear that," said Ioana. "Surely you've

spoken with your family since?"

"No," was Bob's curt reply.

Ioana opened her mouth to speak, but Mihai patted her hand to stop her. "I'm sorry to hear that, Bob, but I'm sure that you aren't here to discuss your family. Except for your missing uncle." Bob gave a slight nod, the expression of his face returning to its normal good humour.

"Alright then. Yes, I found references to those places you had on your list. Most of them, anyway. But the timelines didn't line up. There was no reason for your uncle to be in those places during the dates you mentioned."

Bob held up a hand to interrupt. "The dates were wrong? How so?"

Mihai smiled before answering. His demeanour was falling back into professorial mode. "Some of those dates fell within bad times in our country ... civil unrest, war, and whatnot. Just perhaps an innocent know-nothing might be so unaware of such things as world wars and communist occupation, but you are no fool."

"There are those who would beg to differ," offered Bob, smiling broadly. Both of his friends chuckled at that.

The mood was somewhat lightened by the laughter, and Mihai continued. "Be that as it may, Bob, it was a conundrum that nagged at me. Something about those cities that I could not recall. I had lunch with some old colleagues and mentioned my research. We all had a good laugh at your expense, I'm afraid. Then one of them—you remember Vasile, Ioana—got a strange look on his face. His speciality is Medieval and pre-Medieval history of our country. Many of the places on your list had some fascinating folk legends associated with them." Mihai pointed at the map. "See, I've marked the places on your list in green."

They all looked at the map for a minute. Ioana broke the silence, "It all looks random, my love."

Mihai grinned. "So it does, dear. But Vasile's research put

dates on various legends, with the objective of attempting to find the source of them. All very academic and of interest to very few."

"Until you started asking questions," said Bob, the smile on his face not disguising his honest interest. "How many different legends or stories are we talking about?"

That earned him a nod from Mihai. "An excellent question, Bob. There are dozens at each location. How would you have approached this problem?"

"A semantic analysis," replied Bob still looking at the map. He looked up at Mihai before adding, "Can you adjust your filters to take into account linguistic drift and dialect-based differences?" Mihai nodded, both as confirmation and encouragement to continue.

Bob nodded. "Good. Given that, you can construct a ... well, I'd call it a probability matrix but you may have another term for it ... of the various stories against the locations. Oh, and tag each entry by date. That way you'd be able to track the geographical spread of each story over time. Compare the time-based spread of each story and check for commonalities of origins."

Ioana laughed and clapped her hands. "You sound like one of Mihai's students.

Mihai looked pleased as he beamed at Bob. "Very good. Yes, that's exactly what we did. Easy to say, of course, but somewhat more difficult to implement. That's what took the time, you see. Not much of the source material is digitized, so we had to do much of it by paper and memory. Heh, I even called in some retired colleagues. Offered them a fee, but they were so excited by the prospect of doing some original research that they refused the money. Oh, Ioana, it was like old times again. Good times." He looked at her and beamed.

Bob cleared his throat. "We'll have to do something for them. Perhaps host a party to celebrate the successful end to a research project."

Mihai took the gentle hint and turned to face Bob. "Finished? Oh, my, no. Just begun. But we have enough preliminary results to be worth sharing with you. I've prepared some overlays. Bob, if you'd be so kind as to pass me the briefcase?"

Bob handed the briefcase over with some care—it was heavy and he didn't want his friend to hurt himself. Mihai opened it up, took out a sheaf of papers, then dropped the case onto the floor. Pointing at the map, he began lecturing his audience.

"You'll note all the locations here. We found seven legends or stories that are very probably common to some of the locations. Don't worry about the timelines just yet. Here is legend number one." He laid a thin paper over the map and arranged it so that a dozen of the locations were highlighted.

"This is legend number two." He removed the first paper and replaced it with another. This time seven locations were highlighted, all but two being different from the first page.

One by one, Mihai showed them the results for the different legends. At the end he sat back to let the others think about what they had seen. Bob had an anticipatory grin on his face. He looked at Mihai and said, "There's a focus."

Mihai nodded. "Yes, there is. How can you tell without looking at the timelines?"

Bob felt like a student being tested, but he didn't mind. "Create a combined overlay showing the distribution of each legend." He began to reach for the stack of papers, but was interrupted by a chuckle from Mihai.

"Already done, my boy, already done." He placed another paper over the map. It showed a smeared arc of colour for each of the different legends.

Ioana shook her head. "It looks like a jumble to me."

"No," Bob answered. "Look at it as if each legend were a single event, rather than geographically dispersed. There's a field of activity that encompasses, or at least forms an arc, around that part of the country." He pointed out a section of the map, and twirled his finger to indicate the area under discussion. Then he added, "It's a crude centre, I'll grant you. Mihai, did you do a timeline analysis of these legends?" Looking at Ioana he added, "That'll help narrow the area of interest."

"Yes we did, and yes it does. Here, let me show you." He replaced the paper with another. This new page had a series of arcs. "You'll notice that they all point to the same general area." Both Bob and Ioana nodded.

"Great," said Bob. "That's where I need to go."

"Don't be so hasty," said Mihai. "You'll want to hear about the legends."

The tone in the other man's voice put a damper on Bob's enthusiasm. "Not good stories, I gather."

Mihai shook his head. "Not at all. Now, keep in mind that many of the very old stories were meant to frighten people into obedience. Still, even taking that into account these stories are rather nasty." He hesitated for a moment as he drew a deep breath. "Bob, I have to ask this. What sort of person was your uncle?"

The question took Bob by surprise. "Uhm, as I told you, I always thought of him as a good person. But I was very young and only ever met him a few times. Why do you ask?"

Mihai sighed. "Have you ever heard the stories about vampires?"

"Oh, Mihai," said Ioana, laughing. "Those Dracula stories were all based on Vlad the Impaler. Then those got exaggerated by that English author over a hundred years ago."

"Sorry, my love, but that's not quite true. I'm not talking about Dracula. There are old stories from our own country. Stories that tell, in gruesome detail, of murders committed over decades if not centuries. Bodies stolen from graveyards and dismembered. These stories pre-date the vampire legends by centuries."

"Witchcraft?" asked Ioana, shaking her head in disbelief.

"No, something else." Mihai inhaled sharply and let his breath out slowly. "The stories are all surprisingly clear on that. It is as if something not human stalked the land, periodically attacking and killing many people before vanishing for years at a time. Whole graveyards unearthed and the bodies taken or dismembered. On occasion, entire families were slaughtered. So I must ask again, Bob. What sort of person was your uncle?"

"He came from a family of healers, dedicated to helping people. Although not a healer himself, I can't believe that he would turn feral and do such things."

Ioana said in a soft voice, "War can change people, Bob. So can great loss. You said that no-one has heard from him since the day he came here. That is a very long time to be on one's own."

"A long time, yes, but not the burden for my kind that you seem to think it would be." Bob's face became impassive. "I need to go there," he said pointing at the map. "I need to find out the truth of this."

"And if the worst has happened? What will you do?" asked Mihai.

"Whatever needs doing. Have no fear on that score." He looked at each of them in turn, and they felt the full impact of the fire behind his gaze. "You have my word on that. Now, how do I arrange transportation there?"

CHAPTER SIX
Prince of Darkness

Bob trotted through the dense forest. It was very much as Mihai had described it, a remote and mountainous region that was heavily forested. The sky was overcast, but the dense woods would have made even a bright day seem gloomy. There was an on and off drizzle of rain that left a sheen on everything and made the footing treacherous. A perfect day for infiltrating a mysterious forest that had a dangerous past. Bob was quite enjoying himself.

Getting here had not been any problem. The real problem was convincing his friends to leave him here on his own with no means of communicating with them. He explained that his training and experience were more than a match for anything he might encounter, but to no avail. Finally, he resorted to doing a one-handed lift of the front end of their car. Only then did they grudgingly admit that he might be capable of taking care of himself. After dropping him off outside the forest, they had left him on his own.

Thinking of them brought a happy smile to his face. It had been a while since he'd had a long visit with people, and it was always nice to make new friends. Still, it was time to focus on the task at hand. As he moved through the forest he'd been noting the patterns of the wildlife in the area. That pattern was changing the closer he got to the mysterious centre hinted at by the analysis of the legends.

There were any number of reasons that the local wildlife might be acting differently, and he wasn't familiar enough with the area to know all of them. Still, there were fewer animals around than he would have expected. Pausing every so often to listen, he moved his head around to check for visual clues. There was a light breeze and there were still several hours before local sunset. He could hear birds and the movement of small animals coming from where he'd entered the forest, but there was little near him and even less towards his destination. Which would indicate that he was going in the correct direction. It was time to slow things down a notch and emphasize a stealthy approach.

Given the size of the forest, and the unknown location of his target (assuming the target even existed), he was loathe to move too slowly. He compromised by slowing his pace to a brisk walk, but being extra careful about where he put his feet. That allowed him to move at a reasonable speed while maintaining a silent approach.

After a few minutes of this a faint whisper made him stop and duck behind some cover. He listened intensely for several seconds before realizing that he had sensed not a sound, but the touch of a low-intensity energy field. To confirm this, he moved his head slowly back and forth for a few seconds then grinned. It was the edge of a fear-inducing field, similar to the ones around the portals. Someone was definitely here and trying to keep the locals away.

Swivelling his head allowed him to get a rough bearing on the field generator. He moved very slowly until he was a dozen body-lengths away from his original spot and took another bearing. It was a rough form of triangulation, but more than good enough for the task. The point of origin was within an especially dense part of the forest that nestled at the base of some sheer rock cliffs. The forest made it impossible to estimate a distance accurately, but he figured it couldn't be too far away. The base of the cliffs was probably a good place to start looking so he headed there.

The fear-field was not very strong, but was becoming irritating, so he had his internal systems create a weak neutralizing field. Upon reaching the cliffs he cut it off to get another directional reading. The cliffs reflected the field, making triangulation difficult, but it looked to be coming from his right. Moving with caution he followed the cliff face, which shortly made a sharp turn deeper into the forest. Just ahead was a modest dwelling, the exact nature of which was hard to discern in the gloom of the woods. It was well located, hidden from sight from anyone who hadn't reached this spot along the cliff, which the fear-field would preclude.

He kept very still and scanned the structure at all wavelengths his eyes could discern. It appeared to be a standard cottage for the area, old but well maintained, built with local materials. Viewing in infrared showed that it was warmer than the ambient area, suggesting it was being used by someone. There was only one way to find out if that someone was home.

Bob examined the building again, this time looking for security devices. Nothing stood out as being suspicious, nor were there any reflections that might indicate weapons or monitoring devices. There were no windows of any sort, but there was a door placed just off-centre. A careful look around the perimeter revealed that the house was nestled partially into a cave with only the single door for access. This was a well-designed facility.

Moving with caution he headed towards the door, swivelling his head in a constant sweep for potential problems. Once at the door he examined it with some surprise. There were no obvious locking or sensor mechanisms, just a simple latch. After a moment of indecision, he lifted the latch and stepped inside.

On the inside, the building was to all appearances a snug

little cottage. Off to his left was a small kitchen, to his right a couple of rustic but comfortable-looking chairs sitting in front of a fireplace. That was interesting, as he'd not seen a chimney. There was a short hallway with a couple of door-less small rooms to either side. At the end of the hallway was a substantial looking door, but this one had what looked to be a hefty locking mechanism of some sort. That would no doubt lead to something else that was inside the cave the building was nestled into.

He looked at the fireplace again and frowned. Although there was no fire in it, there were indications of heavy use. Then he looked around and realized that there was another discontinuity from the outside appearance—windows. There were several large frosted windows, each providing a modest amount of illumination. Another interesting datum was that the fear-field was gone. That was the only thing that made sense—who would want to live inside a fear-field?

Bob shut the door carefully, making sure that it latched, and went to examine the fireplace. There was a good draw of air up the chimney. The soot his fingers brushed off looked and smelled real enough. He could feel heat from the hearth, as if from the remains of a fire that had burnt out not too long ago. It was all most peculiar, and Bob grinned with anticipation at the mystery and puzzle it presented.

There was a loud bang as the door at the end of the hallway flew open. A figure flew in, a large cape giving it the appearance of appearing out of roiling darkness. Out of the swirling chaos of the cape reached out a pair of arms, the large hands hooked into claws. A voice boomed out, "Who dares to enter my abode? Prepare to be consumed!"

Bob stood up without haste and brushed his hands on his pants. "Hi, Uncle Sid."

The figure halted its flight and sank to the ground. The cape ceased fluttering and then hung motionless from the figure's shoulders, revealing a man of indeterminate middle age. The man was a head taller than Bob, and had a long, thin face. His shoulders were as broad as Bob's, but the extra height gave him a slender look. He held himself stiffly erect, with an air of great strength held in coiled readiness.

"What? Who?" he spluttered, at a loss at how to react. His voice, no longer booming, was a rich baritone.

Bob laughed. "You used to pull that exact stunt on me whenever you visited us. When I was a kid."

The man had by this time regained his composure, and stared at Bob with an intensity that looked into the soul. Bob returned the stare measure for measure.

"Bob?" he whispered. "Bob! It *is* you! All grown up!" Sid dashed forward and embraced Bob warmly. Then, holding onto the younger man's shoulders, he held him at arm's length. "Oh, it is so good to see you, boy." He enveloped Bob in a hug again, before holding him at arm's length once more.

Sid's voice bubbled with laughter. "What brings you here? How did you find me?" Then he became serious and asked, "Is there trouble? Has the Enemy followed you here?"

"Everything is fine. Everyone is fine. Don't worry," he assured his uncle. Then his own face grew serious as he said, "But we need to have a talk, Uncle Sid. A serious talk."

"Oh. Well, yes, I suppose we do. Would here do? I've got quarters in the cave, of course, but I like to sit in front of the fire. Helps me relax."

"That would be fine, sir." Bob allowed his uncle to lead him to a chair in front of the fireplace.

"Just sit there, my lad, and I'll get a nice fire going. Nothing like a good fire to warm the soul." Sid puttered about with kindling and logs and lit a fire. It started quickly and they were soon basking in its comforting glow.

"Can I get you anything to eat or drink?" asked Sid.

"No, thank you. Please, Uncle, just sit. We need to talk." Bob was sitting upright with his hands on his thighs, as if sitting at attention.

Sid removed his cloak, tossing it over the edge of the chair as he sat. "This sounds rather serious."

"Yes, sir, it is."

Sid met Bob's gaze and sighed. In a soft voice he said, "You want to know why I'm here, and why I've not contacted anyone in all these years. That about sum it up?"

"Yes, sir, it is."

Keeping his voice soft, Sid responded, "You're being awfully formal, Bob."

"Sir, it has to do with how I found you. You've entered local folklore, and not in a good way. Why is that?"

Sid's face creased as he gave a slight lopsided smile. "I'm well aware of the tales. Many of them, at any rate. And, before you ask, yes, there is some truth to them."

"May I hear your side of things, sir." It was not a question, and Bob's tone was flat and emotionless.

"Yes. But first you need some background. You're aware of what happened to my family and home?"

"I know the basics."

"Well, whatever you've heard ... what anyone has heard ... can't begin to tell the whole story." Sid inhaled deeply and exhaled slowly to calm himself. "After all these years the pain still cuts deeply." He leaned forward, resting his elbows on his thighs, his hands clasped tightly. "They came without warning. An entire battle fleet. You know my family, Bob. We're healers and researchers, not soldiers. But, like all families, we had some defences. Those took out a big chunk of the fleet, but not enough. My grandparents had awoken by that point. They were very old and slept most of the time. You never met them, of course." Sid paused, and he looked at something far away in space and time.

"They were raised in a different time, and had battle aspects which they kept even after choosing the Precepts of Healing. They rose up, the two of them, and destroyed the remainder of the fleet before succumbing to their wounds. My cousins—whom you probably never met—went out to replenish and repair the planetary defence stations. My father went out into space to recover the bodies of his parents, my grandparents. There was only my mother, my sister, and myself left at the main household. Mother coordinated the others, and Freida sent out details of the attack to as many other families as she could. I checked our stores for weapons and brought up as many as I could find. Then the next wave hit us."

Sid's voice had become very quiet, and Bob strained to hear him. Then Sid locked eyes with Bob and his voice regained its normal strength.

"The second wave was even larger than the first, and they knew exactly where to hit and with what sorts of weapons. My cousins and father never had a chance. None of us had true battle aspects, you see, as those would interfere with our chosen path. Oh, they hit the Enemy hard, but there were just too many. Their ships enveloped the planet and began a precision bombardment. They had energy weapons, orbital kinetic weapons, missiles ... just like in the histories of the Great Wars. First they took out the offensive weapons, then the defensive screens, and then there was only the household left. All we had were hand weapons against a battle fleet. We managed to do some damage, but not enough to matter."

Sid's right hand flashed out and grasped Bob's hand, gripping without applying excessive force as if he had no strength left. "We had lost, Bob. Totally. Throughout this, mother had stayed at the main control console. During a lull in the bombardment she instantiated a portal and yelled at me to return to the house—I was outside with a battle rifle—and I got inside in time to see my sister enter the portal. It flickered and wavered, but mother managed to restore it and ordered me to leave. I'd always been a contrary child, and refused. She didn't argue, just hit me hard enough to stun me, then tossed me into the portal. Just before entering the transit field I managed to catch a glimpse of what she was setting up on the control board."

Sid's hand fell away, and he sat there as if the weight of the universe were on his shoulders. He was silent for a few moments, and when he spoke again his voice was empty of emotion.

"She had set the portal to overload. Maximum release of energy. That can only be done under manual control. That's the last I saw of her or any of my family."

A look of pity and sorrow flashed across Bob's face before he got his emotions under control. "And then?" he asked in a soft voice.

"I arrived on this planet. Mother must have set up the portal transfer as a bounce-jump, because as soon as I exited, the portal bounced me elsewhere on the planet. Not too far from here, actually." Sid looked up and made a circular motion with a hand devoid of strength.

"Uncle Sid. Your sister, Freida is alive and well. I saw her not too long ago."

"What? Where?" Sid leaped to his feet, his eyes blazing.

"She was sent to another location, but managed to get in contact via the portal network. She had spent some time on a sanctuary planet when my dad found her and asked her to look into a problem on one of his planets. There was a global plague raging and he wanted her to try to stop it. After fixing the problem she decided to stay."

"A plague, you say?" Sid was on his feet now, pacing back and forth. "Your father did the right thing setting her on that problem. She's the talented one, you know. But tell me, she is well?"

At the look of yearning on his uncle's face, Bob forced his own face to soften its expression. "She is well. Helping the planet, and its human population, recover from the ravages of the plague. Doing a lot of gardening, I gather. And raising pets."

"Pets. Oh, I can just imagine. Still going for the more fearsome types, I suppose?" Sid managed to find a smile inside himself.

Bob laughed. "Indeed. Tried to eat me when I showed up."

Sid echoed the laugh, although it was a bit strained, as if he was out of practise. "Hope you didn't hurt them. Or at least hid the bodies if you did."

"Nah. Just a few bruises until they decided they weren't really that hungry."

"And is she happy? Truly happy?"

Bob nodded. "Seems to be, actually. Has become something of a philosopher these days. Keeps in touch with her old gang, some of them at least. Apparently been exchanging notes about philosophy with Aunt Gertrude."

"Gertrude? Philosophy?" Sid's head jerked back. Then his face took on a thoughtful expression. "I could imagine my sister going that route. But Gertrude? Imagine that. But tell me more about this plague she cured."

Bob was puzzled by the request, and asked, "Why the interest in plagues?"

"Ah. There was more than one, was there?"

Bob sighed. "Yes, uncle, there were. Several of them, in fact. Seemingly natural in origin, but Aunt Freida suspects that someone had an active hand in it. She also thinks she has evidence of multiple waves of population arrivals in a culture with no space-travel capability."

Sid surged to his feet and resumed his pacing. "It fits. It fits," he muttered to himself.

"What fits, sir? Uncle Sid, please stop pacing. What fits?"

As instructed, Sid stopped pacing and turned to face Bob. "Plagues, Bob. Shortly after I got here there was a plague. Actually a series of plagues over the years. Then there were the strange readings from the portal, and ... and ... I was all alone and afraid that the Great Wars had returned and didn't know what to do." He buried his face in his hands, weeping softly. It was nearly a minute before he raised his head, wiped his eyes, and muttered an apology.

Throughout this display, Bob maintained a stoic expression despite his inner turmoil. It was one thing to stumble upon a mystery, but quite another when the mysteries insisted on popping up faster than he could solve them. His most immediate problem, of course, was what to do about Uncle Sid. Was he a simple castaway or something much worse?

By this time Sid had recovered his equilibrium and faced Bob squarely, a slight lopsided smile on his face. "You're wondering what to make of me, aren't you, nephew? Can't say as I blame you. It's also your duty, however unpleasant or disconcerting you may find it." His face became blank, and his voice took on a ritual cadence as he added, "Ask your questions and let the truth be revealed."

"Thank you, sir. But this is not a judgement, for I have no authority from the Conclave to conduct one."

Sid had a puzzled look on his face. "But why else would you be here?"

Bob sighed. "As I mentioned earlier, I met your sister. But that was by accident while tracking another mystery—I'll get to that later. She explained about how the two of you had gotten separated. But no-one knew your destination, you see. My dad managed to get some energy readings that hinted at possible locations. After all the most probable ones got checked out, everyone lost hope of finding you. This was one of the few on the faint-hope list and she asked me to check it out for her. So here I am."

"Your father has always been a master portal engineer," Sid said as he nodded. "None better. Still, how did you track me to this place?"

"Dad taught me some of the basics. I checked the portal logs when I arrived and worked out the probabilities of where the portal might have bounced you. That got me to Romania. I stumbled across some local historians, and they correlated legends with the locations that I had gleaned from the portal logs from when you accessed it for data. The sources of the legends indicated this general area as a locus, so I came here and started poking around. Stumbled across your fear-field, and here I am. Straight-forward stuff, all in all."

"Uh huh. Straight-forward," Sid's eyebrows rose slightly at the tale. He shook his head in amazement. "I ... well, never mind. Suffice to say that I'm impressed, Bob. But continue with your questions. I assume they are about those legends that led you here."

"Yes, uncle, they are. They tell of a series of killings and mutilations over the course of decades, if not longer. Also the digging up of bodies at cemeteries, also over decades. Also some very old stories about werewolves and vampires."

Sid sighed. "As I said earlier, those stories are not entirely without some truth." He held up his hands with the palms towards Bob, as the younger man stiffened. "But also not without good reasons, I assure you. Remember that I mentioned plagues?"

Bob nodded.

"Well, when I arrived here the portal bounced me at some height above the mountains. You'll recall that a bounce is an emergency measure and assumes that a person will levitate or apport to safety."

Again Bob nodded.

Sid continued. "My body's energy reserves were low and my emotional state was a mess. Unlike your family, I've never been trained for combat situations. None of us were. Oh, yes, my sister chose a combat aspect, but that was out of respect for our grandparents. Besides, she'd replaced most of the battle functions with medical gear. Anyway, the best I managed was a rough landing. Got banged up rather badly and had to hobble around bent over for a few months while my healing factors regenerated enough to heal me." He chuckled at the memory. "For a while it was easier to walk around on all fours, when I could walk at all. Funny to look back on, but terribly painful at the time."

Then his mood turned sombre. "But psychologically I was a mess. I'd lost everything and everyone I ever cared about ... or who had cared about me. The Enemy from the Great Wars had returned. I ... shut down."

Sid took a deep breath and raggedly exhaled. "I'm not proud of that, Bob. But that's what happened. I roamed the woods in a fugue state for several months. Caught and ate small animals to stave off hunger. The larger predators learned the hard way to leave me alone. For some reason, a pack of wolves sort of adopted me. They liked snacking on the remains of my kills, and decided I was useful enough to hang out with. Truth be told, I rather enjoyed having the company."

"How did this become legend, Uncle?" prompted Bob.

Sid chuckled. "Even in my fugue state I stayed in the deep woods, away from the human population. Still, every so often bands of them would come into the woods. I avoided them without being seen until one day they tried to attack my pack. I rose up and chased them away. Think about it, Bob. Out of a pack of wolves arises a human figure, naked and screaming and running towards them as if attacking."

"Did you attack them?"

"Of course not!" came Sid's shocked reply. "But I couldn't let them hurt my friends, could I?" He sighed before continuing. "After that happened a few more times, the locals stopped coming into that part of the woods. Hence the legend of the fearsome wolfman creature." The expression on Bob's face caused Sid to hastily add, "No-one was harmed by me, I assure you. Well, aside from some minor cuts and bruises received when they tried to apprehend me. My healing factors were getting back to normal by that point, so any injuries inflicted on myself healed quickly. Hence the notion of the wolfman creature being invulnerable to mortal weapons."

"So you avoided the locals?"

Sid shook his head. "Only for those first few months. By the time my healing factors had regenerated and got my body back into shape, I was thinking rationally again. It was time meet my human neighbours."

"Did you have any weapons or supplies with you?"

"No. And by that time my clothes were gone." Sid smiled. "Can you guess what legend that spawned?"

Bob answered the smile with one of his own. "The man-of-the-forest or green man. I assume you made clothes out of the forest materials?"

Sid nodded. "Indeed. And, yes, I'm sure I was the source of those legends as well. Or, at the very least, added some substance to stories that already existed. It's difficult to be sure with these sorts of things."

"Alright, Uncle Sid, but how did you learn the language? The portals logs show periodic accesses to the databases from this area."

"And I thought I was being so careful," said Sid with a touch of irritation. "Didn't realize the portal would triangulate a simple data request."

Bob chuckled. "Don't feel too bad, Uncle Sid. The information is buried in the debugging logs, and not many people know it is even there much less how to interpret it."

Sid gave a small shrug. "Thank you for that, nephew. Well, yes, I downloaded what little information the portal had. The language it gave me turned out to be somewhat archaic, but I managed to communicate. Took a while to figure out the social structure and earn what passed for currency, but I managed to fit myself into things reasonably well. Had to move every few years so people wouldn't notice my lack of ageing, so I became an itinerant fixer of things and seller of nostrums."

"I'd have thought you would have set yourself up as a healer," said Bob.

That got a chuckle from Sid. "Oh, no. It's true that I came from a family of healers but I was the family shame, you see. Could never quite get a handle on the medical studies, or scholarly pursuits of any kind. In fact ended up rebelling against it. Became a traveller and something of a wastrel. Took on this aspect to make it easier to travel among humans. Eventually got homesick, so I swallowed my pride and went home to help out with general chores and such. But it turns out that along the way I had picked up enough to be useful here." Sid's face took on a happy look as he remembered the past. Then after a moment it hardened. "Then the plague came. This planet's history books call it the Black Death. You've heard of it?"

Bob shook his head. "Not until I met up with the local historians. Something rather nasty I gather."

Sid gave a curt nod. "Very nasty. No-one is sure what it was or where it came from or how it spread. Lots of theories, even now. Back then it was considered to be the work of something evil. They didn't have any idea about germs or viruses, you see. And when the people began to die off—it was just a few days from when symptoms appeared until they died—people worried. When whole villages got wiped out, people panicked. It was an ugly time, Bob, an ugly time."

"So what did you do, Uncle?"

"The only thing I could do, Bob. I tried to find a cure or at least something to ease the suffering. But I had no equipment, no staff, no resources aside from what I could find locally. The only thing I had was my interrupted training and a minimal talent for medicine, but that turned out to be enough. It took a couple of years, but I managed to put together a primitive lab capable of doing serious work. Do you know anything about going about finding a cure for a disease? No? I'm not surprised given how effective our healing factors are. Well, to find a cure one needs to isolate the cause of the disease. Determine if it is a bacteria or virus, how it is spread, where it resides in the body, its effects on the body, that type of thing. In short, one needs samples. So I began to examine corpses. That gave me some information but not enough, so I needed fresh samples. Not surprisingly, the locals didn't understand such things and looked upon my work as some sort of dark magic."

"You raided cemeteries?"

Sid nodded, and Bob continued his questioning. "But why were so many corpses needed? The stories tell of whole graveyards emptied."

Sid gave a small shrug. "Not every death was caused by the plague, you know. Those weren't the most sanitary of times. On top of that I needed to understand how their bodies functioned, which meant autopsies. It meant keeping samples of those bodies, too. My lab got discovered a couple of times, forcing me to move and start over. That slowed my progress and started a few more stories and legends going."

"And the attacks on the living?"

"Yes, yes, there were some of those. But only to get a sample of blood for analysis. No-one was seriously hurt, you understand, but it did frighten them. Actions of that sort on top of the plague that was ravaging the continent started people talking. Not surprising, but it forced me to change my tactics."

"How so?"

"I went out at night and took blood samples as they slept. Gave them a light dose of anaesthetic gas, then used a hypodermic needle to draw a small sample of blood. No harm to anyone except for a trifling puncture wound that healed within a few days. That allowed me to get samples from a wide range of ages, sexes, and health. Could sample a small village in a night, and larger towns in a week depending on the population. Travelling around also allowed me to track the progress of the disease. That was the first oddity I encountered. The disease was carried by rats—and there were a lot of those—who were infected by small insects. The oddity was that the progress of the disease often outran the rate of travel of the rats or even humans. But I was too busy trying to find a cure to worry about that."

"Did you find the cure, uncle?"

The look on Sid's face was one of infinite sadness. "Yes, Bob, I did. It took me a few years but I came up with a vaccine. The next trick was to produce and distribute enough of it to make a difference. It was a race, you see. The plague was spreading like a wildfire that threatened to wipe out the bulk of the population. It was too much for a single person, so I recruited and trained several dozen people to help me. It wasn't easy, but we did it. They were a great team, with some of the finest people I've ever known. Smart and dedicated. It was a crude setup, of course, but we made it work. The bulk of the vaccine we put into water supplies and foodstuffs. Not the best way to administer a vaccine, but better than nothing. A couple of my team had a knack for mathematics and figured out the path of the plague. That allowed us to predict which population centres were the next targets, and we focused our distribution efforts there. For areas that needed a more concentrated effort, I went out at night and inoculated people as they slept."

"How did you cover so much ground so quickly?"

Sid shrugged. "I'm very good at levitating and apporting. And, towards the end, I stopped caring if people saw me. The only thing that mattered was stopping the plague. Which we did."

"What was the cost?" Bob asked in a soft voice.

"About fifty percent of the population died, overall. Perhaps more. Whole families and towns wiped out."

"And your team?"

"I was out on a vaccination run one night, the last one we had planned. I came back to our compound only to find it ablaze. Every one of my team was dead. All the equipment and supplies destroyed."

"Locals?"

"No. Someone else. Someone with the training to do infiltration and large-scale targeted killing."

"You tracked them down." It wasn't a question.

"Tried to, but the trail went cold. Found a few things that suggested increases in shipping to places just before plague outbreaks, but nothing specific."

"What did you do then?"

"Shut down for a time. I'd found another family, in a sense, and lost them." He looked around the cabin. "Came here and built this. Or, rather, an earlier version of it. This spot, though. Hidden and defensible. Gathered information and tried to make sense of things. Made up a supply of vaccine. Travelled around, watched and listened. You know how it goes."

Bob nodded.

"Well, things returned to normal quickly enough. Then about a year later the plague returned, but just at a single port town. I went there, distributed the vaccine, and managed to stop the plague from spreading. Then I found out that there was an organization dedicated to distributing the plague and eliminating anyone who hindered them."

His voice took on a harsh edge. "They were a strange bunch, though. Didn't get much information out of them. Only made references to serving a higher power, which they would not name. So I disposed of them. A search of their quarters gave me another location. I went there and met the same sort of fanatical resistance. There were no clues to any other groups of them, but I did find a few artifacts which I'll show to you in a minute." Sid shook his head. "The plague was stopped, and there were no more leads to follow, so I came back here and decided to better secure it. Also encouraged the telling of the old legends." He uttered a soft grunt of amusement. "All those old stories came in handy."

"The fear-field?" prompted Bob.

Sid shook his head. "That actually came much later, just over a century ago. I re-built the cabin,and put my equipment and records in the caves. The only entrance is through here." His hand gave a dismissive gesture. "Not important what I did, but only the 'why' of it. The artifacts I found didn't come from this world, Bob. The tech was far too advanced."

"What type of tech are we talking about?" snapped Bob.

"Communications gear, for one. Hand-sized and permanently sealed. Worse, there were biological reactors. They took a virus and weaponized it, making it more lethal."

"Excuse me?"

Sid shook his head in exasperation. "Sorry. The Black Death was based on a local virus that had been around for centuries, popping up every so often. Common enough on primitive worlds. But these bioreactors modified it, made it much more virulent. If I hadn't developed and distributed the vaccine it would have depopulated the continent, and from there the rest of the world."

"Not local tech?"

"No. Tech of that level was developed only recently. Also, the materials used to construct the bioreactors were beyond even current tech. Definitely an off-world source."

"But who would do such a thing? And why bother using locals as a front for the operation? I can't see one of us doing something like this."

"That was my assessment as well, Bob. There's another player out there, or perhaps more than one. First the attack on my home planet, then this weaponized plague, and now you tell me that my sister stopped another weaponized plague. But there's another angle, too. Why was my family attacked?"

The change in topic caught Bob off guard. "Uhm, luck of the draw?"

Sid nodded. "That was my initial thought. Our home is ... was ... on the fringes. But no more so than a number of other families. No, what set my family apart were our defences. Or, rather, the lack of them. We'd all but put aside the military side of things to focus on medical research. We weren't the only ones to move away from the old ways, but we were certainly the most isolated."

Bob's eyes narrowed. "So you think that your family was targeted? That whoever attacked knew what to expect?"

"Yes, Bob, I do. I've thought about this for a long time. The only apparent surprises for them were my grandparents. Once they were killed, though, the attack was intense and very precisely targeted." His shoulders sagged a bit. "Or perhaps the first wave was considered an acceptable loss to take out my grandparents. Impossible to say for sure."

They were both silent for a few moments. Bob thought furiously while Sid mourned the loss of his family.

"No," Bob suddenly snapped out. "Planetary-level battle fleets, even small ones, aren't thrown away like that. No, the probability is that the first wave was expected to soften you up, with the second wave supplying reinforcements as required. Were planet-busters deployed or just precision bombardment weapons?"

The question caused Sid to look at his nephew in surprise. "Precision bombardment. Why does ..."

"That means it was a neutralize-and-occupy mission, not simple destruction. That fleet meant to use your planet as a beachhead. For what purpose I don't know, but nothing good for us, I'm sure. Instead, they were completely destroyed. A fleet of that size and capability takes a long time to build up, too. Which means that their plans, whatever they might have been, were finished. Probably for good."

To the amusement of his uncle, Bob began pacing as he talked. "As you said earlier, it all fits. Those plagues were planned and initiated before the attack on your home. Both of the attacked worlds are relatively isolated and on the fringe of our space. It looks to me as if these worlds were being softened up for another invasion. Or rather, being depopulated while leaving the planet undamaged."

"But why us? Why hit any of our home planets?" Sid's tone was that of a man worrying at a puzzle.

Bob's pacing came to a halt as he pondered the question. Then his puzzled look was replaced with a grimace. "An in-force intelligence gathering mission, possibly to acquire samples of our tech. A blooding of the troops to prove their invincibility. To eliminate our best medical people. All of the above." He turned to face Sid. "Do you still have that tech you found? I'd like to see it."

Sid sat with folded hands and looked up at Bob, his expression calm. "There's one important thing we need to settle first, nephew."

"Excuse me?"

"What is your judgement?"

Bob just gaped at him, his eyes wide.

"Bob. Focus on your duty. You came here to investigate and make a judgement."

Bob stood upright, his face a solemn mask. "With respect, sir, there is still vital information that needs examining. The alleged off-planet tech, for example. However, I can make a preliminary judgement that you are worthy of trust. There is insufficient information to say beyond that."

For his part, Sid nodded formally. "Well spoken, nephew. I thank you and hope to prove equal to your trust." Then he broke into a large smile and said, "Do you want to see the rest of the facility? I'm rather proud of it, and haven't ever had a chance to show it off."

* * *

Bob looked around in amazement. Passing through the locked door from the cottage had revealed a shallow, wide foyer. Beyond that, shelves filled with books lined the walls. Three book-lined corridors branched off like spokes. Stairs at either end led up to a second level that was equally book-lined with its own corridors. On the far sides of the foyer were sets of sturdy double doors. The construction material used throughout was wood. The design was functional, with nothing ornate about it. In fact, Bob noted that most of the wood had been left without any finish whatsoever.

Sid smiled at his guest's reaction. "This is the main library. There are others deeper in the caves, but this is the nicest."

Bob turned to look at his uncle. "You've got a lot of books."

"Well, I've been here a long time. A book here, a book there, and after a few centuries it tends to accumulate." They both chuckled at that.

"Reminds me of Aunt Gertrude's library."

"Oh, you've seen it?" asked Sid with great interest. "I was there once, but all too briefly."

"I spent a lot of time with her with I was younger. Got tossed out of my house more than once after a fight with Mom, and Dad arranged for me to stay with her whenever that happened. I loved exploring her planet and her library. She sang all sorts of old ballads, too."

"You mentioned earlier that she's still around. She's got to be getting on."

"Oh, yes. Haven't seen her in ages, but send her mail once in a while. I've been, uhm, travelling around a lot and it hasn't been easy keeping in touch."

Sid gave Bob a questioning look, but refrained from asking for details. He knew all too well that family politics could be difficult.

Bob broke the awkward silence. "What sorts of books?" he asked, waving a hand to encompass the library.

"All sorts," came the cheerful reply. "Histories, fictions, maps, science." A corner of his mouth quirked up. "Even some books on local fables and legends."

Bob laughed at that. Then he pointed at the sturdy doors to either side. "Those go to the rest of the complex I assume?"

Sid nodded. "Correct. The library's corridors are all dead ends. It's all something of a maze, of course. Just in case."

Bob nodded his approval. "Where to next, Uncle Sid?"

"First things first. Time to see those artifacts. Let's take those doors on the right." They exited the indicated doors and walked through a short length of bare rock tunnel.

"I left some of the cave system as I found it," Sid said as they walked. "Takes less material, of course, but I rather like the contrast it gives to the wood." Bob agreed that the effect was very nice.

"Where do you get your power from?" Bob asked.

"Locally-produced solar panels, actually." Sid laughed at the startled expression on Bob's face. "You were expecting something more exotic, weren't you?" Bob nodded and Sid grinned. "Think about it, Bob. Stranded on a low-tech planet with no tech of my own ... easier to adapt to local conditions. Started out with candles and oil lamps, upgrading to electric lights when they developed electrical tech. Added a few improvements but nothing terribly advanced. Then, of course, past a certain level of local technology it becomes harder to hide emanations from advanced tech, or strange structures from orbital surveillance. All in all, easier to just blend in."

That got a frown from Bob. "Why not just erect a cloaking field?"

Sid smiled and waggled a forefinger. "And where, exactly, was I supposed to find one of those? I'm not terribly technically inclined. Never was." Bob looked mildly abashed. They followed a bend in the corridor and emerged into a large work area. In addition to bookshelves there were tables with various types of apparatus on their tops. There was dust on most things, to a greater or lesser extent.

"Well?" asked Sid, a smile on his face. "Rather more primitive than you're used to, I'd expect."

Bob walked around to get a sense of what the room held. After a few minutes he turned around and said, "The tables appear to be grouped by function. Not seeing any biological equipment."

Sid nodded. "That's right. I've got a sealed area for that. Cleanliness matters for that sort of work. This ..." he waved an arm to encompass the room, "is my main technology workshop area. There's another area for the dirty work, like woodworking and metalworking."

All in all, Bob found the area delightful and amazing. "You've done very well here, Uncle Sid. I'm really impressed," said Bob in all honesty. "You've got bits and pieces of all sorts of tech here. You said you powered this with solar accumulators?"

"Yes. Nothing as efficient as the sorts we use, of course, but good enough. Before that, I generated electricity with steam engines and water wheels. Still use those when I need some extra power for something. Oh, see that corridor at the end there? Down there is the fear-field generator, close to the electrical generation systems. I use cables to carry the signal to the antenna system."

Bob paused his wanderings to peer at a large piece of apparatus that was standing off on its own. It was taller than him, nearly as wide as it was tall, and looked like an intricate form of sculpture. There were coils of wire of various diameters carefully placed next to, and around, empty glass flasks. He could see a bright light being reflected off of various reflective surfaces and onto the wall. Looking up, he could see a fixed light that was emitting a narrow beam into the top of the sculpture. Unlike everything else he'd seen, there was not a speck of dust to be seen on its surface. He couldn't say why, but it reminded him of something. The more closely he examined it though, the harder it became to focus on some of the more intricate windings. With a start he forced his gaze away, blinking rapidly to regain his mental focus. The whatever-it-was had a strong hypnotic effect.

"What is that, Uncle Sid? It seems vaguely familiar but I can't place it."

Sid shook his head in mock sorrow. "Ah, kids these days. Just don't get the classical education my generation got. That, my young nephew, is a copy of one of the very first alternate energy detectors. Well, as close as I could make it, at any rate. Works surprisingly well."

That took Bob aback, and he was at something of a loss for words. "Those first experiments were done so long ago. I've read brief descriptions of them but never seen one. Not even a representation of one, come to think of it."

That got a laugh out of Sid. "I'm not surprised. In my youth I got fascinated, almost to the point of obsession, with how our people developed the alternate energy technologies. The information is there, just buried deep in the archives. Not many people bother looking it up because there's no real need for it. I loved it for its own sake, though, and that knowledge proved to be useful."

Bob frowned for a moment before asking, "As I recall, setups like this really didn't do much, did they? Just simple detectors—on or off."

"That's right, Bob. But that was sufficient for my needs." He paused for a moment to collect his thoughts before continuing. "After the Black Death, I needed to figure out who was behind weaponizing the virus and how they got to this planet. I monitored the skies with telescopes to check for spacecraft, but there was nothing obvious. That in itself proved nothing, of course, since the ships could have been stealthed. Even so, if ships were involved it meant that precautions were being taken to prevent observation. Since the local humans could offer no resistance, that meant the Enemy was afraid of someone else. Probably us. I cobbled together some primitive electromagnetic receivers, but only picked up emissions from natural sources. That eliminated certain classes of vessels and technologies. That left the portal. I was loath to access it too deeply or often, for sake of security as much as my own superficial knowledge of its systems. But this primitive detector could sense if the portal were ever activated."

Sid paused long enough for Bob to prompt him, "Well? Was it?"

The older man took a deep breath and replied in an even tone, "Yes. Several times over the course of a century after the Black Death. Each time I hunted down and eliminated the human agents of the Enemy—I knew how to find them by that time. Never got details of the Enemy or their motives, but their method of operation always followed the same basic organizational structure. A closed, militant religious order that was fanatically loyal to their unseen masters. That loyalty turned out to be based on a terribly addictive drug. It was like nothing I'd ever heard of. For most people it seems to produce a deep feeling of clarity of purpose, of being powerful. For the remainder, though, it either reduces them to a vegetative state or kills them outright. Combine something like that with the appropriate indoctrination and you can create an army of unquestioned loyalty. The weakness was, of course, that without a continuous supply of the drug an addict would go into a horrible withdrawal. Then, after a day or so, that escalated into irreversible catatonia and death."

A suspicion tickled away at Bob, but he only asked, "Did you ever find what it was?"

Sid grinned "Even better ... I found the source. Or rather, where it came from. Here, let me show you. I've got a couple samples over here."

He led Bob over to a wall of drawers. He opened one, pulled out a long box, and turned to place the box on a table. After opening the lid he gestured for Bob to look inside. Inside were several black feathers the length of his forearm. At the base of each quill was what looked like dried sap, yellowish-white in appearance. He began to extend an arm to point.

"What's that dried ..." he began, but his arm was brusquely knocked away as Sid dashed towards him. Sid's rapid movement created a strong breeze that wafted across the open box and into Bob's face. The room began to spin, and Bob felt his knees buckle.

"Wha ..." he managed to croak out.

"You young fool," snapped Sid, his voice booming from a great distance. Bob opened his mouth to speak, but darkness claimed him.

CHAPTER SEVEN
New Beginnings

Bob awoke with a throbbing pain in his head and body. A quick check of his internal chronometer indicated that he'd been unconscious for only a few minutes. His healing factors were trying to alert him to various issues, but were otherwise in standby mode. That was not normal, so after a brief query to determine the problems he activated them. Within a few seconds the pain was reduced considerably, enough to think more clearly.

While the healing factors continued their work, he took stock of his surroundings. He was on a flat surface, inclined at an angle, and bound tightly with straps. A brief test proved that he was unable to move. He tried to extend his sensorium, but the placement of the bindings prevented that.

"Awake I see. The pain will pass very quickly as your healing factors neutralize the toxins."

"Toxins? What did you do to me, Uncle?"

"I'll ask the questions, Bob." Sid's voice had a dangerously neutral tone. "You reacted to the control drug. Actually, there was only the slightest amount of it in the air within the box. I'd not even considered that until you reacted to it. But it was too small an amount to affect anyone, even the merely human much less one of us. Only an addict would have reacted the way you did. So, tell me. How long have you been an addict? Who supplied it to you?"

Despite the pain in his body and head being almost eliminated, Bob struggled to make sense of what was happening. He wasn't an addict of anything. Then he remembered.

"Uncle, is the processed form of that dried substance on the feathers a white liquid?"

The question startled Sid, but he replied in a neutral tone, "Yes. Why do you ask?"

Bob tried to nod, but was frustrated by the restraints. He grunted in exasperation. "The planet where I met Aunt Freida. Before I met her, I had a run-in with Freddy. Don't know if you ever met him, but you'll know his family."

Sid grunted an affirmation, before adding, "One of your childhood playmates, was he not?"

"Yeah, kind of. Well, he has a dragon aspect now. Seems to be working as an enforcer, but we can get into that later. Important thing is, he had a mind-gem embedded in his forehead. I removed it, wrapped it in iron, and put it into a hot fire to minimize its effectiveness. A white fluid leaked out and the resultant smoke blew into my face, and I blacked out. Took several days before my strength and abilities were back to normal. I told Aunt Freida about it, and she called the stuff 'pure quill'. She hadn't ever heard of it being used in conjunction with a mind-gem, though. Wasn't too pleased about it, either. Didn't know where it came from."

A stern-faced Sid glared at Bob as he processed this new information. Finally he asked, "What did you do with the mind-gem?"

"Tossed it into a volcano," came the prompt reply. "That was before I met Aunt Freida, though. Turns out she lives not too far from the volcano. Saw some cultivated fields from the top and went to investigate. Turned out to be hers."

"Farming? My sister?" Sid shook his head and sighed. "No-one would make up an unbelievable story like that."

Then he became serious once more. "What happened to your friend, Freddy?"

It was Bob's turn to sigh. "He issued a formal challenge. We fought. He lost."

"A challenge? By what right?"

"I, uhm, took the mind-gem from him. He was harassing some local humans and burning their village. So I stopped him and removed the mind-gem. Made him very angry and then he flew off."

"My word. Why ever would he be doing that?"

Bob grimaced. "It's complicated, Uncle Sid."

"Family politics?"

"Yeah. Of the nastier kind. You probably need to know about this, too."

"Oh dear. That sounds ominous. And the sort of thing that made me go walkabout before I ended up here." Sid shuddered. "Family politics. Ugh." Then he paused to look at Bob more critically. "How are you feeling? Any tremors or pain?"

Bob queried his healing factors before answering. "No, everything seems to be pretty much back to normal. Some passing weakness, but nothing untoward. But I could use some water and nourishment. I'm running low on some trace elements and such."

Sid nodded. "Yes, of course you are. I've got just what you need, young Bob. Here, hold still while I undo the restraints." It took over a minute to undo the extensive restraining system. Bob stepped off the table and onto the floor. He stumbled slightly and Sid steadied him by placing a hand under his arm.

"Easy now, Bob. It'll take a few minutes to fully regain your strength. Sit down here and I'll fetch some water and food." Sid guided Bob to a chair, still supporting an arm, and eased him down. Bob felt rather foolish and more than capable of walking and sitting under his own power but felt it would have been rude to say so. He sat and rubbed at the tingle in the arm that Sid had been holding. Then his head snapped down to stare at his tingling arm.

"Wait. What did you do, Uncle Sid?" Bob said while rubbing his arm.

"What? Oh, nothing," Sid replied, a distant look on his face. "Just did a quick interrogation of your healing factors. Yes, you'll be just fine. Now that I know your needs, I can select the proper nutrients. Just wait here. Won't be but half a tick." He walked away at a determined clip but after several steps, stopped and turned to face Bob with a grin on his face. "Oh, and the timeline of your story appears to be consistent with the logs of your healing factors." With that, he turned and continued out of the room.

Bob's face wore a wry expression as he rubbed his arm, which was now tingle-free. It would seem that Sid had more of the healer tech contained within his aspect than he had let on. It also appeared that his long exile hadn't dulled his wits.

Within a few minutes Sid returned carrying a couple bottles of wine and a plate heaped with a selection of cold meats and cheeses. "This should cure what ails you, nephew." Sid opened up the wine, setting a bottle in front of Bob. "Start on the food while I fetch some glasses."

"Oh, no need for glass, Uncle."

"Nonsense, my boy, nonsense. Good wine is best savoured from a glass that shows off its character. And this, I can assure you, is good wine." Sid rummaged about for a moment before returning with two intricately carved goblets. He filled up both, gave one to Bob, and they raised their goblets in silent salute before beginning the meal. As promised, the wine and food were excellent, and not just because of Bob's hunger. For a time neither spoke as they ate and drank their fill.

Eventually every scrap of food was gone, as was most of the wine. They sat finishing up the second bottle, settled comfortably in their chairs.

"I feel much better, Uncle, thank you. Curious to know what you did, though."

Sid acknowledged the complement by raising his goblet and taking a sip. He then placed the goblet on the table as he replied, "After you passed out, I put you in restraints and gave you a nullifying potion that I'd worked out many years ago. Converts the drug into toxins that our healing factors can deal with."

Bob's eyebrows rose at that. "Nullifying potion? Well done, sir. Were you trying to cure the addicted cult members?"

Sid snorted. "Not at all. I got exposed to the horrid stuff myself, once. Rather a larger dose than you got, though. Left me helpless for weeks, and I felt the effects for months. Worked out the nullifying agent out of necessity. Not of any use for the merely human, of course, since they lack the healing factors to neutralize the resultant toxins. Works wonders for us, though."

Then his face grew grim. "Tell me about the politics, Bob. Sounds like something I need to know about."

Bob was quiet for the space of a few heartbeats, twisting his goblet as it rested on the table. "Why did you never leave here?" he asked in a quiet tone.

Sid nodded. "Good question. Well, first there was the Enemy and the weaponized plagues. Those stopped after a century of failed attempts. I had no idea who the Enemy was, and even worried that it might be one of us turned feral." He shrugged. "And, besides ... who could I contact? My entire family was gone, so far as I knew. We'd been attacked, and then someone was attacking the planet I arrived at. It was a very grim time for me." Sid grew quiet for a moment, lost in remembrance.

A few seconds later he gave a small shake of his head and continued. "Now, of course, I realize it was a coincidence. My mother had sent me here to get me as far away as possible. Little did she, or anyone, realize that the Enemy was attacking planets at the fringes. Anyway, at the time things seemed quite focused on me, so I stayed hidden. After neutralizing the attacks there was no activity from the portal for many decades. Then a flurry of activity over a month or so. I checked things out, but found no trace of Enemy agents, so assumed it was someone else. Then twenty-three years later, another month of activity. After that, the only activity on the portal was every thirty or forty years. I never did find out what that was about, but there was no trace of Enemy activity that I could find. The only theory I could come up with was that they were periodic scouting trips to gather information rather than take any action."

Bob interrupted. "Excuse me, Uncle, but was the Enemy activity limited to Europe?"

Sid nodded. "Yes, it was. My theory is that they wanted to use Europe as the basis for a world-wide plague of extermination. The society here had the capability of large-scale, long-distance shipping which would have been useful in spreading the plague."

"What about that semi-periodic activity? Did it stay constant over the centuries?"

"Yes, more or less. And, no, I didn't see any traces of Enemy activity. No untoward plagues or findings of off-world tech"

"So that's why you figured them for scouting missions, yes?"

"Indeed. Couldn't think of anything else to explain it."

"Could it be a different Enemy? Or even just a scientific study by one of us? It's not unknown for scholars to pop in and out to study primitive cultures."

Sid shook his head. "Very unlikely. Interest in that went out of fashion before my time. There were only one or two people doing such things when I was out and about, with no indication of any new interest."

Bob leaned back in the chair with his legs stretched out, his fingers steepled in front of his face. "Doesn't smell right to me, Uncle. The periodicity is close to a generation for the humans here, isn't it?"

Sid nodded. "A bit longer, actually. It was never less than a generation, and rarely more than two generations between visitations."

Bob assumed an upright posture, his hands on his lap. "Alright, here's what you need to know about what's happening now. There's been no trace of the Enemy that attacked your home planet. There were few remains of them, but what little remained apparently indicated one of the ancient invader species long thought extinct. The general consensus was that it was a splinter group that survived the Great Wars and sought vengeance. No further traces of them were ever found so the assumption was you destroyed all there were." He paused to see if Sid wanted to comment on that.

For his part, Sid shrugged slightly. "Perhaps. Attacks of that sort, if on a smaller scale, were a fact of life for some generations after the Great Wars. But it's been a long time since something like that. Never occurred in my parent's lifetime, and I think only once in my grandparent's lifetimes. Strange but possible."

Bob nodded. "Putting that to one side, let's move on to Family politics. My brother, Set, is attempting to set up an empire. Actually, he's trying to re-create the pre-war setup of a large-scale galactic society."

Sid held up a hand. "What about the merely human? They only showed up after the Great Wars, so far as anyone knows."

"Exactly, Uncle Sid. He wants to use them as slaves, in effect. He's set up a network of temples on a number of primitive planets in order to build up a power base. Worshipping himself as a god, of course. Convinced a number of the lesser lights among us to join him as subservient gods in his pantheon. My old friend Freddy was one of those. There are others. Rather more than I would have expected, actually."

Sid gave a deep sigh. "Bob, you've got to understand that this sort of thing happens every so often. It really is no big deal, and burns itself out sooner or later."

Bob made an exasperated snort before replying. "That's what everyone seems to think. But this time it's different. This is larger and better organized than anything that's come before. A lot larger. On top of that, he's beginning to draw in the high-tech planets. Those are harder to do, of course, since very few of those will fall for the godhood scam, but he's gaining ground there. I could never figure out how he was controlling people so tightly. Stumbling across the mind-gems and the pure quill goes a long way to explaining that, I think."

As Bob talked, Sid was slowly tapping his fingertips together, his eyes gazing into the distance. Bob allowed Sid the time to digest the information. After a minute Sid focused his attention on Bob and in a crisp tone asked, "What planets?"

Bob listed the planets where he had detected Set's activities. Sid pondered the list for the space of a few heartbeats before asking, "Your conclusions?"

"The pattern is incomplete, sir. At first I thought the temples and worship were merely an ego-stroking activity. But how does that explain the activity on the high-tech worlds? Those tend to be more trouble to even visit than they are worth. What's more, on a least some of the temple planets the harvests are disappearing. That is, crops are planted and harvested, but I can't find out what happens to them. It's as if they vanish off the face of those planets. On top of that, armies are recruited that no-one seems to ever see again."

Sid's fingertips had continued their tapping. "Which implies?"

"The crops are being sent off-world. The armies are being sent off-world as well. I can't find out where, nor even any hints of actions they might have been involved in. That suggests that troops are being gathered for some major operation."

"So what have you been doing about this, nephew? Just lurking about?"

Bob laughed. "Not really. No-one else seems to care, so I've taken it upon myself to stop this nonsense plan of Set's. Managed to topple a few of his temples. It's amazing how few people want to worship at a ruined temple these days."

A smile tugged at the corners of Sid's mouth, although he tried to keep a stern look. "Anyone else helping you?"

That question wiped the smile off Bob's face. "No, Uncle. No-one wants to take an interest. The ones that do seem to want to help Set, or at least sympathize with his aims. There's a very real and widespread dissatisfaction with the way things are. Nothing solid, just the general sense of a sour feeling."

Sid nodded. "Yes there is, Bob. That 'sour feeling', as you call it, was evident even when I was young. We, as a culture, have been static for so very long. We pride ourselves on our achievements and powers and independence. So much pride in our ancestors' ability to survive in the face of such overwhelming odds. And what have we done with all that, really? There's been an ennui building for generations, Bob, each generation more so than the previous one. That's the reason I left home to wander, if truth be told. Couldn't see the point in it. Probably one of the reasons I stayed here after I'd beaten the plagues, come to think of it. This is as good a place to live as any. Lot of people in my generation felt that way. Suspect it's the same in yours."

Bob nodded. "Yeah, but Set figured out a way to set a fire

under some of them. And managed to build and maintain an organization of them. Imagine that—our people working across family ties for some large purpose."

In a soft voice Sid replied, "Is that such a bad thing, Bob? We've needed something like this for a long, long time."

"No." Bob's voice was firm and adamant. "Not like this. Not built on slavery and rigid hierarchies of control. That's not us, Uncle Sid. I won't let Set to send us down such a poisonous path."

"So how are you going to stop him? Sounds like he outguns you by rather a lot."

Bob's smile returned. "Yes, indeed he does. But I don't have to do anything other than poke fun at him. Make him look silly and ineffectual. That's a much easier task."

Sid harrumphed and was silent for a moment. "You never did get along with your brother, did you?"

"Not really. Never knew why. Just didn't."

"I do," said Sid in a firm voice. "You take after your grandfather, and to some extent your father. Set takes after your mother."

This took Bob aback. "Excuse me?"

Sid chuckled. "A simplistic explanation, but one with a lot of truth. Bob, our kind simply doesn't reproduce at a very high rate. Barely replacement levels, if that, actually. That's offset by our long lifetimes. Yet your family had four children. Did you ever wonder why?"

Bob shook his head.

"Alright, I'll tell you. It's more politics, you see. Your mother and father were an 'encouraged marriage' to mingle the bloodlines. Moreover, both of their families were of the activist bent, always going out and doing things. Your father, for example, was a leading portal engineer ... something that takes long-term focused study. Also something of a rebel in his youth, though not as much as his father. Your mother came from a family that prided itself on its managerial and organizational skills. They've kept the Conclave and Central Archives running since the end of the Great Wars, for example. When they were young—and, oh yes, they were young once—they were part of a movement that yearned to rebuild what we had lost. Well, not so much a movement as a bunch of loosely-organized wishful thinkers. Still, there was talk about building up once again. That, of course, meant increasing the population. Hence, a brief, and not very widespread, fad for having large families. Large by our standards, that is. Your elder brother was groomed from birth to lead that stillborn movement. Your mother had such high hopes, but only she believed the movement would amount to anything. Tell me about your elder sister."

The sudden change of topic confused Bob, and he spluttered for a moment. "Well, not much to say. She has always been quiet and obedient. Does whatever Mom tells her to do. Hung out with the few others of a similar nature." Then his face broke into a mischievous smile as he added, "And has no sense of humour."

"Hmm," Sid answered in a non-committal fashion, recognizing a familial squabble when he heard it. "That may be so, but she was groomed to be a middle manager. Obedience preferred over original thought."

"What about me?" demanded Bob. "And my younger sister?"

That got a genuine laugh out of Sid. "You? You were supposed to be something military, I think. Even though you were very young the last time we met, I saw too much of your grandfather in you to make a good soldier." Then his face grew thoughtful. "As for your younger sister, she was only an infant when I saw her. Still, there was something about her. Depths, I suppose you'd call it. I suspect she was expected to become a scholar or religious leader. How is she, by the way?"

Bob had smiled at the thought of himself as a soldier, but

grew thoughtful when his younger sister was mentioned. "Oh, she's something special, that's for sure. She's got a purity of spirit that is quite infectious. And very smart ... smartest one in our family, I think. Mom refused to allow Dad to train her in anything resembling self-defence. Said it would spoil her talents."

"And?" asked Sid.

"I trained her on the sly, of course. Just the basics, but she'll be no-one's pushover," Bob said with some pride. "Of all my siblings, I spent the most time with her. She's definitely got a mind of her own and that's what has Mom on edge, I think."

"How did Set take to her?"

Bob shrugged. "She was so much younger that he rarely interacted with her. I made sure those interactions didn't escalate to his usual levels." The last was said in a harsh voice that tugged at Sid's heartstrings. Instead he just asked, "Do you get home often?"

The hard look on Bob's face gave Sid his answer. "Ah," was all he said. He knew that look and the pain behind it all too well from personal experience.

Nothing more was said, and the silence stretched out for several minutes. Finally Sid cleared his throat. "Ah, you mentioned seeing some symbols at the portal when you came through?"

Bob gave a slight shake of his head to force his attention on the here-and-now "Yes, Uncle. Do you have paper and something to write with?" Sid handed him a notebook and a pencil, and Bob sketched the designs quickly. He handed the notebook to Sid. "Oh, and there was a small fire. I've indicated it there." He pointed at a mark on the sketch. "Not large, though. May have just been for warmth."

Sid frowned at the sketch. "I've seen symbols like this. Somewhere, but where?" he muttered to himself. With chin in hand he studied the sketch for a minute before snapping his fingers as he jerked upright. "Now I remember. It's a symbology used in the pre-war days, when the portal network was new. Fell out of use even before the Wars. Huh. Haven't seen anything like this since I was very young and reading all those old history archives I told you about earlier. Fascinating to see them in actual use."

"Well, what does it mean?" Bob asked with a touch of impatience.

"What? Oh, this group over here refers to a planet. Think of it as a destination address. These others over here, now those are more interesting. Those were used in the early days of the Great Wars as a beacon or signal. The portal could be remotely activated and the transmitter could probe to see if the beacon symbols were there. That allowed information to be passed securely and safely. Very clever. All sorts of uses."

"What other uses, Uncle? I've never heard of these."

"Oh, used in conjunction with a signalling device it could allow whoever was on the receiving portal to pass through." Then Sid frowned. "Which works well until an enemy figures it out. Which is what happened, and their use was discontinued. Not to mention how easily they were damaged or erased by local weather—a two-edged sword, for sure. I'm surprised to see it being used at all." He thought for a moment, then turned to Bob and asked, "Any signs of people in the area?"

Bob shook his head. "Whoever did it was careful to hide their tracks. Couldn't have been very many, though. If I had to guess, one or two. Coming or going, do you think?"

Sid gave a shrug. "I'll leave that determination to you. All I can say for certain is that it happened nearly a month before you arrived on this planet."

"Can you determine the destination it refers to?" asked Bob.

"Not sure, not sure," muttered Sid, already trying to remember. "Probably need to do deep meditation to access the memories. I'm going to go up to the cottage for this, though. Chairs there are more comfortable and I like the fireplace. Helps me concentrate." He stood up and waved a hand absently around. "Amuse yourself, nephew. Just don't break anything. Wine and food are in the other room." With that he wandered off.

Bob smiled fondly at his uncle's retreating form. Then he looked around ... the idea of food sounded good. Unfortunately his uncle had neglected to say which of the many rooms the food might be in. Which, to his mind, was as good an excuse to explore as any.

* * *

Several hours passed before Bob felt a directed communication from his uncle telling him to meet in the cottage. Bob was in the library section examining the books. He felt sure his friend Mihai would love to see the collection, which spanned many centuries.

Moving quickly, Bob reached the cottage in a handful of seconds. He strode through the door. "Uncle, did you ..." he began before being interrupted by Sid's upraised and waggling index finger. When Bob halted, Sid wordlessly pointed to the other chair. It was only when Bob was seated that Sid began speaking.

"Nephew, you have given me a pretty problem. Or, rather, set of problems. Yes, I managed to recall enough to be useful. Yes, I think I can give you the modern portal address of the planet." Sid had slouched back into his chair, hands steepled before him, the fingertips of one hand lightly tapping against the fingertips of other. "I'll give you that in a moment, never fear."

He paused for a moment before continuing. "While recalling the old records I'd scanned, I came across yet another symbol that tickled my recognition. After some further contemplation, I recalled seeing it in a local book.

Possibly predating my arrival, but I cannot be sure about that. All I know is that it is very, very old. This book—a manuscript, actually—mentions it as being a copy of something from an even earlier time. Like the one you supplied, this symbol can be converted into a modern portal address. Adding to the strangeness is the description the manuscript makes of the symbol. It describes it as part of a powerful spell that opens what the author called 'a doorway to another realm'. Ah, I see that got your attention."

Indeed, Bob's eyebrows had risen up to their limits of travel. Before he could speak, Sid hurried to add, "And, yes, I believe the author to be a local human. That section, along with the rest of the book, reads like something reported after many generations." A lopsided smile played on Sid's face. "Interesting on so many levels, no? But hold on, it gets more interesting."

Bob leaned forward, his face now a study in the focused concentration of a hunter on the trail of a new mystery.

"There's a vague description of the other place, but what there is indicates that it contains many halls devoted to battle. Weapons and treasure await those of the true blood. Mind you, that's standard enough for that era ... except for some of the auxiliary illustrations. They strongly resemble battle badges from the human forces engaged in the early portion of the Great Wars—possibly as early as the second or third wave. Those records are scant, at best, but I think the resemblance is too strong to be a coincidence."

"An old military base of some sort," breathed Bob. "There's never been an intact one discovered that's been that old, has there?"

Sid shook his head. "No, there hasn't. And the few ruins we know of are in poor shape. This could be an important find, Bob. But why there's a record of it on this remote planet I can't even begin to understand."

Bob sagged back into the chair, his mind whirling. "That's

amazing, Uncle Sid. If you broadcast this widely, there's no doubt a Conclave would be convened. They'd give you pretty much anything you might ask for. If this base is intact, the historical value would be ... inconceivable." Then his eyes narrowed and his face hardened. "It might even have clues as to the identity of the Enemy who destroyed your home," he said in a soft, dangerous voice.

"Thought of that, Bob," Sid replied in a conversational tone. "But there's something else that it could be used for. Something more important."

That caused Bob to snap to an upright position. "What? What's more important that learning more about our ancestors and the Great Wars?"

"The here and now. You've all but declared war on Set and his followers. Without help, it's a war you'll lose. Been thinking about this quite a bit ever since you told me about Set's plans. This goes deeper than just his need for being worshipped, you know. Deeper in time and deeper into our society than you realize. You're correct in thinking that the whole thing is a dark and terrible path for us. People want change, and right now Set's the only one who is offering a new path. In the short term, he needs to be stopped. That's your job, I'm afraid. But what he's offering needs to be replaced with something better. Freida was always the deep thinker, so hopefully she'll have some ideas."

"I could use your help, Uncle Sid."

"No, nephew, I'd only be a hindrance in any fight." A wry grin came to his face. "I make a fair layabout and do-nothing, though. Been doing that most of my life. But on this planet I realized that I make a decent enough researcher. We've no shortages of enemies facing us. You deal with Set. I think the best use I can be is to research these feathers and see where that leads me. If Set is handing out mind-gems laced with pure quill, he's getting them from someone who's hiding in the shadows. You're not on your own any more, Bob."

Bob's throat tightened with emotion, and he didn't trust himself to speak until he regained his self-control. "Uncle Sid, that ... that means a lot to me. More than I think you know."

Sid gave a sympathetic nod and grinned. "I know something about facing terrible odds all by myself, nephew. Better to have someone at your back. Isn't there something in the Precepts of Survival about many hands increasing the odds towards victory? Something along those lines, I think. What's more, I think Freida and I could contact some of our old acquaintances, too. Put out some careful feelers. But in any case, that old base, if it still exists, is yours and yours alone. I won't tell anyone about it without your approval."

Bob laughed. "Alright, Uncle Sid, we'll do this your way. Indeed, having a secret military base could be very handy." He shook his head as his mind threatened to get lost in an expanding series of decision matrices. "Well, there's two of us now. So let's do some planning to coordinate our actions."

* * *

After nearly a day of debate, broken only by trips to Sid's well-stocked wine cellar and kitchen, the two men had hammered out a plan of action. Sid and his sister would work on the social issues side of things, and as a side project work on tracing the Enemy behind the pure quill. The latter would be kept between the two researchers until they recruited more people to help. Bob's role was to work in the field, attempting to slow or neutralize Set's plans. That didn't sit too well with Sid, who was becoming rather more protective than Bob was comfortable with.

"Bob, I'm still not convinced that you should be rushing off to confront your brother and his organization on your own. Given time, I'm sure that a sufficient number of people will decide to join us."

"That's the sticking point, Uncle Sid," replied Bob in a patient tone, even though they'd argued about this before.

"We don't have the time. Don't forget that I'm not going up against his organization as such, just making him look like an idiot so that people leave him. That's not a very difficult thing to do when one knows how ... and I've had many years of practise at that." A happy grin split his face at the memories of those good times.

"Harrumph," answered Sid, trying to look stern. "And many of those times required you to pay a heavy price, judging from some of the stories you've been telling me. Oh, you've been very careful not to mention that," Sid held up his hands to forestall Bob's retort. "But I know how such things go even in the happiest of families. And yours, I'm afraid, was never the happiest. I saw the beginnings of that, and now have no doubt that things got much worse. My fear is that you're beginning to underestimate your brother. From what you've told me, I suspect he's become far more dangerous than you realize."

Bob looked pained. "Uncle Sid. Please. If there's one lesson that Dad beat into me was to never underestimate your opponent. And, yes, earlier on I did make the mistake of underestimating how dangerous Set was, and paid a price for that. Never again. Still, as you've pointed out, his plans are getting more extensive. That means someone needs to gather intel, if nothing else. And that someone has to be me." At the look on Sid's face Bob hastened to add, "Until you and Aunt Freida can convince others to help, that is."

Sid looked slightly mollified, but only slightly, so Bob pressed his advantage. "Time is of the essence here, Uncle. There's something—probably several somethings—in play out there. More so than I realized, it would seem. Now that I have hints about what to look for, that should help me quite a bit."

Sid restrained himself from heaving a sigh, and settled for a slight snort. "Very well, nephew. You aren't wrong, but I don't like it. But with that settled, have you decided how to go about checking that old military base?"

"Been giving that some thought. Need to find a quiet, unused portal to use as a transit point. On the other hand, I need to be circumspect about getting there. Set's got watchers on some of the most commonly used portals, and watchers on the planets along the best routes. Makes things tougher, but I've had a lot of practise evading him. Just means it takes me a little longer to get to where I want to go. Given that, I thought I'd pop over to the planet addressed by that symbol I found. Never even heard of it before, so it'll be off the routes Set will expect me to be. Worth checking into. From there I'll bounce around a time before heading to the military base. I'm looking forward to seeing that."

"Assuming it still exists. That's not a given, you know," Sid admonished.

Bob refused to allow his enthusiasm to be dampened. "Hope for the best, Uncle, and plan for the worst. Right now, I'd settle for a working portal on an airless ruined planet. Even that much would give me a base of operations that could be hardened against intrusion."

Sid looked askance at his nephew. "How can you harden a public portal? Those are open to everyone, by design."

That got a laugh from Bob. "Oh, Dad taught me a few tricks, Uncle Sid. They're open, yes, but one can play games using the diagnostic modes. Not many people know about those any more. And keep in mind that the portal, if it exists, will be one of the more primitive ones. I can deal with that, never fear."

This time Sid allowed himself a small sigh. "If you say so, nephew. Now, have you had any more thoughts about how we should communicate?"

Bob shook his head. "Still think it has to be as little as possible, I'm afraid. Sending physical items via the dawn boats is totally out of the question until you have a secure base of your own. Messages via the portals requires access to a portal, and leaves a trace even if the message is safely encrypted. That's probably not an issue when you send messages to me, unless you need to go into hiding. If things get that bad, head to that old military base if you can. When I get there, I'll set things up to allow you and Aunt Freida to transit in and have full control access."

"That's a lot of trust you're placing in me, nephew," said Sid in a soft voice, his eyes glistening slightly.

Bob's response was equally serious. "Things are getting serious, Uncle Sid. You and Aunt Freida are among the few people I feel that I can trust. If my trust is misplaced, I'm dead and I accept that. But unlike most of us, you've lived through what happens when things go horribly wrong. It's changed both you and Aunt Freida, but only for the better I think. I don't believe you'll allow that sort of horror to spread."

"Belief, nephew? Isn't there something in the Precepts of Survival admonishing against mere belief?"

Bob gave a hearty laugh. "Oh, yes, of course there is. But they also say not to be an asshole about it."

That got an amused grunt out of Sid. He was old-fashioned enough to be discomforted by the mocking of any of the Precepts, but had enough of a sense of humour not to get too upset. "I'm sure that's not quite how it goes, Bob. What would your father think if he heard you say that?"

Bob grinned as he replied, "Who do you think it was who taught me that phrasing?"

Both men laughed, and decided it was time to toast to the success of their undertaking. As they sat enjoying the companionable silence, Sid looked around the cottage in an attempt to remember everything about it.

"As much as I'm looking forward to seeing my sister again, I shall miss this old place. Hardly a speck of tech in it, but it's been a good home. Still, you've made me aware that I've been away too long. It's time to go back."

"Decided what you want to do with this place, Uncle?"

Sid looked around fondly. "Not really. Could keep it as an emergency redoubt, I suppose. Some sense in that. I'll take all the biological samples and off-world tech with me, of course. My journals and some of the books, as well. As for the rest, though ..." his voice trailed off into a sigh.

"There's something special about a physical book, isn't there, Uncle Sid?" Bob smiled as he spoke. "Totally impractical for an advanced society, of course, but lots of fun."

That got a pleased smile from Sid. "I'm glad you think so, Bob. Yes, I've grown rather fond of them. Hate to just leave them here to rot."

That gave Bob the opening he'd been waiting for. "Well, about that. Remember I mentioned that some local historians had helped me to locate you? Well, I'm sure that they would consider your library to be a treasure worth caring for. I can ensure that they will have the financial resources to do the job right, too."

Sid looked puzzled, then brightened. "Oh, yes, the portal will have links into the planetary financial system. I'd forgotten about that. Never used it, and all these years had to earn the money myself. Speaking of which, I won't be needing that anymore. Why not use my funds instead of the portal's? No records."

"An excellent idea, Uncle Sid," opined Bob. "Hadn't thought about that aspect of your operations here. I've always used portals to tap into a planet's financial systems."

"Not surprised, Bob. Any of us who travel do the same thing. Still, might be worth setting up an alternate funding source here. If only for the practise."

Bob nodded. "Your point is well taken. Still, are you alright with donating your library?"

Sid nodded. "Did you want to give them this site as well, or just the books?"

Both men pondered the question for a minute. Finally Bob spoke. "Do we really need a base of operations on this world, do you think? I'm not convinced, but you've lived here for a long time."

"How do you usually handle such things when you travel around?" asked Sid.

"Never had a base of operations before, to be honest. If I needed to stay somewhere for any length of time I just set myself up after creating a string of false identities. Easy enough to do once you've done it a few times. I guess the only question would be whether or not you might have enemies who would want to know about this place?"

Sid frowned as he pondered the question. Finally he shook his head. "Not that I can think of. If the Enemy who created the plagues knew about this place, they would have attacked it. I've kept a very low profile during my stay here. Travelled the world numerous times, of course, but always disappeared into the crowd. Lived in a lot of cities over the years but, as you say, that was easy enough to set up." He was quiet for a moment then added, "I guess it is only habit that wanted me to keep this place. It's been a good place to call home." Then he added in a firm voice, "But it is time to move on. To get on with my life and duties. Your historian friends are welcome to this place." He chuckled. "You could easily pass it off as the home of a reclusive and secretive old man. Not too far from the truth, I fear."

Both men shared a laugh over that.

"Any tech that needs to be taken away, Uncle? You said you'd be taking the biological stuff. What about the lab equipment?"

Sid shook his head. "Leave it, for the most part. Oh, we'll need to destroy the fear-field generator and medical lab, but other than that there's nothing here that would raise an eyebrow. And the power generators will make things easier for your friends ... it's all local equipment, anyway."

"What about the alternative energy detector?"

"Oh, I forgot about that." Sid paused in thought. "I'd hate to destroy it, actually. Took me ages to build and I'm rather proud of it."

Bob nodded. "Take with you when you go to Aunt Freida's planet. It'll help you detect when the public portal gets used. Give you some warning if anyone decides to show up."

"Good idea. Well, we're going to have something of a packing job to do before I can leave. Not exactly travelling light, I'm afraid. It'll be something of a feat to get everything to the portal in Wales."

"Hmm, perhaps not. My historian friends should be able to help with that. Don't their sort typically have experience in moving large, fragile things around?"

"Now that is a good thought, nephew. Yes, indeed. Best to get in touch with them before we start crating things up, as I seem to recall that shipping companies have strict preferences as to what they want to see."

The next morning Bob headed back to Bucharest, leaving Sid to get ready for his move. The area was populated enough that Bob decided that apporting wasn't the best of ideas. Besides, he was in no rush. It took more than a day of walking and transit before he arrived back at the hotel in the wee early hours. He was looking somewhat worse for wear and the desk clerk, whom Bob hadn't met before, was loath to believe that he was a guest.

"Get the manager, please," said Bob in a pleasant tone. "He can vouch for me."

"Perhaps if you returned in the morning, sir, and we can sort this out. The manager is very busy right now."

It had been a busy few days, and Bob was in no mood for nonsense. He reached across the desk, grabbed a fistful of the clerk's jacket and did a straight arm lift until the clerk's toes were just off the floor. In an even voice that showed no sign of strain, Bob repeated his request, adding a single word,

"Now." To emphasize things, he added a touch of subsonics to his voice. When released, the hapless clerk dropped to the floor and scuttled off in a rush. In a minute the clerk came back preceded by the manager who recognized Bob at once.

"Bob, it is so good to see you back. I hope your trip was rewarding. What seems to be the trouble?"

"Your clerk seems to find my ragged appearance distressing, and refused to give me the key to my room. Suggested I come back in the morning."

The manager's face darkened. "My deepest apologies, Bob. I'll take care of it immediately. Do you have any baggage?" He alternated between beaming at Bob and shooting dangerous looks at his cowering clerk as latter passed over the key with shaking hands.

"Not this time. But I do need to clean up and rest. By the way, I assume that your aunt and uncle will have their restaurant open at the usual time later?"

"Oh, yes. They've asked about you. Quite concerned, actually."

"That is very nice of them. I'll drop by later for breakfast. There's some good news that I want to pass on to them. Good night." Bob went up to his room, and smiled slightly as he heard the manager berating the clerk. Honest mistakes were one thing, but minor functionaries abusing their authority always rubbed him the wrong way. He got to his room and had a long, hot shower. The dirty clothes were put into one of the hotel's bags and placed outside his door for housekeeping to gather up and clean. He'd be needing rugged clothes again soon enough, and didn't want to waste time buying new ones. Those chores done, he lay on the bed and decided to sleep until the sun came up.

The sun had been up for at least an hour before he awoke. That annoyed him, but a query of his healing factors revealed that his body was still dealing with the last of the toxins created while neutralizing the pure quill. That was good information to know, even if it was gained the hard way. It'd probably be worthwhile getting a supply of the antidote from Sid. The more modern portals could synthesize many medicines, and perhaps this antidote could be added to the available pharmacopeia. That would certainly make things easier, he thought.

That was something for another day, though. Right now he needed a hearty breakfast. In his experience there were few problems that couldn't be solved after a good meal. He dressed in the local business casual attire, and headed out to the restaurant. It was a pleasant day, if a bit overcast and cool. Spending time in the forest and Sid's caves allowed Bob to see the city as if returning to an old friend after a long absence.

He got to the restaurant and was not surprised to find the door locked, as it was well before opening time. However, he could see glimpses of activity in the kitchen, and knew that the day's prep work was underway. He grinned as he sauntered around to the alley where all the local businesses had their deliveries. As expected, there was a constant flow of fresh goods being delivered to the various establishments. He always enjoyed watching professionals at work, especially when seeming random movements resulted in an orchestrated dance. There were warm greetings exchanged among the workers, but no shouting or wasted movement.

Bob arrived at the back door of the restaurant in time to see the day's produce being delivered. As the deliveryman was passing a heavy box to Mihai, Bob intercepted it and said, "Need a hand, my friend? I could sure use some coffee."

Mihai was at first startled, then grinned broadly. "You know where it all goes," was all he said before he turned and went into the kitchen. Bob spent the next little while taking boxes off the truck and stacking them in the pantry. He had just finished that when the dry goods delivery van pulled up, so he took care of those boxes as well. That was the last delivery of the morning, so Bob went inside to the kitchen. On hearing Bob come in, Mihai called to him from the dining room. Bob went there to find Mihai and Ioana sitting at the table with a pot of coffee, a hearty breakfast, and a plate of fresh pastries. They greeted him warmly and urged him to sit with them. Little was said until after he had finished off a cup of coffee, the meal, and a couple pastries.

"Your explorations went well?" asked Mihai in a conversational tone.

"You look tired, Bob," said Ioana. "Did you not eat properly while you were away?"

Bob grinned at them. "Yes, Mihai, it went very well. Yes, Ioana, I ate but came down with a slight illness. I'm fully recovered, though."

Mihai leaned forward. "Did you find what you were looking for?" Ioana swatted his arm. "What?" he said in injured tones. "You're as curious as I am." That earned him a glare from his wife.

"That's alright, Ioana. I don't mind," replied Bob as he laughed. "Things went very well. So well, in fact, that I might have a way to repay you for your kindness."

Both of his friends looked started. "You have already paid us, Bob. In money and in helping us here," said Ioana. "And friendship," added Mihai, to which his wife added a nod.

"Thank you both for that, but this is more on the lines of a bequest for your university I think. There's a rather large collection of very old books that needs someone to look after it. Not just books, actually, but manuscripts and scrolls on all sorts of topics. Just the thing an historian might enjoy delving into and organizing."

Mihai looked thoughtful. "That's very generous, Bob. Something like that, though, requires staff and facilities. Certainly an organization of some sort. I'm not sure the University could take on that level of responsibility."

Bob nodded. "Exactly. A staff of trained professionals who

can do a proper job of things. I can help on the financial side, if I can get some help setting things up." He paused briefly. "In exchange I'll need some help in transporting some artifacts."

Mihai and Ioana exchanged looks. "Is this regarding your uncle?" asked Ioana in a soft voice. "Did you find him?"

They both looked so serious that Bob had to grin. "Yes, I found my uncle. He cleared up some mysteries and is going to help me clear up some more." His face grew serious. "I'm not sure how much of this you want to know, actually. Perhaps you should ask questions about what is troubling you. There is very little I won't tell you." He leaned back in his chair and sipped his coffee.

After a moment Mihai asked, "Why the secrecy?"

"Not really secret. It's just that in my experience many people don't like anomalous events. This is a rather big one, I think."

"So you're asking us not to tell anyone?"

Bob had to laugh at that. "You can tell anyone you want about all of this, Mihai. But keep in mind that there is no proof for any of it. Oh, I can show you a few things if you like, but it'll still just be your word. There will be an old cottage with lots of very old books of interest only to historians. Nothing more."

"So, you found your uncle?" asked Ioana.

Bob nodded. "Yes, I did. We did a lot of talking, and caught up on a lot of things."

Mihai took a deep breath before asking, "What about those terrible legends, though? Did he explain about those?"

"Yes, he did," Bob answered in a serious tone. Then he sighed softly before continuing. "He became trapped on this world just before the Black Death hit. Managed to come up with a vaccine, which he distributed in time to stop it."

"It killed at least half the continent, Bob," said Ioana in a soft voice.

"Yes, it did. Would have killed everyone in Europe and then the rest of the world if he hadn't stopped it."

"But there were subsequent waves, Bob. In Europe and the rest of the world. What about those?"

"Yes, but those were natural enough. That first one, though, was a weaponized plague based on a local virus. That's what my uncle stopped. That and the organization that was spreading it. Do you still want to know about this?"

Mihai and Ioana exchanged looks, then nodded.

"Alright. Uncle Sid—that's his name, by the way—spent a century foiling attempts to spread the weaponized plague here and around the world. Then all the attempts stopped. He stuck around to make sure that nothing else happened, and after a couple of centuries decided that he liked the planet enough to stay here."

"There's more to it, isn't there?" said Ioana. "Is that the secret part?"

Bob shook his head. "Not really. Look, I don't want to worry you. But since you asked, here's the rest. We don't know who was behind the attack on this planet or why they did it. There are two other anomalous attacks that I know of. One was a planetary plague that was stopped by Uncle Sid's sister. The other killed off Uncle Sid's family and destroyed his world. Both happened long, long ago with nothing since. I'm going to find out what's going on, and my uncle is going to help."

"But all those horrible legends, Bob. What about those?" asked Mihai.

"All have a grain of truth in them, I'm afraid. Uncle Sid needed to find out about your physiology, so he raided graveyards. Then he needed blood samples from the living. Then he needed to distribute the vaccine. Lots to do and little time to do it in. Oh, and he had to create all of his equipment from scratch since he arrived here literally naked."

"Was there no-one he could call for help? Do your people

not have government agencies, or at least police?"

"Sorry, no. Besides, the only communication device looked to be under the control of, or surveillance by, the Enemy. He was on his own."

"And he has stayed here alone for all those centuries? Oh, that poor man," exclaimed Ioana.

Bob laughed. "Once the danger was over, I gather he spent quite a bit of time seeing the sights all around the world. It's the sort of thing he did before he came here, just limited to a single planet."

Everyone was silent for a few minutes. Ioana poured everyone more coffee, and Bob ate a couple more pastries. Finally Mihai broke the silence.

"So. Your uncle is leaving with you and needs to move a few trinkets."

Bob nodded. "Mainly a few books and journals, actually. Things he needs to show other people. A large, fragile sculpture that he made and wants to keep. Everything else is yours. Plus a fund to help with expenses. That was his idea, actually. It caused him some distress to think of his library rotting away after he left."

That caused both of his friends to wince. As much for the loss of physical books as for the information they contained.

"You're convinced that your uncle is on the side of the angels?"

That caused Bob to grin. "Pretty much. Although he plans on giving the Enemy that attacked his home and adopted planets a taste of Hell if he ever finds them."

His friends nodded at that. Then Mihai shrugged and asked, "So, where do we need to send these ... artifacts?"

"Wales. I'll need to arrange details with people on the other end, but that won't be a problem."

"When did you want to get started?"

"As soon as possible," Bob replied. "Uncle Sid is sorting out what he wants to take. You'll have to tell me what types of crates the shippers will be wanting, and I'll arrange to get the appropriate materials to him."

"It's somewhat irregular," grumbled Mihai.

Ioana swatted his arm. "Just like old times, you mean." Then she turned to Bob and added, "But first we need to get ready for the morning rush. Some things just won't wait."

CHAPTER EIGHT
Tracing Echoes

Bob stretched and grinned at the sun peeking above the horizon. It had been a busy two weeks and he was glad to finally be on his own again. It had taken several days to arrange for crates to be made and delivered to Uncle Sid. The memory of the look on the faces of the truckers when told to drop everything off at the edge of the forest still brought a smile to Bob's face. Even more so the look on their faces when they picked up the fully-loaded crates from the same spot several days later. Mihai had helped get the paperwork in order, and had been invaluable in knowing just who to call when issues arose. Sometimes personal contacts were more important than mere money, a lesson that Sid reminded Bob of more than once.

It turned out that Sid had his own contacts that were of immense help in setting up a scholarship trust fund for the preservation of his library. That required Sid to visit Bucharest to sign some papers, which prompted a visit to Mihai and Ioana's restaurant. Bob had been doubtful of the wisdom of that but Sid had insisted. His worries, however, turned out to be unfounded. Sid was a charming and urbane guest, and found a kindred scholarly spirit in Mihai. The two chatted for several hours, and Sid drew a map of his library showing where the different types of books were. After finding out Mihai's historical preferences, Sid went into some detail about certain manuscripts that Mihai had thought existed only by rumour. As the two men talked, Bob had helped Ioana in the kitchen and handled the walk-in customers. When Bob made off-hand mention to some of Sid's collection of artwork, her eyes lit up. All the more so when Bob pointed out that the fund was certainly large enough to provide for an art curator.

All in all, it had been a good visit that was all too brief. Sid summed it up best when he said, "Goodbyes are when we discover all the things left undone and unsaid. But my nephew and I have work to do and time is not our friend."

So goodbyes were said and everyone went their separate ways. Bob had accompanied Sid and the crates to Wales. The only problem occurred when British customs agents insisted on viewing the contents of the crates. That caused Bob some concern, but the agents found nothing untoward. They did, however, make some unkind comments about the large alternative energies detector, calling it "a neo-postmodernistic mess with steampunk influences". After he found out what those terms meant, Sid swore he was going to have that phrase engraved on a nameplate for the device.

All in all, Sid had been a good travelling companion but both were glad to be going their own ways. After a final goodbye, Sid left for a long-delayed reunion with his sister. He hesitated only long enough to mention a minor puzzle. "I just remembered this, and offer it as a minor mystery. A few days before my home was attacked, one of my cousins mentioned seeing crows in one of the central forests. They're common enough throughout the galaxy, of course, but never seen on our world. No-one thought of it as anything other than a minor mystery to be looked at some day." A look of loss flashed across his face, but vanished in the space of a heartbeat. Then he said goodbye and left.

Bob had stayed behind to deal with some financial details but now it was time to head out. He had a quick breakfast, then trotted to the portal glade. Once the portal was instantiated, he did an examination of the usage records over the past thousand years. The analysis confirmed that the only times it had been used correlated with the events sensed by the crude detector of Sid's.

To get further information would require that he do a deep scan of the portal's diagnostic logs, which would in turn alert whoever had travelled here. He had initially thought that he would grab the information and dash away, hoping to lose himself. Now, faced with the moment of decision he wasn't sure that was the best choice at the current time. There was something to be said for letting the Enemy, and there appeared to be more than one, believe themselves to be anonymous. As he sat there in a rare state of indecision, an idea came to him. There was a way to probe the diagnostic functions to determine the basic access code of the travellers without revealing the actual identity.

What was revealed was interesting, if not terribly informative. The access codes used by the Enemy incursions during the Black Death were very old. The later periodic incursions used a modern code, which suggested that there were two separate Enemies. As a working hypothesis, the new ones represented Set's organization. Which begged the question as to what they were doing. Those old codes, though, were something else again ... a deeper mystery. Whoever they were, it would probably be a very good idea not to alert them just yet. At least not until Uncle Sid had looked into them from his end.

On the other hand, Set's group would bear looking into. If only for a quick scouting trip while passing through to muddy his path prior to checking out the old military station. The thought of giving Set another tweak brought a smile to his lips. Thinking happy thoughts, Bob did what he could to delete traces of his poking around in the diagnostics menu. It wouldn't do to leave a mess behind as he headed out.

* * *

Bob arrived in the middle of a pleasant-looking forest that was lush and green. The local flora was similar enough to Earth's that he experienced a moment of disorientation until he recognized the differences. The air was fresh, without the tang that all industrialized planets had in one form or another. Looking around, one of the first things he noticed was an old campfire surrounded by intricate symbols carved into the ground. Some were identical to those on Earth, but a couple were different. A chill ran up his spine when Bob recognized one of the new symbols as a simple non-specific summoning symbol used by very young children to contact a parent.

He could detect nothing untoward in the area, so he turned to the portal and acquired knowledge of the new world. He examined the information and discovered that there was a second public portal located further inland. With the basics taken care of, he had the portal make him some local money, a knife, and a hatchet. He hesitated when it came to selecting suitable clothing. He decided to stay with his current hiking boots, but replaced the rest with something more suitable to the locale. With the addition of a hooded cloak, the boots should pass muster. If worst came to worst he wanted solid footwear that could be used in battle or rough terrain, both of which were common enough. He kept his staff, as such things were common enough here. After a moment's consideration, he added a traveller's pack and a length of rope. The rope and the bulk of the money went into the pack. Clothed and equipped, Bob headed off to the nearest town.

As usual, the portal was located some distance from the town, with rugged terrain forming a natural barrier. The forest surrounding the portal blended into a regular forest, but there were enough glades and game trails to make his passage reasonably easy. There was a fast-running river not far north of the town that wound its way towards the second portal. There was also a decent road leading from the outskirts of the portal glade to the town, but he decided to bypass that as a simple precaution and stick to the woods. He started off at a run but the terrain soon forced him to reduce that to a trot, and at times a careful walk. He slowed to a human-normal pace when he got close to the town and stepped onto the road.

As expected, the town itself was of a common-enough style for a low-end, low-tech planet. The streets, however, were made with crushed gravel and were well-maintained, allowing heavy carts to make use of it in most weather. There were no sidewalks, so he walked in the middle of the street. Bob had been to enough similar worlds that he knew the dangers posed by walking too close to buildings where the contents of a chamber pot might be tossed out at any moment.

The streets were busy but not crowded. The strange thing was that the closer he got to the centre of town, the more people began walking next to the buildings. That seemed strange until Bob noticed that the sides of the buildings had channels attached to them to allow refuse to be transported without being tossed onto the streets. These drained into square tubing that he had initially assumed to be decorative, but were now revealed to be drain pipes. It was an interesting way to add plumbing without tearing apart a building. Then he noticed the increased number of carts and horses, which explained why people were walking alongside the buildings. It was a very neat arrangement, and not usual for a planet at this stage of development. What was very strange about it all was that the portal had no knowledge of it. Another interesting piece of information.

The layout of the streets, however, matched the information the portal had given him, so he headed to the town square. This was supposed to be the main gathering place for merchants. However, the closer he got to the square the more merchant stalls he encountered on the street. Glancing over at other streets, he saw a similar pattern. When he arrived at the square itself he discovered the reason. Where the city governor's building had been now stood a tall gleaming ornate structure. The town square had been converted to a semi-open place for worshippers to gather.

Bob sighed—this was another one of Set's temples. A little more gaudy than most, but he recognized some of the carvings. The other carvings, though, were not something he recognized. That meant he'd stumbled into the middle of another of Set's merry band of idiots.

He turned around and at a steady pace walked back the way he had come. At the first side street he turned to his left, then at the next side street a right. When he was sure that he was out of line-of-sight of the temple he stopped to think. Approaching one of Set's temples was always tricky, but to simply walk into one was inviting trouble of the worst sort. He'd attacked enough of them—successfully for the most part—that they tended to be on the alert for his presence. Still, this was one he'd never even had an inkling of, and that made it worth checking out for that reason alone.

Bob began walking once more, if only not to draw unwanted attention. As he walked he began to catalogue the differences between the information the portal had and reality. The closer he got to the temple, the greater the differences, in a roughly circular fashion. He also noted the changes in the types of shops. Where the portal information indicated a somewhat random assortment of types with the occasional grouping, the trend now strongly suggested an organized grouping by type of wares being sold. The only exceptions were the tithing stations set up at regular intervals.

From the looks of the hard-looking individual manning the booth ahead of him, they probably functioned as enforcers whatever their other duties were. That impression was reinforced by the leather armour the man was wearing, as well as the shortsword that hung at his side.

This was confirmed when his travels forced him to walk by the booth. A club swung out to block his passage, resting lightly against his chest.

"Alms for the Goddess, stranger."

Bob turned to look at the well-muscled tough. "What makes you think I am a stranger, blessed monk?"

"I'm a guardian, not a monk. That'll cost ya extra as penance. Make that mistake in front of a real monk, and ya'll be whipped as well as fined—they's right proud of their rank. Ya should be thank'n me, stranger."

"Blessings upon you, guardian, sir. My pardon for not knowing the proper forms. What be the alms and penance?"

"One gold plus one silver." The club had not moved from Bob's chest.

"Of course, guardian, sir." Bob fumbled at his pocket and removed the required coins and passed them over. The goon grunted and handed over a coloured strip of cloth. Bob recognized it as something he'd seen dangling from many people's shirts or coats.

"Be sure ya put that on before gettin' to the next tithin' station."

"They'll let me pass if I wear it?"

The goon guffawed loudly, but not unkindly. "Ah, a newbie. Goddess love ya. Nah, ya gotta pay 'em. But they know ya'd have to come by here to get there, so ya better be wearin' it. Traders or market-goers just go to the section they do business in. Pilgrims, now, many like to make a point o' gettin' the flags o' every tithin' station. O' course, not many can afford it." He eyed Bob speculatively.

Bob gave the man a harried look and rushed to say, "Oh,

I'll stay here, gentle guardian. Many thanks for the assistance."

"Goddess bless ya," intoned the man, moving his club down to his side. His attention had returned to scanning the crowd.

Bob shuffled off and tried to blend in. He had a lot to think about. The local temple religion was not only organized, but fiscally militant in a way he'd never seen before. Whoever Set had in charge here had considerable organizational talent. Which made it strange that he'd not heard at least rumours of such a person. In any event, it was time to pull back and think about what he'd seen and decide whether or not to continue his reconnaissance.

He began moving outward towards the older sections of the town and away from the heavy presence of the temple's watchers. It was only when he was a short distance from the outskirts that he began to relax fractionally. The area was a warren of narrow streets, alleys, and dead ends. The stench was rising, too. That made him yearn for the nearby forest and got him thinking about which portal to use as an exit. The path to the first portal lay on the other side of the city, whereas the new portal could be reached through the forest ahead of him.

His musings were interrupted by a clanging bell and a volley of shouts that seemed to be getting closer. There was an undertone of leather on leather, indicating someone wearing leather armour. The temple goons were after some poor soul. It was time to fade into the woodwork and not draw any attention to himself. Seeing a dead-end alleyway he ducked into there and trotted towards the high wall—almost three times his height--at the end. Not only was this almost at the edge of town, only the most idiotic of fugitives would run into a dead-end alley.

The sounds of the pursuit seemed to move away, and he was allowed a moment of relief before the sounds began drawing closer. He shook his head as he uttered a soft sigh. Turning to the wall he paused for a moment to gauge the height, then leapt to the top. The leap was good enough that he could grab the top with his hands and pull himself over. Tempting as it was to drop to the ground and continue on, his curiosity got the better of him. He hung on the far side of the wall, raising himself just enough to see what happened.

Within a few seconds a hooded figure dashed into the alley, skidded to a halt, and began looking around desperately for non-existent escape routes. Then the pursuers showed up--four well-muscled men in leather armour, holding clubs. The fugitive turned to face them and backed away slowly. The squad of enforcers moved forward as a group slowly, with one of them in the lead.

"Easy, now, yer ladyship. We's not to hurt ya. Just want to take ya back to temple. The Goddess forgives all. Ya need to come back and help Her Glory give blessin' to the worshippers." The man spoke in a low, soothing voice as if to a child or a pet.

The response of the fugitive was to let loose with a string of invective, followed by a handful of stones tossed with enough force to draw blood. That invoked snarls from the guards. The leader shrugged as he grinned. "We tried to be kindly to ya. Captain said to bring ya in gentle if we could, but to bring ya in. Ya be comin' with us, ladyship. Hard or easy be your choice." Their target had by this point backed up against the wall. She assumed a fighting stance and let loose with another stream of invective. The leader signalled his troops with a slight motion of a hand, and they sauntered forward, smacking clubs against open palms. Their leather armour creaked slightly as they moved.

This sort of brutality, although not uncommon on such worlds, had never sat well with Bob. What startled him was the invective used by the young lady. She spoke not in the language of the locals, but English with a distinct Welsh accent. Stopping an assault was reason enough to intercede, but her language decided it. Taking care to make no noise, he pulled himself to the top of the wall and leapt down. He landed between the woman and her attackers, and immediately did a tuck and roll towards them. Springing upright just in front of them, he used his staff to knock them aside using a single blow apiece. They each hit the walls with some force and collapsed in a heap.

The leader spat and advanced towards Bob with the cautious moves of a trained fighter. For his part, Bob smiled and walked towards the man with the casual attitude of one taking a quiet stroll. The leader snarled as he lunged forward with surprising speed, using the club as a rapier. Bob moved the bare minimum required to avoid the blow, grabbed his opponent's arm, and used the momentum to send him crashing into the wall. The unfortunate thug hit with a loud *crunch* and fell to the ground without uttering a sound.

Without sparing a look for his downed opponents, Bob turned to face their target. Putting on his most dazzling smile he said, "Hi. I'm Bob. You're not from around here, are you?"

The young lady had been gaping at the unexpected turn of events and his use of English, but resumed a stern face and fighting stance. "I ain't goin' back to that temple. Won't serve the Goddess nor her priests. Never again."

Bob replied, "I'm not from the temple. And I don't blame you for not going back. I can help with that, if you'd like. Get you back home. To Earth, if that's where you want to go." The look she gave him would have curdled stone, if she'd had any powers. He stood there smiling at her, attempting to look trustworthy.

Their standoff was interrupted by the sound of shouts and the clanking of plate armour. The sounds grew in number and volume and came from multiple directions.

"Hear that?" asked Bob. "That's the backup for this sorry

lot of thugs. We need to get moving."

"You seem to be a good fighter. Why not do to them what you did to this lot?"

Bob chuckled. "No-one's that good, and you know it. Too many of them and too many weapons. We need to go, and quickly. They're getting close."

"Close be damned," she snarled, "they're nearly here. How're we goin' to escape?"

"Over that and into the woods," he replied, pointing at the wall.

"Ye're daft. I can't climb that."

The sounds of pursuit were getting closer, so Bob sighed and walked towards the wall. The young woman, who looked to be in her early twenties, tensed as he grew near but he simply moved to one side. He turned to face her with one side against the wall, squatted, and held out cupped hands. "Allez oop?" he asked. The woman continued to stare at him but the sound of rattling armour coming closer forced a decision. With a final glare at him she put her right foot into his hands.

"On the count of three I'll toss you up. Just hold on once you get there. If you drop you'll probably hurt yourself, and we've a long run ahead of us. Ready? On one, two, and three." With that he stood up and heaved. Without sparing a glance at her, he trotted back a few steps then ran at the wall and jumped. She was lying astride the top as he scrambled up and into a sitting position. Checking to confirm that they hadn't yet been discovered, he held out one end of the staff to the woman.

"Hold on to this and I'll lower you."

With the briefest of hesitations she wrapped a hand around the end of the staff and eased herself off the wall. Bob lowered her quickly but with care. Once she was down, he tossed the staff off to the side so it wouldn't hit her. Before the staff had hit the ground, he eased himself over to hang one-handed for a moment before dropping. He hit the ground, rolled, grabbed the staff, and was on his feet in an instant. Pointing to the forest he said, "That way. Run, but quietly." An urgent jerk of his head served to emphasize the command and she trotted off.

Bob spent a few seconds clearing the ground of any signs of their escape before trotting off to join her. He made sure that their trail wasn't obvious, but knew that wouldn't fool anyone with any tracking experience. At least their escape route wouldn't be obvious to a casual observer. With luck, that would be enough to buy them some time.

CHAPTER NINE
On the Run

Bob and his companion made it out of sight of the town without being seen. Or, if seen, without any obvious sign of pursuit. Given the loudness he'd witnessed earlier, though, he doubted than any pursuers would be worried about stealth. They kept to the roadway—which was little more than a wide path—for nearly an hour. The topography was slowly changing, with more outcrops of rocks becoming visible. The woman's breath was becoming laboured, although she'd not spoken since her few words at the wall.

"See that rocky hill up ahead?" asked Bob. The woman gave a short nod.

Having made sure she was listening, Bob continued, "The road gets rocky alongside it, so without breaking stride I'm going to pick you up and toss you onto the rock. Climb up to the top and over to the other side. Rest there for a few minutes until I come back. Stay out of sight, of course."

Her snort of derision was soft but audible. "Keep yer hands to yerself, if you know what's good fer ya," came a growled response.

Bob sighed. "We need to lay a false trail and not give away our true path. Can you do that?"

The woman was silent for a few seconds before giving a grudging negative shake of her head.

"I've got the training and experience to do just that. Don't worry, I won't toss you very far ... just far enough to be beyond jumping distance. We're almost there. Are you ready?"

She gave a curt nod.

"Keep walking normally. I'll pick you up on three, walk two paces, then toss you. Ready? One, two, three." As promised, he put his hands to either side of her waist and lifted. Taking two steps on the rockiest sections of the road, he lifted his arms and tossed her forward and to the side. His aim was good and she landed on a relatively flat section of stone. For her part the woman landed on her feet, caught her balance by squatting low, then stood up and carefully moved to the top of the outcropping.

Bob watched her without breaking his stride. He continued on up the road, taking care to add extra scuffs to give the impression of more than one person walking. After a minute, he took a short hop to his left and entered a copse of brush. There, he carefully broke up a leafy branch then worked his way back, swatting carefully at the tracks. He got back to the outcropping where the woman waited, but kept moving back along the way they'd come. Some distance back, he repeated the hop and entry into some low brush. He returned to the outcropping, swatting with the leafy branch as he came back.

Once back at the outcropping, he carefully stepped onto it and climbed up to meet his companion, taking care to remove all traces of his passage. When he finally dropped down beside her, he turned to her and said, "Feeling better after a rest?"

To her disgust, Bob's breathing was as even as ever and he showed no sign of physical exertion. For herself, her breathing had returned to normal, but she was still wiping sweat off her forehead. Her response to the enquiry was a terse, "Yeah."

Bob allowed himself a slight smile as he replied, "I'm sensing some hostility here. Look ... if I'd wanted to harm you, I'd have done so before now. Or turned you over to those temple thugs. Now they're after me as well as you, and have no special reason to treat me kindly. Growling at me won't help things. We've got a long way to go, so we might as well be civil."

As he spoke, she examined him carefully, obviously unsure of how much to trust him. Then she gave a tired sigh and rested her head on her knees. "Not got much of a choice do I? What's this going to cost me?" she said in a toneless voice.

The lack of hope in her voice took him aback. He gentled his voice and said, "It's not what you fear, I can assure you of that. This temple is one of many, just as this world is one of many. I've been trying to shut them down for a long time."

She turned her head without raising it and said, "You some sort of cop?"

He gave an amused snort. "Me? No. Think of me as, oh, a concerned citizen."

That caused her to raise her head, and there was a semblance of her original fire in her eyes. "Uh huh. So you know this lot, do you?"

He shook his head. "Not this particular group, no. But I do know the organization they are part of. A very nasty thing. Needs stopping."

"Why you? Why not someone official?"

Bob sighed. "It's complicated. Look, we need to get going. We've got at least a week's travel ahead of us, and lots of time to discuss this. For now, though, we need to put some distance between us and the temple. To increase their search area and make it harder for them to find us."

She stood up and Bob followed suit.

"Fine. But the way home is that way." She pointed back towards the town.

"That's the way you came, yes, I know. But there's another

way, further inland. We'll head there. Let's go." He moved a few steps but noticed that she wasn't following.

"What's wrong now?" he asked.

"You never said what the price was." Her voice was firm, but her face showed a trace of fear barely held in check.

"Information," he said in an even tone. "The setup of this temple is something new to me, and I need to find out what's going on. That, and to get you back to your home. So, are you coming?"

She gave a shrug that seemed aimed more at herself than him, then began walking. Bob nodded, turned, and led the way deeper into the forest.

After a few minutes she asked, "What was with all that hopping around and dusting with the branch back there?"

"Laying a couple of false trails and hiding ours."

"Yeah, but you didn't do much of a job. I could see the odd place you missed."

"That was the point. Can't make it too easy, or the enemy will get suspicious. I laid two trails to make it look like one was the real trail and the other a decoy. Both are aimed roughly to one side of the town, as if circling around."

The woman gave a thoughtful harrumph. "Leading back to the way home. Clever. So this new way home ... you know the spells to unlock the magic?"

He gave her a startled look. "Spells? Magic? I know how to work it, if that's what you mean. Was that you who scratched those symbols into the ground?"

The woman nodded. "Of course. That's how I let the Goddess know that I was ready."

"Ready? Ready for what?"

"For the summoning, of course. For such a clever man, you seem dim about so much."

"Hmm," replied Bob in an amused tone. "You're not the first to say that of me. Still, it wounds me to the quick."

That got a chuckle out of her, the first sign of good spirits

Bob had seen. Pressing the moment he asked, "So, what's your name? As I said earlier, I'm Bob."

After a moment of silence she replied, "Celcilia."

Without breaking stride, Bob looked at her with a somber expression and gave a respectful nod. "Pleased to make your acquaintance, ma'am. I wish the circumstances were better, though."

Celcilia grinned. "You and me both, bucko."

The exchange had lightened the mood considerably, and they marched along in companionable silence for over an hour. Celcilia now allowed Bob to give her a hand to cross obstacles. Finally they came to a stream and Bob called a halt. Celcilia groaned as she sank to the ground.

"Blessed rest," she said in a weary voice. "And there's you not even breaking a sweat. I'm slowing you down, aren't I? No, don't be playing the gentleman, Bob. Truth's truth."

Bob gave her an encouraging smile. "Got any water or something to put it in?"

She shook her head.

"Hang on," he said. Going to the water he took a handful and tasted it carefully. His healing factors detected nothing that would harm him or anyone merely human. Looking around, he saw some large leaves. He plucked one, licked it, and again his healing factors declared it to be safe. Forming the leaf into a crude cup, he scooped up some water and took it to Celcilia who smiled at him as she accepted it. Then he went to the stream, squatted, and took a long drink.

Celcilia watched him as she sipped. When he was done she said, "Ta for the water, Bob. But is it safe? I'll drink it regardless, mind."

Bob nodded. "Wouldn't have given it to you otherwise. The leaf is safe, too."

She regarded him through narrowed eyes. "And you'll be knowing that how, exactly?"

He gave her a broad smile. "It's one of my many gifts. I'm

a handy person to have around, you know."

"Uh huh." She drained the water from her improvised cup and held the leaf out to Bob, who took and refilled it. Accepting the water with another smile, she asked, "So, Bob. What is that you do when you're not fightin' evil?"

Bob chuckled. "I travel around a lot. Pretty much all I'm good at, I guess."

"Got a home to go back to?"

"Used to. Left it."

The matter-of-fact tone of the response kept Celcilia from digging into that topic. Instead, she stood up and gave the leaf a shake before tucking it into a pocket. "Best to be moving on, I think. It'll be dark in a couple of hours," she said.

With that the pair moved on. Bob helped her across the stream and pointed to their next waypoint at the crest of a hill. The sun was about to set by the time they reached their destination, so Bob decided to call it a night. Celcilia protested that she could keep going, but Bob pointed out that, unlike him, she couldn't see very well in the dark. There was a nice spot a little further down slope, so Bob guided Celcilia there. It was a small area nestled into some large boulders on three sides, offering a cozy shelter.

"Any chance of a fire, Bob?" Celcilia asked, shivering in the chill air.

"I'd rather not, given we're not that far from any searchers. Smoke can be smelled for a long distance away. Here, take my cloak." He wrapped his cloak around her. "Wait here a minute while I gather some dry bedding. That'll help keep you warm." He trotted out to gather up some of the copious dry vegetation and branches. Returning back to the shelter, Bob had Celcilia stand up while he spread it on the ground and part way up the sides of the rocks. After she was seated, he put more of it around her. He gathered some larger branches and laid them on top of the area to form a crude shelter.

"There. Snug as a bug in a rug."

She uttered a small grunt that sounded very much as if she was unconvinced. Bob could see micro-tremors indicative of shivering.

"Give it a minute," he urged. He sat in front of her, blocking the entrance to act as a windbreak. To help heat the shelter he boosted up his body temperature a notch. Within a few minutes her shivering stopped. A few minutes after that she whispered, "Is it OK for us to talk?"

Bob listened intently with all his senses, but could detect nothing untoward. A moderate breeze had started up, rustling the trees and shrubs. "Sure," he said. "Just keep it to a whisper and it should be fine."

"You hungry? I've got a bit of cheese."

"I'm good, thanks ... you eat it. Want some water to wash it down with?"

"You got some?"

"No, but it's easy enough to get. Give me that leaf you kept. Back in a couple of minutes. Bon appétit." With that he silently moved out of the shelter and into the gloom of night. Celcilia stared hard at where he'd been, then dug into her cloak and brought out the cheese and began nibbling on it. It wasn't much, but better than nothing.

For his part, Bob was glad for an excuse to do a little scouting. He'd noticed a spring not too far off, but detoured to the top of the hill. He used that vantage point to take a thorough look at the surrounding area, with extra attention paid to the direction of the temple town. Everything he could sense was what he'd expect from this type of ecosystem at night, with no sounds of pursuit. He trotted to another hilltop and repeated the exercise with similar results. Satisfied that there was no pursuit, he went back, gathered up some water, and returned to the shelter.

"Thought you'd maybe decided to go walkabout." Celcilia's

tone was light, but Bob detected tenseness in her voice.

"Nope. Took a good listen to see if there was any pursuit. We seem to be in the clear. Here's the water ... hold out your hand and I'll pass it to you."

She took the water with a murmur of thanks and drank it slowly. Once finished, she said, "Saved some cheese for you."

Bob smiled, even though he was invisible in the darkness. "Thank you, Celcilia. But I'm good. Save it for breakfast. We've got a long day ahead of us tomorrow."

"Yah. So, how's it that you know where we're going? You don't act lost."

"I'm a man of many talents. Besides, I saw a map."

"Uh huh. Saw a map. Not using it now, I noticed. Good memory."

"Training. And natural talent, of course."

He heard the rustle of the bedding as she settled back. A quick infrared scan revealed that her body temperature was back to normal and that she was grinning.

"Of course," she said in a tone that was only slightly mocking. "So, you said you'd be trading information for saving me. Guess I owe you something for the effort you've made so far. Any questions you'd like to ask before I fall asleep?"

As one who always tried to pay his debts promptly, Bob appreciated the same in others. "Tell me about the Goddess. How is it that you know her?"

"Ah, I come from a long line of Goddess worshippers, me. Raised to believe it was the true faith. I was the high priestess of the group, like my mam before me."

Bob interjected, "Was leadership passed from mother to daughter?"

"Oh, no. There were special tests to be passed every generation. Tweren't common to have a daughter succeed the mam, but not rare."

"Tests? Who administered the tests?"

184

"The Goddess, of course. Came to us once a generation. The histories tell that sometimes it was a longer or shorter time of waiting, but she always came."

"You actually saw her? Not someone else?"

"Oh, it was her. I were but a wee one the last time she appeared. The histories say that she wore many aspects, but that time she looked human. Scared the ever-lovin' piss outa me, despite me mam bein' there." Her voice took on a faraway tone. "We'd been raised with the worship stones, of course, and the ones who could make them glow were tested. She smiled at us all, the Goddess did, and blessed us. We knew her to be the true Goddess when the high priestess, me mam, tested her by cutting her with the sacred knife. The wound healed in seconds without a scar. Her strength was beyond human, and her voice could be a whisper or thunder. She chose me as the next one." Her voice trailed off.

"The next high priestess, you mean?"

Celcilia nodded despite the blackness in the shelter. "That and more. Every so often the Goddess would choose someone worthy 'nuf to return with her to her high temple. Worthy 'nuf to ascend to the higher planes, I were told." Bob noted that her grammar and accent thickened the more she remembered.

Then she shook her head and snorted. "Spent me life bein' told how special I were. What a blessin' it were. How lucky I were. Pfft. All it did was force me friends to keep at arm's length, those that twaren't consumed by jealousy."

The bedding rustled as she moved to hug herself. Then she added, "By that time I were in school. Locals didn't take kindly to kids not bein' in school, so all us did it. The parents called it a masquerade, and tried to make it out to bein' a game. But there were harsh punishments for those who broke the rules. So many rules. Rules of our Order, rules of the school, rules of the Goddess. Then one day I decided that I was tired of all the bloody rules and left. Went walkabout to see the big wide world that everyone talked about but I weren't supposed to ever see." She fell silent.

"How old were you?" asked Bob.

"Fifteen. Nearly, anyway. Old enough to make a life for m'self."

"How'd you end up here?"

"Everything was fine, more or less. The big wide world wasn't so invitin' to a young lass on her own as I had figured. Learned to take care quick enough. And to take care of m'self if needed. Travelled around, north and south. Had some good times, too, for a few years. Then I started hearin' the voice in my head. The Goddess spoke to me, that is. T'were the same voice I'd heard as a child. First it came only sometimes at night when I were close to sleep, but then more often. Started as a faint whisper barely heard, but got louder as the days passed. The words themselves began soft and kind, turning harsher and commanding over time. Didn't take kindly to that, me. Tried to ignore it, but how can you fight voices in your head? Almost went to a clinic for meds to make the voices stop, but I'd seen folks start those meds and never be the same again. Didn't want to end up like that. So I decided to do what the Goddess wanted. I was her chosen one, after all."

"What did she tell you to do?"

"Go back home, open a sealed chamber, and extract a gem. Then she told me to go to her sacred grove and draw the symbols of worship and invocation. Then I was to meditate as penance for my sin of disobedience and wait for her coming. After a couple of days she arrived and brought me here." Her voice changed to a hissing sneer. "High temple for ascended beings, my ass. Fucking slave shop." She lapsed into an angry silence.

Bob let her sit for a minute, and when she'd calmed down somewhat he asked, "The leader of those thugs in the alleyway said something about you giving a blessing. What

186

was that about?"

Celcilia took a deep breath and let it out in a whoosh. "That's what they were usin' me for, since I got here just over a year ago. They'd have these worship sessions, I guess they were. Hundreds of people packed in. All sorts, too. Peasants, nobles, and some real hard-looking types often in uniforms of some sort but sometimes in smocks. It would start out loud and noisy, and the priests would lead them in chants. Then the drums would start, first low then buildin' up. Tempo about that of a heartbeat at rest, gradually speedin' up until it filled your head. Just like some of the heavy metal concerts, but without guitars. Then the priests would bring me out and sit me on this throne made of crystals and metal. Looked hard and chill, but felt soft and warm after a few seconds. Then the Goddess would make her entrance, floating down from the sky. Her hair would be streaming, and she'd be smiling at the crowds. The drums picked up the beat and volume and she'd stare at me. Stare *into* me, into my head. I could feel ... it were like tendrils of electricity rippling through my brain. Made me body go rigid like a convulsion. The throne would glow and pulse, so strong that it filled the temple with light. She'd float around, smiling and flinging wisps of white smoke that curled around their heads. The drums would be slamming away, but the crowds would gradually grow silent and stand there staring. Just ... staring like they was lookin' at somethin' that weren't there. Seen that look when folks took some of the stronger drugs back home. Same sort of droolin' ecstasy." Her voice trailed off again.

"What happened then?"

In response, she shrugged and closed her eyes. Using infrared, Bob could see tears moving down her cheeks. Her voice, though, betrayed none of that. "Then she would rip herself out of my mind and fly away. I'd be saggin' in the throne, barely conscious. Those folks in the temple? They'd be all passed out and droolin'. The priests would lift me out of the throne and haul me away to my tiny room and drop me on the bed."

"Did it cause you any pain?"

"Not really. But I always felt so dirty afterwards. Like I'd been forced to do something vile. Like I'd been violated. Cried the first few times. Never cried again."

Bob could see that her tears had stopped. "How often did you do this?"

"At least once a week, often more."

"Was it just you being used to do this?"

"Far as I could tell, yah. But I weren't the first. Not by a long shot. There were names and dates scrawled into the walls of my room. Some of 'em were in languages I couldn't read, but others I recognized as the names of those taken from our Order over the years. Swore to m'self I'd leave when I could. Better to die free than live violated like that. So I learned what I could of the language and area, a little bit at a time, and waited for my chance. The day you found me there was an alarm. Buncha guards headed out down the road towards the sacred grove. I saw my chance and ran. The rest you know."

Bob sat digesting what he'd heard. Then he realized that Celcilia was whispering at him. He whispered, "Sorry, was thinking about what you said."

"I said, do you know what they were doing with me?"

He sat still for a moment, wondering what to tell her. "In truth, I can't be sure. But from the description you gave, I'd say you were being used as a psychic transmitter. Probably to brainwash or indoctrinate those crowds. For what purpose, I can't say ... but was probably to reinforce obedience to the Goddess. Give them a taste of ecstasy after seeing, or experiencing, the punishments. Very nasty business, but quite effective." He paused for a moment then asked, "Other than those ceremonies, how were you treated?"

Her mouth twisted into a snarl, then relaxed as she became thoughtful. "All in all, not too bad, I suppose. Room wasn't fancy, but it was clean and kept so by staff I never saw. Saw other folks in the common eating area, though. Food was plain but lots of it, and it varied every couple of days. Even had health care, of a sort."

Bob's eyebrows raised at that, which got a small laugh out of Celcilia.

"Truth. When I got there, a priest gave me several potions to drink. Not an unkind man, but stern, and made sure I drank 'em all down. Came around with a new potion just before each new lot of worshippers came through. Asked him about it when I'd learned a bit of the language, and was told it was a gift of the Goddess to keep the evil spirits out of my body. Took me a bit to realize he was going on about germs. Never got sick, at any rate. Been worried about that, if truth be told, this being an alien world and all."

Bob nodded. "Sounds reasonable that they'd want to keep you in good health. But you need to get some rest. We need to leave at first light."

"I'm fine. Too keyed up to sleep."

"No problem. Just sit back and I'll tell you something about myself." As he talked, Bob pitched his voice and tone to be both soothing and dull. For good measure he modulated the sonic content to induce a mild trance. In less than a minute she was asleep. For the rest of the night he kept watch, troubled by the story his companion had told him. There was something more at play than mere ego gratification from playing god.

* * *

At the first glimpse of sunrise, Celcilia was awake. She stretched as far as the limits of the shelter allowed her. "Ow. Damn rocks. Oh, g'morning, Bob. How'd you sleep? I slept like a rock. Heh."

Bob smiled and eased himself out of the shelter, and Celcilia followed shortly thereafter. She shook out the cloak and handed it to him, nodding her thanks. Then she brushed what she could of the bedding material off her own clothes. "Where's a place that I could pee?" she asked looking around.

"Best to do it inside the shelter, then bury it under the leaves," replied Bob, grinning.

Celcilia harrumphed. "You coulda told me before I crawled out," she grumbled as she went back in.

While she was occupied, Bob jogged to the top of the hill and scanned it once again. There was still no sign of pursuit. He chose to accept that as a good thing, and scurried back to the shelter. Celcilia was brushing the remaining debris off her clothes, and looked up as he approached. "Oh, there you are. Any signs of pursuit?"

"Nope. We seem to be in the clear. For now, anyway."

"Aren't you just the positive bunny today. So which way, oh man of many talents?" She punctuated her words with a broad smile.

After the disclosures she'd made last night, Bob was pleased to see that her mood was good. He hoped that his post-hypnotic suggestions had helped, but he suspected her own strong nature played the biggest role in her good spirits.

"That way," he said as he pointed. "There's some water about a half hour away. We'll stop there for breakfast." And off they went.

His estimate of the distance proved to be correct, and they sat on some rocks next to the stream. Celcilia pulled out the remains of her cheese and offered Bob some, which he refused. "You gotta eat something," she insisted.

"That's true. Been looking at the creek and think there's some fish," Bob said, nodding at the waterway at their feet.

"Ooh, I like fish," she said.

"Raw, I hope. Still too soon to have a fire. Maybe for

supper, but not right now." Her disgusted expression was all the answer he needed, so he chuckled and bent to his task. Within a few minutes he'd caught two medium-sized specimens of aquatic nourishment. He offered one to Celcilia, but she said, "Ick. No, thanks. Uhm, I'll just go over there to the little fugitive's room and water the horse, as it were. Try to be finished by the time I get back." She rose up and looked once more at the fish, shuddering before walking off behind some bushes.

Free from her watchful gaze, Bob devoured the two fish in short order. In truth, he had been getting somewhat peckish. He bent over the water to wash up, and managed to catch another fish, which he ate. He saw that Celcilia was still occupied so he also ate a couple handfuls of leaves. By the time she returned he was washing his hands and face. When he was finished and had stood up, she squatted and had her own wash-up.

"You ready to go?" asked Bob.

Celcilia nodded and said, "Onward, faithful guide."

As commanded, Bob led the way. He kept his pace constant but moderated to what it appeared his companion was capable of. She was no weakling, but wasn't hardened to outdoor life. And, of course, she was merely human.

After a couple of hours Bob called a halt. Although Celcilia had made no complaint, it was obvious that she was beginning to tire. In spite of that she urged him to continue, claiming that she was still good to go.

"There's water here," said Bob, "and none for a few more hours. Best to rest now so we can push hard until sundown."

Celcilia sat heavily on a rock, obviously relieved to rest. "If you say so. Look, if you're tired feel free to stop any time you need to. I don't mind. Really."

To his credit, Bob didn't crack a smile at that, despite not showing any sign of fatigue. "I will, don't worry," was his only response. He checked the water and pronounced it safe to drink. They each took a careful sip, not wanting to risk bloating by drinking too much at one time.

The day was warm but not too hot, with patchy clouds in the sky. "What season is this?" asked Bob.

"Thought you knew everything," said Celcilia, adding a soft snort at the end.

"Didn't think to check on that. Hadn't planned to stay very long. Was supposed to be just a quick look-see and scoot," Bob replied. Then he grinned as he added, "Not complaining, mind. It's a lovely day for a stroll, and the scenery's lovely."

Celcilia stared at him with a crooked smile. "You really love this tramping about, don't you?"

Bob nodded, his face becoming thoughtful. "Didn't used to, quite so much, back when I was younger."

"So what changed your mind?"

"Good question." He paused for a moment to consider it. "Went through a bad patch, and decided to do something different. Found the woods offered a peace that I'd been looking for everywhere else." He looked around, his features calm and showing a contented smile. "Always lots of interesting things to find in the wild areas of any planet. Then when that gets boring, there's the towns and cities." He looked over at Celcilia to find that her mouth was pursed and tilted to one side. "Something wrong?"

She kept her eyes on ground as she said, "So, you wander around the universe playing the tramp. And sometimes interferin' with this temple-building group. Who's the Goddess? Where's she from?" She began poking at the ground using a stick she'd picked up.

Bob was silent for a moment, trying to decide how much to tell her. "Well, she's not from Earth."

That earned him a snort and a glare as she raised her head to look at him. "Figured that much out myself, thank you. An alien, then."

"Not really," answered Bob, shaking his head. "Human

enough, just ..."

"Better," she finished the sentence for him.

Again he shook his head. "Not better, just been around longer. Learned a few more tricks."

"Like you." It was a flat statement, uttered with her head high and staring straight at him.

"Celcilia ..." he began.

"Oh, don't lie to me. I've seen the way you move." She held up her hands, which were covered with a network of fine scratches. "Can't help but get these when moving like we do through the brush. But you heal right away. Just like her. You're strong, too. First I thought maybe you were SAS strong, but you're more than that. So what are you, exactly?" There was no trace of fear in her voice, just curiosity.

Bob sighed. "It's complicated. Yes, I am not from Earth. Still human, but my kind has been around longer than yours. As I said, long enough to learn a few more tricks. But still human."

"Huh? How do figure that? Humans come from Earth."

"Heh, my kind used to think that we were the only humans around. Then we started finding them on other worlds. It's a mystery—one of the many mysteries—that we haven't figured out."

"So these powers of hers. Everyone like you has those?"

He shook his head and grinned. "We're all unique, you know. Not stamped out of the same mould."

That got a chuckle out of her. "All special little snowflakes, are we?"

"Something like that," Bob answered, laughing. "Anyway, we need to get moving." He stood up and extended a hand to assist her own standing. She ignored it and stood on her own efforts. He pretended not to notice, and pointed to the direction they needed to go.

They had walked for about half an hour in silence. Finally Celcilia spoke. "I'm slowing you down." It wasn't a question.

When Bob didn't reply, she continued, "You could be flying out of here if it weren't for me. Safe and sound. Yet here you are."

"I won't leave you behind, Celcilia. I said I'd get you home, and I will."

"Why?"

"I gave you my word."

She nodded her acceptance of that and was silent for a minute. "So, if the Goddess is one of yours, do you know her?"

Bob gave a dismissive snort. "She's no goddess, and you've got to stop thinking of her as one. And as for knowing her, I don't know. Probably. Would have to meet her to know for sure, and I don't think that would be a good idea. She's probably not too happy about your leaving, and would be even unhappier about my helping."

Celcilia gave a soft chuckle. "Oh, I can guarantee that she'd be more than unhappy." Then she became grim. "Saw a server spill some wine on her once. She punched him in the chest and pulled out his heart." Celcilia shuddered at the memory. "Once she caught a priest skimming from the alms collection, and had him skinned alive." She was silent for a moment then added, "Glad to hear she's just human, though. Now I can think of her as just another psychotic bitch. Met a few of those in my day. Still, none of the nasty sorts I met could talk into my head. How'd she do that?"

Bob thought for a moment. "All on her own, she'd have to be close up. Even then, that's a rare talent to have. Hmm, otherwise there'd have to be some tech involved."

"Tech? Like a machine?" she asked.

He nodded. "Could be small, though. Or small-ish at any rate. Tell me, when you left home, did you take anything with you?"

"My clothes. A knapsack. Some food. A few pounds in bills and change."

"Anything else? Uhm, a special keepsake or magical object?"

"Nah, nothing like that. Just my badge of summoning."

"Your what?" Bob snapped at her as he stopped dead in his tracks.

Caught off guard, Celcilia took a couple of steps before stopping. "What? Is that important?"

"What's this badge of summoning?"

"Oh, a gem on a necklace. Got it when I passed the tests. Been wearing it forever. Would you like to see it?" She put her hands to either side of her neck and began to lift up a previously-hidden necklace. It was revealed to be a large, red gem with what looked like silver and gold filigree attaching it to the gold necklace.

"Here." She handed it to Bob who stared at it wide-eyed. "It looks like gold, but it ain't. Tried pawning it once, and the guy laughed at me after he tested it. Dunno what it is, though. Is it important?"

"This could be very bad, Celcilia. Very, very bad. I'm an idiot." Still clasping the gem, he began gathering dry wood. "I need to make a fire right away. Look for small kindling, punk wood, or dry grass. Hurry, hurry." The urgency in his voice was obvious, and Celcilia hurried to obey despite her confusion. Within a minute Bob had a small fire going and was trying to make it larger and hotter as fast as he could.

"What's wrong, Bob? You look scared," said Celcilia in a tense voice.

"I'm an idiot. I'm an idiot. Uncle Sid told me there'd be an identification mechanism to go along with the summoning symbol. When you told me about the artifact you were told to extract, I figured that was it."

"What are you talking about? Dammit, Bob, tell me what's going on. What the hell has got you so scared?"

The fire was burning well and only needed time to reach peak heat, so Bob sat back on his heels and turned to face

Celcilia. "I've made a mistake. Worse, I made an assumption. This gem of yours ..." he held up the gem, now with the necklace wrapped around it. "This gem is a special kind of tech. Like that artifact that you took to the 'sacred grove' as you called it. That artifact, combined with the symbols you drew, let your Goddess know that you were in place and ready. But there's more to the process than that, and I forgot about it."

"I don't understand what you're talking about. What's my badge got to do with anything?"

"That sacred grove. Inside is the ... doorway that brought you here. We call it a portal."

"Yeah, it started like a faint glow that slowly became solid, forming out of the air. Very impressive. Scared me until I heard her voice inside my head."

"Right. But the portal protects the grove ... every portal does that for the area it is in. Emits a special field of energy that makes most creatures want to stay away. Get close enough and it induces outright waking nightmares and eventually it kills. Yet you walked right in without any problem. I thought it was that old artifact of yours, but I was wrong. It was this gem that told the portal to give you safe passage. It was this gem that allowed her to talk to you inside your head. And right now it is allowing her to home in on us. I need to destroy it."

"No!"

The vehemence of refusal startled them both. She held her hands to her mouth. "Sorry, but ... I believe you ... but ... but ..."

"You've had it all your life, haven't you?" Bob asked in a gentle voice. "Been told it shows how special you are. Even when you stopped believing, it still made you feel special."

Celcilia nodded. "Yah. Never been without it. Even when I tried to pawn it, it was like giving up part of m'self."

"Celcilia. Unless we destroy it, it will lead her to us. Please.

Let me do this."

She wrapped her arms around herself, shivered, and gave a curt nod.

"Thank you," he said.

He put the gem, wrapped in the necklace, into the fire and banked the hot coals around it. Then he squatted and began blowing into the mound of coals, heating them up as much as possible, as quickly as possible. The extended effort of furious huffing and puffing made him feel dizzy, so he sat back to allow the carbon dioxide and oxygen levels in his bloodstream to even out. Then he felt a strong breeze and realized that Celcilia was using her cloak to fan the fire. She saw him watching her and gave a wan smile.

After several minutes in the fire, Bob brushed the hot coals off the gem. They could feel the heat radiating from it as it glowed. Using a stick, Bob fished it out of the fire and placed it on a rock. Picking up another rock, he hammered at the gem repeatedly until both rocks shattered under the impact.

"It looks undamaged," Celcilia whispered. "You sure it ain't magic?"

Bob put the gem back into the fire and heaped more hot coals around it and added some more wood. Once again, Celcilia fanned the flames with her cloak. Over the exertion she panted out, "Why not just leave it and run?"

The heat of the fire was beginning to build and they both stepped back a pace to cool off. "First of all," said Bob panting a little from his efforts, "it is attuned to you. Would still work at a distance, and I don't know what that might be. Second, making it stop transmitting is better than simply tossing it aside. Creates more confusion. Oh, and there's no magic involved, I assure you. Just advanced tech and metallurgy."

"Whatever it is, it's not breaking when we hit it," she pointed out.

"Don't need to smash it so much as scramble the inner

workings. Here, give me your cloak and let me fan for a while. Save your strength for running." She gave him the cloak and sank back onto the ground, grateful for the rest. Bob fanned at the fire for another minute before handing her back the cloak.

"That should do it, I think. Now, I want you to run that way ..." he pointed slightly to one side of where they had been heading, "just as fast as you can. Run till you drop, rest for a minute, then run some more. Keep doing that until it gets too dark to run. Then find a good hiding place and tuck yourself in."

"What about you?" she asked as she shrugged into her cape.

"I need to lay some false trails and erase all our traces around here. Don't worry about me, I'll catch up."

"But you buggered up the gem, didn't you?"

Bob shook his head. "Not soon enough. They'll know roughly where we are." Then he flashed her a bright smile. "But don't worry. We've still got a good chance to beat them. And she'll never be able to control you again."

"What if she wraps another gem around my neck?"

"It'll take years to attune itself to you enough to be useful to her. And a strong adult mind can fight the process ... like curdling the milk."

She gave a barking laugh. "My head feels like curdled milk, that's for right sure."

"That's the spirit. Now off with you. Run hard and fast, but not so hard that you injure yourself."

"Yeah, yeah. Yer not me mam." Then her voice softened. "Don't get caught."

Bob flashed her another smile. "I've been doing this for a long time. I'll be fine. Go." Without another word, Celcilia turned and trotted off.

While the gem roasted in the fire, Bob began digging a pit. When it was as deep as his forearm, he stopped. Using a stick he dug the gem and necklace out of the fire and placed them to one side. Then he shovelled the fire into the pit using sticks and stones. Once buried, he covered the pit with loose stones and dried plant material until it resembled the rest of the area.

Using another leafy branch, he carefully wrapped it around the gem, which was still glowing with heat from the fire. He used some thin, flexible branches to create a sturdy package. All this had taken no more than a couple minutes.

Juggling the increasingly warm package in his hands, he trotted back the way they had come. When the heat became unbearable, he tossed the enclosed gem as hard as he could slightly to one side of their path. Then, as before, he created several false trails while taking great care to erase all signs of their actual travels. Eventually he picked up Celcilia's trail and followed it, all the while doing his best to erase it. It was twilight when he finally spotted her, and gave a soft hiss to get her attention. The sound startled her, but there was obvious joy on her face when she saw it was him.

After trotting up to stand beside her, she gave him a short, fierce hug. "We safe?" She looked up at him as the light began to fail.

"For now, I think. Found a hiding place yet?"

She shook her head. "Still some light, so I kept going. Like you said."

"That's good, but you can't see in the dark like I can." He pointed towards a spot not too far away. "We'll camp there. Here, hold my hand and I'll guide you. You just concentrate on watching where you step, and I'll be your eyes." In a few minutes they were safely tucked into a small sheltered area, similar to their previous night. Bob noticed that his companion was still puffing from her day's exertions and looked rather worn.

"You drink enough water?" he asked.

"Some. Didn't see much, though. I was focused on just

running."

"Got any food left?"

She shook her head.

"Stay here. There's a stream nearby. Back in couple minutes."

It took a little longer than that, and Celcilia's exhaustion was beginning to cause her to fade when Bob returned.

"Here's some water. Found a piece of wood with a depression in it, like a shallow bowl. Hold out your hands." She did as commanded, and greedily sipped at it, careful not to gulp it too quickly.

"That's enough for the moment," he suggested. "Here's a platter with some fish pieces on it. I took care of the bones, so just eat it. You need something."

He could hear her sigh as she balanced the bowl on one knee and reached out for the platter. After some fumbling she grabbed a handful of fish pieces and began nibbling. Her hunger soon got the better of her and she made short work of the food. Suppressing a grin, he offered her some more which she eagerly accepted and wolfed down. With the edge taken off her hunger, she took another drink of water and gave a contented sigh as she leaned back.

"Tasted better than I expected." Then she chuckled. "Toffs pay good money to eat raw fish at fancy restaurants. Never tried it till now. 'Spect being famished helps."

Her breathing slowed, and she was soon asleep. Bob smiled at his companion, and leaned back to keep watch. There were still some pieces of fish left, so he nibbled on them as he listened to the night sounds and kept alert for any sounds of pursuit.

CHAPTER TEN
Wrath of the Goddess

The first hints of dawn were making themselves known when Bob nudged Celcilia awake. She stifled groans as she moved stiff, overworked muscles and joints. "Goddess, I could eat a horse," she muttered.

"Can only offer raw fish and water, I'm afraid," answered Bob. "Room service at this hotel isn't very good."

That earned him a grunt, which he chose to accept as praise for his thoughtful attempt to lighten the mood. He passed her a slab of wood with the fish, as well as the shallow bowl which he had refilled with water.

"What's the plan for today?" she asked, her voice slightly muffled from her eating.

"We run hard and long."

That tone of his words got Celcilia's attention, and her head snapped up. She swallowed the food in her mouth with a gulp. There had been no trace of humour in his voice.

"Uhm, do we have time enough to take a quick pee?" she asked in a quiet voice.

That got a small smile out of Bob. "Sure, but don't take too long."

A minute later they were jogging through the woods. By this time they'd gotten the rhythm of running as a team, and were making good time. When they encountered an obstacle, such as a log or large rock, Bob would leap over it then lift Celcilia in a swinging motion that allowed her to continue running as soon as her feet hit the ground. Bob set the rhythm, allowing Celcilia to set the pace. They ran for fifteen minutes, walked for fifteen, and once an hour he allowed her to rest for five minutes. When that short rest stopped being sufficient, he changed the running pace to a jog.

Every so often he would point and tell her to continue to the designated waypoint while he doubled back and erased their trail. A couple of times he was gone for nearly half an hour before returning, explaining that he'd been laying some false trails. By the early afternoon Bob realized that his companion needed an extended break to recuperate. She denied it but Bob knew it was only out of an innate refusal to be a burden. He let her run for a few minutes more until she stumbled to a halt, stooped over with her hands on her thighs, puffing like a locomotive.

"Just a bit further," he urged, taking her by the arm. There should be a stream or creek just over the next rise. We both need the water."

She nodded, too tired to talk, and plodded gamely on. A minute later they were sitting by a stream, sipping water and catching their breaths. Celcilia's breathing was still heavy, but not as ragged and desperate as it had been. She'd been resting her head on her knees, and lifted it up to see Bob sitting quietly with his eyes closed. To her shock she could see bumps on his neck that hadn't been there before. Then the bumps began to slowly move, some withdrawing into the neck and new ones emerging. There were even movements underneath his clothes. Her sharp inhalation of shock was heard by Bob, who opened his eyes and looked at her. Celcilia didn't say anything, but just tapped her own neck and then pointed at his.

His puzzled look was replaced by sudden realization. He smiled and the bumps vanished.

"What in the name of the Goddess were those?" she breathed.

"Ah. Yeah. Sorry to startle you like that. That's my sensorium. That's some extra gear we all have built into us. I was listening using the passive sensors to see if I could hear anything out of the ordinary."

"So it's like a bunch of tentacles or something?" she asked in dubious tones.

Bob looked thoughtful. "Never thought of it that way, actually. It's ... complicated."

She gave a soft snort. "I'm sure it is. Like everything else about you. So, does everyone like you have those tentacle sensie-thingies?"

"Sensorium," he explained in a tone of infinite patience. "And, yes, more or less. That is, some have more. Mine's a more basic set, but optimized for sneaking around." He grinned as he said the last.

They heard a soft *plop* sound coming from somewhere above them, followed by a rich, contralto female voice saying, "And you are oh so good at sneaking around. Aren't you, Bob?"

Bob and Celcilia sprang to their feet and looked at a woman floating above the treetops. Her arms were stretched wide, and her hair formed a writhing halo around her head. Her low laugh echoed all around them.

"The Goddess," whispered Celcilia.

The new arrival floated slowly down towards the pair until she was two body lengths above them and three in front of them. She was nearly a head taller than Bob, with shoulders not quite as broad. In form, she was well-proportioned with features of flawless beauty. Her outfit was a diaphanous tunic with matching pants that emphasized her figure without hindering her movements.

Bob just frowned and stared at the so-called Goddess, his eyes boring intently into hers. She matched his look with one of her own that was equally soul-piercing. Then Bob laughed and said, "Hi, Katie. Fancy meeting you here. You've changed."

"Don't call me that! My name is Kydos, and I'll thank you to remember that." Her voice cracked like a whip, rich in harmonics and a barely-restrained anger. Her face was briefly contorted by strong emotions until she got herself under control. Bob just kept a polite smile on his face. Celcilia hadn't understood the language, but stood very still trying to be invisible.

Within a few seconds Kydos's face once again radiated godlike serenity, and she beamed down at the two. When she spoke again, it was in English wrapped in velvet tones of tranquillity and grace. "Be that as it may. It is good to see you again, Bob. I was worried about my acolyte. There are so many unsavoury sorts passing through these days, and before they have learned to achieve communion with me some of them can be a little rough around the edges. But then I heard how a single man had disabled a squad of my guardians, somehow passed over the city wall, and vanished into the forest. My finest trackers went in pursuit, but got confused by all the conflicting traces. It was only at that point that I was informed about what had transpired." Her visage darkened and her voice took on a dangerous edge as she added, "A mistake that has been punished most severely."

Then she brightened and continued in her sweetest tones. "I tried to reach out to my acolyte through her focus gem, but then it went silent. At first I thought it was one of Set's council come to test me, but none have that combination of skills. Except, perhaps, Set himself. Or you. And here you are, keeping my acolyte safe. I thank you for your service, but I shall take her off your hands and let you continue on your way."

"Sod that."

The words, spoken with some heat, surprised both Kydos

and Bob. They turned to look at Celcilia, who had pushed back the hood of her cloak and was glaring at Kydos with unrestrained anger. She had assumed a fighting stance and her fists were clenched. "I'm nobody's property. Goddess or no, ye have no claim on me. I'm free of you and free I'll stay." Her voice was strong and determined, with only a trace of anger. Then she added, with just a touch of sarcasm, "Your Glory."

Kydos drifted lower until she was just above arm's reach. "Oh, you think so, do you my little apostate?" Her voice was low and menacing.

"When did you get the new aspect, Katie? Funny, didn't see any public notice of that." Bob's voice interrupted the standoff between the two women, and Kydos slowly turned her head towards him.

"Your brother can offer many gifts to those who ally themselves with him."

Bob snorted. "You had an unauthorized aspect change? Must have done it at an off-the-books medical facility; something abandoned from just after the Great Wars. Not the brightest thing you could do, Katie. Very dangerous." His tone had changed to one of honest concern.

Kydos looked at Bob with contempt. "Who are you to pass such a judgement on me. Look at you! Crawling on the ground like a mere human." She turned to face Celcilia. "Girl—how did I convey you to the temple when you first arrived here? We flew! Like a true god I carried you while soaring through the air! Now look at you. Allied with Bob the Cripple. You think him your saviour who will lead you home? From childhood he has been the least of us. An embarrassment to his family, the entire Family of Humanity, and to his ancestors. Now he skulks about like a pitiful thief, extracting petty revenge by creating minor inconveniences for his betters. As pathetic now as he was then." Her face had twisted into a snarl.

Celcilia's resolution began to waver and she cast several looks at Bob, hoping he would say something. For his part, Bob stood there looking rather bored, a polite smile on his face throughout the rant. Celcilia found this less reassuring than she was hoping for.

Kydos turned to look at Bob, her face a study in barely-repressed anger. "Return my acolyte to me and I'll let you live."

Bob shrugged. "She's not much use to you without that gem. That was a rather low trick to play on her, you know. Her and all those others. Not to mention that it's the type of low-level scam I'd have expected from someone like Freddy. You used to be better than this." He shook his head and gave her his best "more in sorrow than in anger" sigh.

"You have no idea what I've invested in her and others like her," Kydos said in a low, dangerous voice. "Generations of breeding, on a dozen worlds. The planning, the coordination."

Bob nodded as if in agreement. "Playing god on multiple worlds instead of just one? So what? Oh, sure, it's a complicated scam. But still just a scam." Bob waved a hand in a dismissive motion. "And that temple of yours? It's not your name on the top tier of the frieze, is it? I couldn't recognize all those symbols, but the top one I did—and it isn't yours." His left hand stroked his chin, his right one moved up and down as he made each point, and he began pacing back and forth. A small arc of travel, but it gradually moved away from Celcilia.

"And for what?" Bob continued. "You're set up to process a lot of people. Move 'em in and out. Not for *your* purposes, that's for sure. Oh, you've organized things pretty well. You always were a good organizer. But look at you now—a middle manager defending her little piece of the action. And you call *me* pathetic? Pfft." He had taken great care not to look at Celcilia, but he managed to catch a glimpse at the big-eyed look of astonishment on her face.

He stopped his pacing and turned to look up at Kydos. "So, really, Katie. After all your big plans, is this the best you can do?" He spread his arms to encompass the woods. By this time he was several additional body-lengths away from both women.

Through gritted teeth Kydos ground out, "Your brother manages the Great Plan, so it is only right that his name be at the top."

"And those other names? Some of them are above yours."

Kydos began to hiss, then caught herself. In a voice thick with anger she replied, "Your brother has forged new alliances. Diplomacy requires compromise. Now. Give. Me. My. Acolyte."

"Nah."

Her face writhed and contorted into a snarl as Kydos pointed a hand at him. A beam of force rippled the air as it tore towards Bob. He twisted slightly and the lance of energy missed him but scorched his cloak. Bob grinned and waggled his eyebrows at her as he resumed an upright stance. That earned him another snarl and another blast of energy. This time he dodged by kneeling with his hands flat on the ground, and the blast rippled over his head. His right hand flicked up and an instant later Kydos uttered a short, sharp sound of pain as a pebble bounced off her head. Her face hardened and she prepared to send another blast when a second stone bounced off her face, forcing her to twist her head.

"Play nicely, Katie," said Bob in a warning tone.

"I told you to call me *Kydos*," she growled as she turned to face him with both hands raised. A pair of clots of dirt hit her open mouth, causing her to choke and cough. Her hands batted helplessly at the air in front of her.

"I'm asking you nicely ... Kydos. Play nicely. Truce?" Bob tried to sound like the voice of reason.

Kydos was spitting dirt out of her mouth as the wounds on

her head healed themselves. She gave a grudging nod, which Bob accepted with good grace. That is, he wisely refrained from cracking a joke or smiling.

It took her several seconds of coughing and spitting before she managed to clear the dirt out of her mouth. Her expression, initially dour, softened just a fraction as a wry smile lifted one side of her mouth. "You've not lost the knack of those little tricks of yours, have you? Impressive dodging, too." Then her voice hardened. "But will you be as good at saving my apostate acolyte?"

The look on her face sent a chill of fear along Celcilia's spine. The Goddess had an array of incredible powers. Bob had amazing reflexes and irritating jokes. It seemed an uneven match. Still, she allowed none of her doubts to show.

Kydos moved up and back away from the other two before alighting on the ground. Her hair, once a radiant halo, now hung like normal hair. "You want to save her, Bob? All right." Her voice had grown lilting and girlish. "I'll give you a half-hour head start before I come after you. Just like when we were children. Won't that be fun?" Then her voice changed into something much harsher. "My love."

Bob ran to Celcilia, grabbed her hand, and half-dragged her away from where Kydos stood.

"What?" Celcilia gasped as she struggled to keep up.

"Don't talk, just run," said Bob in a grim voice.

The brush and trees soon hid them from sight, but they could hear Kydos's laughter following them for several minutes. Bob released Celcilia's hand. "Just like before, run then trot. We need to put as much distance between us and her as we can."

"But she can fly," gasped out Celcilia.

"Don't waste breath talking," said Bob who was still breathing easily. "These dense woods will impede her levitation. She let us go because she needs time to rebuild her energy reserves. It'll be less than that half-hour she promised, but not by much. Levitation takes a lot of energy, and combined with those blasts depleted her reserves. Did you notice how slowly she healed? That gives us a chance." He glanced at her and said, "A good chance, I promise you."

"How?" said Celcilia, packing a lot into that single word.

To her surprise Bob chuckled. "She makes assumptions. Assumptions lead to mistakes. Just like me and that gem of yours."

They jogged in silence for a time, then switched to walking. The change of pace gave Celcilia time to catch her breath. She was embarrassed that it took longer than it should have, and knew it was because of the fear from meeting the Goddess. Bob sensed her mood. "I was very impressed when you stood up to her."

"Pfft," she snorted.

"No, really. You've lived with her, seen what she is capable of, and yet you stood up to her. That's rare and not to be dismissed lightly."

She felt a flush of pride at his words, which she quickly tamped down. Especially since that pride was very likely to get her killed.

"So, you can't fly?" The words came out before she could help herself. Then she quickly added, "Sorry."

To her relief Bob just chuckled. "That's OK. Most of us can, to some degree or another. She's about average. I'm one of the rare ones who just can't do it. It is what it is."

Celcilia was sure that there was more to it than that, but kept those thoughts and questions to herself. Instead asked, "How much time have we got left?"

Bob replied, "Enough, I think. There's a grove up ahead. Run as fast as you can and stop when you get to the far side."

She picked up speed and Bob matched it. Within a couple of minutes they had reached their destination. Celcilia was panting heavily, and Bob pointed to a pile of boulders not too far away. "Go sit behind those. Stretch out if you like, but stay low so you can't be seen." She wearily trotted to where he had pointed and slumped to the ground, glad of the rest.

Bob surveyed the area with a critical eye. He climbed a tree then tied the rope from his pack to a branch. Dropping back to the ground, he pulled on the rope until the tree was fully bent down with the top touching the ground. He walked towards the boulders and tied off the rope against another tree using a slip-knot. He noticed Celcilia poking her head above the boulders to see what he was doing. "I thought I told you to stay down."

"She'll be coming soon, you know."

"Yep. Floating in, making a grand entrance. She always was something of a drama queen. But to do a proper mocking hover she has to pass through that gap in the trees."

"How does that ..."

Celcilia's question was interrupted by a faint laugh. Bob held up his hand to signal for silence and motioned for her to drop back into hiding.

The laughter got louder, and soon Kydos came floating into the glade, wrapped in a shimmering veil of radiance.

"Drama queen," muttered Bob. He stood in a relaxed stance, legs slightly apart, the staff hanging horizontally in his left hand.

"Oh, you disappoint me, Bob," said Kydos in a gloating tone. "Giving up so soon? But my acolyte slowed you down, didn't she? Is she around here, or are you making a noble last stand? No matter. I shall dispose of you and then punish her. I'll ..."

Gauging the angles carefully Bob swung his staff at the end of the rope, releasing the knot, which in turn released the bent tree. It flew up at considerable speed and hit Kydos. There were sounds of breaking branches and breaking bones, and Kydos was flung against another tree. The angle of impact was such that she hit it with her back. The force of the impact wrapped her body around the trunk of the tree and her neck seemed to extend as it twisted. The sound of cracking bones was loud and sharp, and echoed for several seconds. Her body dropped to the ground and bounced once, coming to rest with her head and limbs twisted at unnatural angles.

Bob grunted with satisfaction. Then he turned to see Celcilia standing behind the boulders.

"You killed her," she whispered.

"Nah. Our kind are tough and very hard to kill. Not impossible to do, of course, but it takes quite a lot to do it. That'll just slow her down for a while. Let's go."

"Go where?"

"Told you I'd get you home. We need to get to that inland portal."

"So we're safe?"

He snorted. "Far from it. She'll be up and about in a day or so. Not moving too well, but up and about. Hopefully she'll take the hint and give up."

It was Celcilia's turn to snort. "Not bloody likely."

Bob grimaced. "You may be right. I've bought us some time, though, but probably not much. So time to run, my friend. That way."

Off they trotted. Behind them the body of Kydos twitched and moaned, puffs of breath stirring up the leaves.

* * *

They had been trotting at a good clip for almost fifteen minutes when Bob declared that it was time to slow to a walk. "We need to make good time but can't allow it to become a panicked run."

"You've got a plan?" asked Celcilia.

Bob grinned as he answered, "Always. That's why we're going this way. It leads to a fast-running river that we can use to get to the portal faster. Not my first choice. Lots of rapids and rough water."

"It runs into the sacred grove?"

"Close by. I'd hoped to walk along it, but now the plan is to make a raft and ride the waters downstream."

"Sounds like fun ... something toffs would do for sport. So, that'd be faster than going on foot?"

Bob nodded. "I think so. The information I have on it indicates that it's moving at a speed of your jogging for much of its length. That'll cut our travel time by a lot."

Celcilia sighed, and not from exhaustion. "I'm slowing you down." It wasn't a question.

"Stop thinking like that," Bob said sharply. "We're a team, now, and we have think like one."

"One for all and all for one. That sort of thing?" she answered, grinning in spite of herself.

"Exactly that. Speaking of which, how are you doing? Be honest, please."

"A bit tired," she admitted. Then was quick to add, "But good for a while. Would like a break for lunch later if we can afford the time."

He gave a small laugh. "It'll be time well spent. Trust me, for situations like this you've got to think about the long haul."

"A marathon, not a sprint," she quipped.

"Exactly. By the way, I've noticed you looking at my staff. Any reason?"

"Nah. Just thought it looked like something handy to have for hiking. Maybe we can find a staff for me along the way."

"Take it. No, really. I don't need it and you do."

"Oh, ta. Say, it's heavier than it looks, isn't it? Good feel to it, though." It took her a few steps to get the rhythm of the staff, but within a few seconds she was swinging it as if using it all along. Seeing the questioning look on his face, she laughed and said, "Learned to appreciate a good staff when I were young. Kept the boys in line and at a safe distance." She giggled at the memory of that. Then her mood became more sober as she added, "And kept me safe when I were on the road."

Bob digested that without comment. He allowed the silence to stretch for a few seconds before saying, "Time to run."

They had done another run-walk cycle before either spoke again. They were about to cross a small stream, so Bob called a halt. After testing the water he nodded to Celcilia, who gratefully sank down to refresh herself. The day was warm enough that physical exertion would raise a good sweat, and the few clouds in the sky offered little relief from the sun. They could hear chirping and buzzing from the local wildlife. Everything seemed to be a peace.

"This'd all be delightful if we weren't running for our lives," commented Celcilia as she looked around. "Are those birds that we're hearing?"

Bob nodded. "Something similar." Using an arm he gestured around them. "Ecosystems where humans can exist all follow a similar pattern. Not identical, of course, but similar. Sometimes the bird-like things are reptilian, sometimes insectoid, but always performing a similar niche in the ecosystem."

Just then something went "caw" in the distance. "Crows?" asked Celcilia. "That sounded just like a crow."

Bob frowned. "It could well be. Crows just like you have on your planet are found on many human-inhabited worlds. No-one knows why or how."

"Well, no time for wonderin' 'bout such mysteries, lazy bones. Time to hit the trail and make tracks before noon." Cecilia levered herself upright with the staff and stood there grinning at her seated companion. In reply, Bob laughed and bounced to his feet, and the two continued their trek.

At their next walking-cycle Celcilia asked, "You sure she's not dead? I'd swear I heard her bones break. And the angle of her head ...", she shuddered at the memory.

Bob shook his head. "She's not dead. Far from it. And you'd better hope those bones did break as badly as that. That's our only hope of buying enough time to get away." To change the subject he said, "You're holding up well. Better than I would have expected."

"T'were one of the rules of our Order. A strong body is a tribute to the Goddess, I were taught. Been livin' on the rough for most of my life, too. Thought I was in good shape, but this ... this is something else."

Bob chuckled. "This is military level of physical exertion. I was trained for this since childhood."

"Really? What sort of upbringing did you have?" asked Celcilia.

"No more questions," Bob said. He grinned at her and added, "Save your breath for the running." With that he broke into a trot that she had to work at to match.

The sun was past its noon peak when Bob finally allowed them to halt next to a stream. Celcilia was gasping for breath, so Bob helped her to sit without collapsing.

"Wait here and I'll get something to eat. Catch your breath and drink a little water." He trotted downstream while she lay back sucking in air.

A few minutes later he was back carrying several fish and a couple slabs of dry wood. "Give me a minute to deal with these, and we'll have lunch." He took out his knife and quickly separated the meat from the bone and organs. Chopping the meat into cubes, he gave Celcilia her share on one of the platters. At seeing the wry look on her face, he laughed and said, "I think we can risk having a fire for supper, if you like."

She took the platter, sighed as one much put upon, and began eating. The sweat dripping from her face added some welcome seasoning to the raw meat. She was too tired to ask questions, and concentrated on eating. When the edge was finally off her hunger, she asked, "You're giving me the largest share of the fish. Again. 'Preciate it and all, but what about you?"

"Kind of you to worry, Celcilia, but I'm fine. Ate some while I was gathering these." She gave him a disbelieving look, so he hurried to add, "Truth. My body can handle a wider range of foods than yours. Don't worry about me."

She gave him an innocent look. "Worry? Hey, you're my ticket out of here. Don't want anything to happen to you, is all." Then she flashed a smile and began chuckling. Bob joined in, and their moods brightened considerably.

Celcilia closed her eyes, smiled, and lay back for a few seconds before she jerked upright. "We need to keep moving."

Bob shook his head and said, "We've a few minutes yet. Lay back and rest." She looked reluctant at first, but lay back and within a few seconds was asleep. His smile slowly changed to a frown as he thought upon their slim chances of success and how to improve them. Better to let his companion regain her strength for the hard slog ahead. Riding down the river was going to be harder and more dangerous than he had let on. But that was a problem for tomorrow. As the Precepts of Survival said, "Don't let worries about tomorrow interfere with surviving today".

While he waited, he kept his senses alert for signs of trouble but detected nothing untoward. Hopefully that meant that Kydos was healing and planning to return back to her temple, although he doubted that. The Katie of old was a vindictive person, and not one to let even the smallest slight pass by. He'd given her more than a small slight and was sure she'd do her best to repay him. Much depended on what her current aspect was capable of, and that unknowable bothered him rather a lot.

Some minutes later he detected from Celcilia's brainwaves that she'd had the optimum amount of rest, and woke her up.

Within a minute they were back on the trail doing a fast walk that escalated into a run. They continued with their run-walk cycles until the sun began to set, and Bob began looking for a good spot to spend the night. Celcilia was stumbling along in a haze of exhaustion but never complained.

Finally Bob said, "We'll make camp behind those boulders on the other side of this stream. They'll shield us and allow a small fire."

Within a few minutes they reached their goal. They shed their gear, then Celcilia sank to the pebbled ground. She gave a soft groan as she lay against the cold stones and closed her eyes.

In a quiet voice Bob said, "I'll be back in minute." She nodded without opening her eyes.

A hand touched hers, and she jolted awake. "Just me," said Bob.

"Sorry," she said. "Must have dozed off."

"Not to worry. Here, I brought some leafy branches to use as bedding. They'll be softer and warmer than the cold stones. If you stand up I can get things arranged."

She stood up with the aid of the staff, and stifled a groan. Bob arranged the branches on the ground and against the stones, forming a leafy nest. He dragged some larger branches and formed a rough roof. He urged her to sit, and she flopped down.

"Damn, that's nice and soft. Thanks," she said. Then she sniffed. "Smells like cedar." After running her hands through it she muttered, "Feels like it, too."

"Yep," said Bob. "Seems to be common on many human worlds. Another one of life's mysteries. Hold on while I get the fire going."

He put together a small pile, flicked his knife against the hatchet, and used the resulting sparks to start a fire. It was soon a small, but cheery, blaze that offered real and spiritual warmth. While Celcilia warmed her hands, Bob moved out then returned carrying a rough wooden bowl filled with water.

"Sip on this while I get us some fish. As I promised, tonight you'll eat cooked food. Keep the fire going." With that he left Celcilia alone with her thoughts, vanishing into the night as silent as a cat on the hunt. Although tired, she was now too keyed up to fall asleep. Hunger pangs helped with that, too, as did the nighttime chill. Within a minute, though, the warmth of the fire had taken the edge off her chills. She stared into the fire, occasionally feeding it but otherwise just staring.

She'd spent so many years taking care of herself, when suddenly all her hopes and dreams—and freedom—had been taken from her. Now she was caught up in a whirl of forces beyond her ken. It was not a feeling she enjoyed, and she despaired of ever gaining control over her life again. A soft sound snapped her attention to the here and now. She didn't give any outward sign other than to move the fingers of one hand slightly closer to where the staff lay.

"Good reflexes," said Bob as he moved into the light of fire without making any other sound. "You didn't give away that you'd heard me. Well done." He sat across from her, squatting on his heels. "Hope you like fish. Tried to find something else, but figured food now was better than food later."

He had already cleaned and spitted the fish, so they arranged them over the fire to cook. Once they'd finished eating and had disposed of the remains, they both settled back with contented sighs. The fire, although small, cast just enough light to highlight both their faces. Celcilia watched her companion and Bob matched her stare for stare. Finally he said, "You have questions. Now's the time to ask them."

"Who are you?"

"Told you—my name is Bob."

"Asshole," she said without heat. "Not what I meant, and

you know it."

"Ah," he said, not bothering to hide a mischievous grin. "You need to be more precise with your questions."

Celcilia began tapping a knee with her index finger. "I'm beginning to understand why the Goddess got so pissed with you."

Bob shook his head. "Not a goddess. Not by a long shot. Don't call her that, don't ever think of her as that."

"Kydos, then. How does ... Kydos ... know you?"

After a moment's pause he said, "We used to date."

"Excuse me?"

Bob sighed. "It was a long time ago and we were young. It's complicated."

"Uh huh. Alright, if she's not a goddess and you're not a god, what are you, exactly?"

"I told you. We're humans. Been around a lot longer."

"So you're better. Superior. Better than the 'merely human' riffraff like me."

"No." He said it with a vehemence that surprised her. "No," he repeated in a softer voice. "We're human. Our enhanced abilities come from genetic engineering and technological augmentation, based on discoveries that our ancestors made. We've been around longer and learned a few more tricks." Then his voice lowered to a whisper as he said, "Made more mistakes, too." He closed his eyes and sighed deeply. Then he grunted a laugh and turned to face Celcilia, a smile back on his face.

"Sorry, not trying to be mysterious. That's the short version, is all."

"So what's the long version?"

"Heh. That's complicated." He thought for a moment. "Let's try this. Human life started out long ago, in a solar system you can't detect from here or your own Earth. Eventually they learned enough to explore and populate their own solar system, then those around a few of the nearer stars.

Eventually they met another sentient species. A nasty one that saw humans as competition to be eliminated. That was the first of the Great Wars. Half of humanity was wiped out, but we won. Out of that came better control of the alternate energies, access to the alternate spaces, and from those came the technology behind the portals."

"Wait, the what spaces?"

"Uhm, not sure what else to call it in your language. Well, the closest I can find are terms used in your speculative fictions. You might call it hyperspace or subspace. Does that help?"

"Not really, but I've seen enough movies to get the idea. So, your ancestors figured out how to travel faster than light?"

"Not until that first war. Before that they had fast sub-light ships, but used their limited knowledge of the alternate energies to produce faster-than-light communications and very powerful weapons. That's what allowed them to eventually win. Then came portal technology ... a very fast way to travel between the stars. Not at all efficient or cost-effective over shorter distances, but perfect for interstellar travel. The real work was to create the network. For that they sent out both manned and unmanned ships carrying a small portal. When it got to its destination, it contacted the home world. A team of specialists transferred out to the ship, explored the planet, and if it was of any use they'd build a full-sized permanent portal. Once established, travel between portals is nearly instantaneous. With the modest speeds available to them, it was the work of many centuries to establish a really effective, if limited, interstellar network."

"So, travel by portal is instantaneous?"

"Not really, but close enough."

"But ... isn't the speed of light the fastest anything can go?"

Bob nodded. "Yes, it is. In this universe, anyway. Accessing the alternate energy spaces gives us access to other ways of travelling, and the massive amounts of energy required to do so."

"Alright, so how did all that lead to you and Kydos?"

Bob got a faraway look on his face. "We attracted the attention of yet another aggressive alien species. That was the second of the Great Wars. Before it was over, and we had won, three quarters of the human race had been exterminated. Out of that came more scientific breakthroughs and more technologies. The greatest of those were the discoveries of the means to mingle the alternate energies together to create all sorts of useful effects. Like truly effective faster than light spaceships. Faster ships allowed us to greatly expand the portal network. You had a question?"

Celcilia looked uncomfortable. "Ah, yah. Why are you telling me all this? Isn't this the sort of information that the spy services kill people for?"

To her surprise, Bob laughed uproariously. "Oh, Celcilia. Think about it. What, exactly, have I told you that's at all secret? And who would believe you? You've got nothing except a story. Even if someone did believe you—and there are a few who would, I assure you—there's nothing in what I've told you that is of any use. Your speculative fictions have talked about such things for many years."

Celcilia blushed, but looked a lot less tense. "Yeah, alright. Okay, what about these Great Wars of yours? I get the impression there were more than just the two."

Bob's face became sad. "Yes, there were. But no-one knows for sure how many. It was very, very bad, Celcilia. Not just worlds, but entire solar systems destroyed. Our records of the time are fragmented and incomplete."

"Holy shit. Why?"

"No-one knows for sure, any more. As far as we can tell, humans were late on the cosmic scene. We didn't know about the others, but they knew about us. We stumbled upon and began to investigate the alternative energies ... something no-one else had done. Turns out greed and fear are common to all sentient species. So they came after us. Fought each other, too, but only in their eagerness to rip our discoveries out of us. Wave after wave of attacks. At the end of it, we won but there were only a few hundred humans left."

Celcilia whispered, "The aliens?"

"Gone, for the most part. A few scattered remnants here and there. It's a big galaxy, after all."

"Then you all went to Earth?"

"What? No, no." Bob took a deep breath before continuing. "No, we had our own planets. Lots of them, by this point. Many more than we had people, in fact. More than enough for everyone." He fell silent for a time, and Celcilia was loathe to interject. Finally he continued, "We'd acquired a tremendous amount of science and technology by that time. Our ancestors decided to use it to enhance themselves and their descendants, to make us all but impossible to kill. Mighty in power but exhausted as a society, we became insular and family-based. As we became very long-lived, the birthrate plummeted to barely replacement levels. Some suspect not even that." He fell silent.

Celcilia waited for a time, but Bob remained quiet. Struggling to control her impatience, she blurted, "But what about us? Earth and here?"

"Hmm? Oh, yes. Sorry. Well, the truth is we don't always know how planets like yours came about. How the humans got there, I mean. Overall, there are a lot of human-inhabited planets, some more advanced and some less. And, yes, some where they've wiped themselves out."

"But how do the portals fit into all this? You said you lot had more planets than people. Did the Great Wars have something to do it?"

Bob puffed out his cheeks. "You know how I keep saying there are mysteries we don't understand? Well, people like you are the biggest mystery of all. You see, at the end of the Great Wars, the Home Worlds—where we were—had it all. All of the human survivors, the best tech, the portal system, everything. Then a few itchy-footed souls went out exploring and stumbled upon a world with humans on it, then another, and another. Humans, but not like us."

"Primitives," she interrupted, a bitter edge to her voice.

"Unenhanced," he corrected firmly.

"So how'd they—we—get there?"

He shrugged and looked embarrassed. "We don't know. Some of them were obviously started by old military bases that somehow survived the waves of exterminations. Others seemed to be founded by refugees. Some were, perhaps, former colonies that got lost in the shuffle. But some of them couldn't be accounted for. Many, but not all, had portals. It was our greatest mystery for several generations. And then ..." he paused, unsure how to continue.

"And?" she prompted.

Bob sighed. "When no answers were forthcoming, my ancestors stopped wondering and began to use those worlds as sightseeing destinations."

"What?" her voice was low and had a dangerous edge to it.

His voice took on a pleading tone. "You've got to understand how it was, Celcilia. My people had barely recovered after being nearly exterminated as a species. They—we—had become incredibly insular. These new worlds of new humans began as wonders that forced us to look beyond ourselves. Then ... things changed. People became outward looking, but only as a way to experience a temporary amusement. Many of us, when we achieve formal adulthood, take a trip to a few of the Outsider Worlds, as we call them." His tone became bitter. "Some use the failed societies as bad examples, proof of their inferiority." Then his voice lowered to a pained whisper. "A few use them as training grounds."

The look on his face stopped the questions she was about to ask. She waited a minute in silence, then cleared her throat. He turned to face her, but said nothing.

"Uh, okay, but what about the Goddess. Kydos, I mean. And this other person she mentioned. Set, was it? What's this organization you were talking about?"

Bob looked away and scrubbed at his head with his hands for several seconds. Celcilia had never seen him look so stressed. When he looked at her once more, his face had a neutral expression. "Set is setting up an empire. He uses temples on low-tech worlds as his power base. He's convinced others, like Kydos, to join with him in this idiotic venture of his. I've managed to interfere with his operations on some worlds, but am still working to understand the big picture."

"So you dated Kydos once upon a time. Does this mean you know this Set, too?"

Bob sighed as his shoulders slumped. "Yeah. He's my brother. Older brother."

Celcilia could only gape at him. Then she closed her mouth with an audible snap. It took a few false starts before she finally got out, "So where do you fit into all this?"

"Me? I'm putting a stop his nonsense."

"Oh. So you're like a policeman or something?"

"Nope. Just me. No-one else cares enough to get involved."

"So, he has allies among your kind, temples on lots of worlds, and armies. You have ... what?"

Bob assumed an expression of innocence as he placed a hand on his chest. "A pure heart."

"You're a bloody idiot."

"There's many people who'd agree with you," he said with a laugh. The grin on his face faded as he added, "It's getting late, and you need to rest. Morning is going to come all too soon."

She opened her mouth to argue but was betrayed by a

yawn. Her mind was reeling with questions but her body was sagging from exhaustion. She nodded, settled back, and within moments was asleep.

Bob watched her for a time, envying her the balm of sleep. He banked the fire so it would keep going for at least a couple of hours, then closed his eyes and tried to relax. Celcilia's questions were reasonable ones, but had awoken unpleasant memories. As had the arrival of Kydos. She'd always been something of a wild child, but he'd thought something like this beneath her. So many wheels within wheels, so many incomplete puzzles competing for attention. Just like one of his father's many tests that he'd endured as a child. The memories of those, and resulting pain, caused a slight shiver. He could still hear his father's voice, calmly listing Bob's many faults while Bob struggled to escape from some painful trap or other. Then beating him when the test wasn't done to perfection.

His breathing became ragged and it was only through an effort of will that it evened out. This was a trap as nasty as any his father had devised, and the stakes were higher. His hands clenched at the thought of the price of failure. Then he inhaled sharply, exhaled slowly, and forced his body to relax and his mind to stillness. Experience had taught him to examine any problem and treat with the respect it deserved.

A frown of concentration eventually became a smile as a soft chuckle burst forth. There might not be a solution, but there were certainly steps that could be taken. It was time to stop wallowing in self-pity and get back to work. After checking that Celcilia was still fast asleep, he once again ensured that the fire would keep burning for several hours. Then, silent as a shadow, he slipped into the night.

CHAPTER ELEVEN
Furious Race

Celcilia awoke at the first hint of light, with the smell of cooking meat teasing her nostrils. She felt a little stiff and sore, but reasonably well rested. After a thorough stretch she sat up rubbing at her eyes. Then she remembered where she was, uttered a soft curse, and grabbed for the staff.

"Good morning, sleepy head," Bob's mirth-filled voice said. "Ready for some breakfast? The kitchen can offer cooked fish, raw fish, and squirrel. Well, sort-of squirrel. It's a change from fish, at any rate. Eat hearty—we've got a busy day ahead of us."

She opened her mouth to speak but Bob held up a finger to interrupt her. "Eat now, curse me later."

Celcilia decided that it was foolish to curse on an empty stomach, so she merely grunted and held out a hand for a skewer of meat. She decided that it was possible—just barely possible—that he had a point. In between bites she glanced over at him. "What's that you're eating?" she mumbled through the food.

"Berries," he replied. "Not sure it's something you can handle, though. Needed the trace elements."

"Harrumph," she mumbled, tamping down a flash of jealousy at his enhanced metabolism. Then she noticed several sticks with cooked meat on them, more than they'd be eating for a meal. "What're those?" she said, pointing with her chin.

"For later. Eat on the trail or a cold lunch, whatever. It's good to have options."

She noted with surprise that his attitude was on the casual side. "What about Kydos?" she asked. "Still worried about her?"

"Oh, yes. That's why I went out last night, while you were asleep, and laid some false trails."

"Shouldn't we get on the move, then?" Celcilia said, her voice betraying some nervousness.

Bob shook his head. "She'd just catch us. We need to funnel her attentions ..."

He was interrupted by a howl. It sounded like a very large predator on the hunt, but wasn't anything they'd heard before on this planet. Bob cocked his head and held up a hand for silence. Celcilia saw writhing on his neck that indicated activity by his sensorium. The intermittent howls were getting closer, and she could hear the faint sounds of something crashing through the brush.

Celcilia would have been worried except for the smile on Bob's face. It was a predator's smile of satisfaction.

He moved towards the fire, picked up a large stone that had been sitting getting warm, and tossed it into the woods far upstream and to one side. There were a couple seconds of silence broken by a howl of triumph, a brief moment of crashing brush, followed by shrieks of pain. Several heartbeats later, the shrieks became words in a language that Celcilia had never heard before. The only word she could make out was "Bob".

On hearing that, the target of the ranting turned to her and said, "Grab your gear. Time for us to go. That should slow her down for a while."

They began to trot into the forest. Celcilia couldn't contain her curiosity. "Those false trails of yours ... they were more than that?"

"Yes, indeed," said Bob, his face split into a wide grin. "Put myself into her position, and decided she'd be after us despite her injuries. Anger tends to make people stupid—don't forget that. And she was very, very angry."

"Will these traps stop her?"

"Nope. But between these injuries and her old ones, at best she'll only be able to move as fast as we can. Probably slower, but we won't count on that."

"Probably?" Celcilia's voice hinted at the incredulity she felt.

Bob turned to grin at her. "Makes things more interesting, don't you think? So let's beat feet. The usual pace—it's a true marathon, now."

"Why are we going this way, then? That way's a more direct path to the river." She pointed downstream along the creek they'd just left.

"You've got a good sense of direction. Yes, that's the direct path, but there's some very nasty terrain that way. If we're lucky she'll take that direct route and get bogged down. The way we're going will avoid that and get us to the river faster. Now, stop talking and run."

They continued the routine of run-walk cycles until noon, when Bob called a halt. "Brief break. Here's some of this morning's meat." He passed her a couple skewers, keeping one for himself. The munched their meal in companionable silence, listening to the sounds of the wildlife going about their normal lives.

"Mind if I ask a question?" Celcilia asked in a quiet voice.

"Never stop asking questions, Celcilia," said Bob.

"How is it that an advanced being like yourself is so good at bushcraft and stealthy stuff?"

Bob chuckled. "That's my Dad's work. Trained me to survive and thrive, as he used to say, anywhere. Very big on thorough and rigorous training, was Dad."

"But your powers?"

"A central tenant of Dad's training was making sure I could survive with minimal use of my enhancements. He was adamant that depending on enhancements made a person weak, made them vulnerable. Not a common attitude, I should point out." Seeing that Celcilia was struggling not to ask the obvious question, Bob added, "Yes, my own powers are in some ways less than the average. Dad made sure that I could make optimum use of what I had, though, including my regular human abilities. Made me appreciate the subtle approach over brute force."

Celcilia blushed. "Didn't mean to pry."

Bob grinned at her. "That's alright. Better to ask, better to know. But family is complicated."

She rolled her eyes, puffed her cheeks, and said, "Tell me about it."

After a few seconds of shared laughter, Bob declared it was time to move out.

* * *

After pushing hard, they reached the river at sunset. The far side was lost in the gloom of the approaching twilight, and the roar of the raging water was like a blow to the senses after the quiet of the forest. They looked at each other and with nods agreed to retreat to the forest for the night.

"What do you think?" asked Celcilia. "Walk along it or risk a raft?"

Bob shook his head. "It's worse than I imagined, to be honest."

"If it were just you, you'd do it."

He nodded. Then added, "Maybe. Yes, I heal quickly but injuries still hurt us as much as they do you." He pointed at the river. "That's a nasty piece of water for anyone. I think we should run alongside it. It'll take an extra day or so, but it's safer."

Celcilia nodded. "On the other hand, the riverbank is rather rocky. Easy to twist an ankle. Can we just go through the forest?" She thought for a moment, then answered her own question, "It's pretty thick next to the river. That'd slow us down. Rather a lot, I'd say."

"Agreed," Bob said. "Let's find a good shelter for the night and see what things look like in the morning."

They found a spot away from the spray and noise of the river and made a sketchy camp. Bob had kept a couple sticks of meat, so they ate those and turned in. The next morning they went back to the river and agreed that walking alongside was the prudent course of action. It turned out that while the riverbank was rocky, there were stretches that were easy walking. That allowed them to keep to their normal run-walk rhythm, more or less, and they managed to make reasonable time.

Along the way, Bob taught Celcilia how to throw a short stick with enough force to knock down small game. This allowed them to hunt as they travelled, cleaning their catch as they walked. These were a welcome addition to the fish which formed the staple of their meagre diet. They paused only for brief rests breaks during the day, sleeping at night when there was no longer sufficient light for safe travelling.

Most of the time the noise of the river precluded conversation, but there were stretches where they were forced to make short detours away from it. Those welcome periods of silence were the highlights of their day. During once such interlude, Celcilia asked, "Is the temple here similar to the others you've come across?"

Bob helped her over a log before answering. "Well, this is certainly one of the larger ones I've seen. The best-organized setup, too. Not just for the temple, but for the general population, too."

"Excuse me?" she said in terse tones.

"Hmm, well Kydos certainly does bad things, no doubt

about that. But much of what she's organized has improved the lot of people here. Better sanitation, better roads, a better variety of food and better distribution of it, new buildings and not just temple-related ones either. Yes she's harsh, but a lot of people have better lives in spite of that."

Celcilia spat and snarled a curse. It was several minutes before she spoke again. By this time her fury had cooled to be replaced by a thoughtful look. "Hate to say this, but you may have a point. I've no love for her, but I never heard tell of anything like the sweatshops back home. From what I could tell, most of the production of everything was in private hands, although she was always the biggest customer." She paused for a moment before adding, "People worked hard, but I still saw lots of smiles and laughter." She let her breath came out in a whoosh and she was silent for a few steps. In a quiet voice she said, "Maybe she did some good."

Bob's eyebrows raised. "You never fail to impress me, Celcilia. Even after all you've endured, you can see things in a larger perspective. That's a rare quality, I assure you."

She shrugged. "What is, is. T'ain't easy to come to terms with it, but I'm tryin'. Seen people dig a pit of woe so deep they couldn't get out." She was silent for the space of a handful of steps. "So, are all those other temples so helpful?"

"Not at all. Kydos, for all her many faults, seems to want these people to worship her for her ability to make their lives better now and in the future. Most of my kind might start with good intentions, but few have the managerial ability or tenacity to pull it off. They end up ruling by force and threats of force. My brother is a mixture of both."

"Why do people follow them at all? Oh sure, putting on a big show will impress people, but what you're talking about means creating a larger organization."

"Good question. My brother came up with a system. First he establishes a small shrine in an out-of-the-way location.

Once or twice a day, the shrine emits an energy field that stimulates the pleasure centres of the brain and produces a feeling of mild euphoria. That helps to attract a modest following, including the beginnings of a priesthood. The priests get an extra small burst of euphoria outside of the regular ones. Then he alters the shrine to emit only when the size of the congregation exceeds some minimum size. Also, the bigger the crowd, the greater the intensity of euphoria. All that serves to modify behaviours for those susceptible to such things."

"Nice, but seems a thin gruel to base an organization on."

"Ah, but then come the miracles—medicines, money, special gifts. That gets the attention of the local power structure. The influence of the priesthood spreads and deepens."

"Won't that step on a lot of toes?"

"Indeed. That's why starting with the shrines is so important. Start small and seemingly innocuous, then over time increase the reach and depth of influence. Keep in mind that this is done over a span of many years, often decades. It's a long game, you see. Set got the idea from one of our popular stories, which called such a gambit 'the dagger of eons'."

"To what end? That's a lot of effort, Bob. What's the payback?"

"For some, it's a just a way to lord it over someone weaker." He shot her a look. "We aren't gods and we aren't perfect, Celcilia." Then his shoulders slumped. "We used to be better, something special. Or at least so we're taught." Then he inhaled and exhaled sharply before continuing. "Our entire culture is based around how amazing our ancestors were before the Great Wars. About how magnificently they fought against overwhelming odds to emerge triumphant at the end. How they overcame the threat of racial extinction to rebuild our species." His tone had taken on a bitter tinge.

"We're awash with their history and literature and art and tales of their great deeds. It's drowned out our own voices, I think."

It was several seconds before he spoke again. His voice was moderate, but his face was pained. "It's bad enough that we lose ourselves in the past ... but that's our problem. Trouble is, every so often one of us decides that they are as good and wise as the ancestors and sets themselves up as supreme ruler on some planet of humans. For the good of the lesser races, of course. It never ends well. But Set seems have changed all that."

"How so?"

"He managed to set up a large-scale, stable organization. Once established, the shrines act as centres to build full temples. That's when the organization really get their hooks into the social structures. In a surprisingly short time, the temples become the centre of what amounts to a planetary government. Get a few of those going, establish trade with other temple-worlds via the portals, and that locks it all together. Putting something like that together takes skill and focus. That got the attention and admiration of his friends, so Set taught them how to do the same sort of thing. Some set up their own organizations, but most found satisfaction in serving within Set's. By this time, you see, he'd gotten the idea to re-recreate the pre-War civilization of our ancestors. Using the resources of the younger races makes the task of building up a new civilization a whole lot easier and faster. Also gives him a good-sized empire with himself as the head." Bob shook his head and looked as if he wanted to spit. "That re-creation holds a great deal of attraction for a lot of my kind, I'm afraid. So people either go along or turn a blind eye to the excesses and foulness."

Celcilia was a bit startled at the venom in his voice. She kept silent for a time, then in a carefully neutral tone asked, "So how are you stopping this ... this ... dagger of eons, you called it."

She was grateful to see Bob's normal good humour return as he thought about his response.

"Heh. Shrines are easy. I tweak the euphoria field to be sour. Just a little bit at first, then ramping that up over time. Planting foul-smelling plants in the area helps, too, though I save that for when the sourness peaks. Sowing aggressive vines along the structure makes it look run down and ugly. It all helps to get people thinking."

"Why not just smash 'em?"

"Nah. Someone in Set's organization would notice it and investigate. On the social level, it just makes them out to be martyrs. Far, far more effective to make them look like fools and bunglers." He turned to look at Celcilia and grinned. "Tyrants of all stripes hate to be laughed at. One of the things that makes it so much fun to do."

The look of mischievous joy on his face caused Celcilia to giggle. "All right, but what about the temples? They'd be harder to crack, I'd think."

Bob sighed. "Very much so. By the time I find them, they've been established for centuries and control the planetary economy. Like Kydos, but typically a lot more repressive. Often brutally so. Yet simply smashing them would cause more problems than it solves." His face became grim for a moment, then he forced a grin. "But the principles of attack remain the same. The first step is to make them look silly. That allows me to work with the local resistance ... and there's always a resistance. That's where the hard work begins, you see. The mockery gets people thinking, which leaves them open to the possibility of new ways of doing things. Eventually, that leads to neutralizing the temple's control of the social and economic systems, at least to the point where they can be openly challenged. After that, it's up to the locals to choose their own fates."

"Sounds like the work of years," she said in a soft voice.

"Yes, it can take quite some time. Of course, the hard part is finding the shrines and temples in the first place. It's a big galaxy, and Set tends not to advertise. Well, at least not anymore."

Celcilia laughed as she gave him an appraising look. "You've been doing this for a very long time, then."

Bob shrugged. "I suppose so. It needs doing, and everyone needs a purpose in life."

"Any chance that some of that purpose involves sibling rivalry?" she teased.

"Just icing on the cake, I assure you," he said through a grin.

By this time their path had taken them closer to the river and its noise. By unspoken agreement they put off any further discussions to concentrate on their footing.

* * *

After four days of hard marching they arrived at the grove where the portal was. They were half a day's march from the river, through dense forest, and reaching the grove was like finding a calm pool after shooting the rapids.

"It's beautiful," she said in measured tones, constantly scanning the surroundings for danger.

Bob nodded. "That's the idea. Supposed to create a zone of serenity."

After a few more steps, Celcilia slowed her pace, her face tilted to one side in obvious pain. She soon was forced to pause, grunting with the effort to continue. Bob grabbed her by an arm and escorted her back a dozen steps.

"Sorry," she muttered. "Like walking into a brick wall."

"My fault," he insisted. "That's the repelling field around the area. You got through it before, so I'd forgotten that it would affect you."

"So how'm I getting to the portal?"

"Leave that to me," said Bob in a confident tone. "I'll

instantiate the portal and tell it to let you in. Sit here and rest."

Fifteen minutes later, Celcilia called out, "Still waiting."

The prompt reply came back, "Still working."

A few minutes later Bob came trotting back to where Celcilia waited. She looked up at him with a wry expression. "You're having problems." It wasn't a question.

Bob sighed. "Sorry, sorry. This is an older type of portal. Very adamant about not letting just anyone through."

"Would it let me through if I still had my jewel?"

"Not sure if even that would do it," Bob admitted. "It's a stubborn old thing. Probably the reason the other one is used instead. However, unlike the more modern ones it can link with other local portals and perform some diagnostics of them. A nice piece of craftsmanship, actually."

"Lovely. So how does that get me in there?"

"It doesn't, actually," said Bob in a cheerful voice that did nothing to improve Celcilia's mood. "But I queried the other portal and discovered that its energy levels are somewhat depleted." At a glare from Celcilia he hurried to add, "That means it has been used to transport large payloads of something or other over a considerable period of time. From what you've told me of the operation of the temple, I can only conclude that it is people being ferried in and out."

Celcilia nodded. "I coulda told you that. And did."

Bob gave a courtly bow. "Yes, you did. But now I can confirm that it has been happening for several centuries, in fact, with traffic building over time and spiking over the past year."

"So whatever the Goddess—Kydos—is doing, she's doing more of it."

"Exactly," said Bob.

"Interesting," she admitted. "But how does that get me home?"

"Well ...", began Bob before he lapsed into silence.

Celcilia sighed. "Just tell me the bad news."

Bob grimaced. "The good news is that I can get you in. The bad news is the how of it."

"Meaning?" she said, drawing out the word in feigned patience.

"I apport you in"

"Excuse me?"

"Ah, think of it as, uhm, teleportation. Yeah, that's it." He paused for a moment before adding, "Not exactly, but close enough."

She considered that for a moment. "Why not just carry me in?"

He looked pained as he said, "You'd be dead before we reached the portal."

"Ah."

"Well, I did say that we installed these things after a time of war. Security was very, very tight. And for good reason, I might add."

"Fair enough, fair enough. So how do I get in? What's this aporty thing?"

"It's 'apporting', and is, as I said, sort of like teleportation."

Celcilia rubbed her forehead. "Look, I don't need a detailed ..."

Bob hurried to interrupt her. "I move you from here to there without moving in between. Teleportation uses a machine; apporting is a skill we learn."

Celcilia pursed her lips in thought. A few seconds later she asked, "And the portal won't mind if I just kinda show up next to it?"

"That's it, exactly. Not happy about you approaching it, but quite content if you just happen to show up beside it with me."

She looked at him through narrowed eyes. "There's a price to this, isn't there?"

He sighed. "Yeah. I can apport well enough. Couldn't do it

at all as a child, but turns out I was just a late bloomer."

Celcilia nodded. "Kydos called you a cripple. Sorry, but she did. Wondered what she meant. You don't seem crippled to me."

Bob gave her a lop-sided smile. "Thanks, Celcilia. But that's okay. In some ways I am a cripple among my own kind. Can't levitate at all, and my apporting is limited. But I can do other things the other can't, so it all evens out."

"When you say limited, that means what?"

He gave a small sigh before answering. "I can apport myself and a small payload ... like the clothes I'm wearing and a bit more. One of the reasons I've learned to travel light."

"And I'm something more than 'a bit more', aren't I?"

"Yeah. What it means is that it'll take a lot out of me. In practical terms, I'll probably pass out for a few seconds and then be not much good for anything for up to a few minutes."

Celcilia snorted. "Typical man. Do a little work and then lay back and moan about the effort." Her smile took the sting out of her words, and they both laughed. Then she became serious. "So we leave and Kydos keeps on doing her thing? What does she do with all those people she had me indoctrinate?"

"Good question," said Bob, "and one that I've been giving considerable thought to. I've managed to convince both portals to lock down after we leave. In fact ..."

Their discussion was interrupted by the sound of something crashing through the forest coming towards them.

Bob turned to Celcilia and snapped, "Hold on to me tightly. We've run out of time."

Celcilia ran forward and hugged her companion. There was a brief moment of intense cold and disorientation, then things were normal once more. The only difference was the structure standing in front of her. It had strange angles that hurt the eyes to look at, and a cold sheen of oily writhing wrongness coated it. She felt something at her feet and looked down to discover Bob's prostrate body. She knelt to check on him and for the first time saw a shimmer of sweat coating his face. That, and his lack of consciousness, worried her, but not nearly as much as the rapidly-approaching shrieks from the forest. Within a few seconds the shrieks began to take the form of words. Or, rather, a single word screamed over and over again, "Bob."

The Goddess had arrived.

"Wake up. Wake up," she urged her companion, shaking his shoulder with increasing firmness. "Time to go." She was rewarded by a soft moan, but his eyes remained closed and his body limp.

A bush next to her exploded into flames, and a heavy weight landed two body-lengths away from her. She looked up to see a vision out of the most horrific stories of her youth. The Goddess had been a being of transcendent beauty and full of life. The naked creature before her was little more than a ragged collection of poorly-assembled skin and bones. The skin was mottled, with some areas black with rot. The configuration of her skeleton no longer looked human. The rib cage had bulges and dents that no human could have survived, and the spine had a definite s-curve to it. The head wobbled on a neck that was both stretched and had odd angles to it. The face was broken and shattered into something not human, with a mouth twisted into a permanent scream. Sections of skull poked through the skin, and the head itself looked battered and dented.

But it was the arms that drew Celcilia's attention. On one arm the hand was missing but the wrist bones thrust out like twin knife blades. The other hand was replaced by a hollow tube that began to point towards her.

Still squatting, Celcilia lashed out with her staff and batted the tube-arm away. The knife-arm lashed out and hit the staff, almost knocking it out of Celcilia's grasp. Uttering a low growl, Celcilia sprang to her feet and lunged at the demon-figure before her, hitting at it with her staff. She managed to parry a blow from each of the hideous arms before a downward blow knocked the staff out of her hands, bouncing it across her shins and onto the ground away from her. The demon-figure grinned at her and hissed. Celcilia sneered and assumed a fighting stance. Time seemed to stand still as the two women glared at each other.

Then a blow from the staff slammed up against the chin of the creature. That was followed up by a flurry of blows against the head, arms, and body. Bob was awake and had entered the fray. He spared a quick glance at Celcilia and snapped, "Back up." She hurried to obey.

What followed transpired faster than her senses could follow. Bob and the demon—Celcilia could no longer think of it as the Goddess—traded blows at speeds that were faster than the merely human eye could sense as anything other than a blur. What she could hear, however, were a succession of what sounded like tree trunks snapping as the staff hit against the limbs of the demon. Finally she saw Bob flick the staff against the chin of the demon, throwing the creature into the air. Several seconds later it landed heavily at the edge of the grove.

Bob turned towards the portal, leaning heavily on the staff as he stood upright and closed his eyes. He was breathing heavily and was obviously attempting to concentrate. A sound, more felt than heard, coming from the portal caused her to look towards it. A blackness was forming to one side. A blackness that was deeper than anything she'd ever seen. It was folding in and around itself, attempting to wrap itself into her mind.

"Don't look at it," snapped Bob. "It's a transdimensional construct."

Celcilia shook herself and turned to look at Bob. "What?

Oh, not for the sight of the merely human, is it?"

"Pfft. No-one can look at it for long without getting a headache," he panted. The blackness filled with symbols that pulsed and writhed as if alive before being absorbed by the darkness. "There, I've set the destination. Hold my hand and we'll walk through it."

A wordless shriek from behind them caused them to pause. They turned to face the snarling demon as it hobbled towards them. Its mouth clattered and frothed, but no words came out.

"You didn't take the time to heal properly, Katie. That'll take a very long time to heal, now," said Bob in a soft voice.

In response, the demon lifted its tube arm and a shimmering stream of bright objects raced towards them. Bob threw the staff at her, spun around, then placed himself between the stream of darts and Celcilia. He felt several impacts on his arm and torso. From the spreading numbness, he realized the darts contained a toxin of some sort. He picked up Celcilia and ran into the safety offered by the blackness.

Author's Afterword

Although authors are to blame for the final product, none of us are an island when it comes to inspiration and assistance.

The original inspiration came from pictures posted on Twitter as writing prompts ("write a sentence based on this picture"). I started making up strange and silly responses around a character named "Bob". I'd especially like to thank @DougWallace1973. He not only posted interesting pictures, he encouraged my silly micro-stories and jokes.

Many thanks to my beta readers : Janice, Lynn, and Trit. Your encouragement helped keep me going.

Thanks to Steve for his pointers regarding the speech patterns in Wales.

A special thanks to Trit for making many editorial comments.

About The Author

Brian retired from the software development rat race to take up the carefree life of an author. He lives with his wife and two cats in Ontario, Canada.

For the latest news about this and forthcoming books, the occasional commentary on life, or to leave a comment (we love feedback), check out Brian's blog at

www.BrianGreiner.ca

Books by Brian Greiner

All books are available as e-books and paperbacks from :

kobobooks.com
amazon.ca
amazon.com
overdrive.com

The Ascending Darkness series
#1   Darkness Creeps Forth
#2   Darkness Comes Reaping

The Accursed North series
#1 The Werewolves of Winter
#2 The Final Doom

The Saga of Bob series
#1 Ancestors and Descendants
#2 Dagger of Eons

Ancestors and Descendants

Bob has spent much of his life crisscrossing the galaxy
trying to protect people from the ancient evils, horrors,
and demons that lurk among the stars; fearsome creatures
that consider humans as mere nothings, if they bother with
humans at all.
Some call them monsters.
Bob calls them family.
Now he has discovered evidence of an insidious and
corrupting influence spreading across the galaxy,
threatening his family and all of humanity. Unsure of who
he can trust, Bob must fight to uncover the truth and find a
way to save everyone. He will discover there are no perfect
solutions, and all come with a price.

Darkness Creeps Forth

A terrorist attack that leaves Toronto's financial district in
shambles and the country's economy vulnerable. An
investigative reporter who uncovers a major national
scandal and then dies of apparent natural causes before his
story can be published. Investigating these seemingly
unrelated events draws small-time private investigator
Yancey Franklin and his friends into a century-old web of
corruption and deceit that threatens the security and
independence of Canada. In a desperate race against time,
Yancey and his friends rush to prevent an attack by a
ruthless opponent on an ageing secret military facility in
northern Ontario that holds a deadly secret.

Darkness Comes Reaping

Small-time investigator Yancey Franklin has thwarted the plans of a ruthless enemy to unleash biochemical weapons in Northern Ontario. Now he is on the run and trying to uncover the secrets behind a century-old web of corruption and deceit that strives to eliminate Canada as an independent nation. In a desperate race against time, Yancey and his friends struggle to stay alive as they rush to stop their enemy's latest plan – the deadly "Harvest of Souls".

The Werewolves of Winter

The werewolves were created by the Change Plague—the result of ill-considered biotechnology. It was only their annual winter die-off that saved humanity. But every spring the Change Plague returned to create a new and more deadly crop of werewolves.

People adapted and managed to carry on despite the increasingly precarious situation.

One man, trapped on his farm north of Toronto, began to piece together hints of a deeper and more dangerous threat. With werewolves closing in, time was running out in a desperate race to uncover answers.

A novel of modern horrors, ancient prophesies, data analysis, and nerds who save the world.

The Final Doom

Felix Kurtsius discovered that the Change Plague was being dispersed as part of a deliberate attack. Toronto appeared to be the epicentre for the infection, which targeted Canada preferentially. He escaped to Toronto after werewolves began purging the rural areas of humans, only to discover insidious forces at work. In a race against the clock, Felix and his friends must use all their skills to unravel the forces behind the werewolves, and prevent the destruction of humanity.

A novel of modern horrors, ancient prophesies, data analysis, and nerds who save the world.

www.ingramcontent.com/pod-product-compliance
Lightning Source LLC
Chambersburg PA
CBHW050028180626
46810CB00002B/628